REBELS OF RUIN

RUIN OR REDEMPTION TRILOGY BOOK 2

MARTI M. MCNAIR

Hope You Enjoy
Marti. M. McNair
x

REBSAM PUBLISHING

In loving memory of my beloved mum and stepdad, Martha and Jimmy Ferguson. I am grateful for all the love and encouragement given throughout the years.

To Mum, for encouraging me never to have a book out of my hand, and for all the childhood stories that sparked my imagination. To Jimmy, thank you for being there, and for being a part of our lives.

CONTENTS

1

Time dissolved into nothingness. Having sailed across the treacherous Pewter Sea, I found myself in a bleak existence within the mines. The darkness pressed in from all sides, thick and suffocating. It clung to my skin like a second layer, stifling every breath.

The noxious reek of sulphur hung in the air, a toxic grip refusing to dissipate. Death hovered over me, a phantom reluctant to relinquish its hold from this wretched prison. Each breath stabbed into my lungs like a dagger, as if each gasp might be my last.

The mine wardens and their masters were ruthless, weaving a tapestry of cruelty with their whips. Their faces twisted with sadistic pleasure as they tore welts upon our skin, leaving behind scars bearing witness to the brutality we endured.

Within the prisoner's quarters, a clear hierarchy emerged, with Saxon positioned at its core as our wise and trusted linchpin.

He served as a beacon of sanity amidst the horrors we suffered. Despite the weariness etched into his aged bones, he carried the burden of leading us forward and dispensing hope. His failed attempts to escape had brought harsh beatings which took their toll. Nevertheless, he stubbornly held onto life, refusing to meet his end.

'How're you faring today, Jasmine?' he asked, passing a cup of water from a sturdy wooden barrel.

I knelt beside his dust-layered body, swirling water around my mouth before spitting it back out, ridding it of the black layer that coated every tooth and membrane. 'I'm fine. Concentrate on yourself and don't worry about me.'

'Is that light still blinking under your skin?' he asked, his eyes wandering towards my upper left arm. He was referring to the microchip, which I believed Aspen, a medic from Ruin, had implanted before my transfer from the island to the mainland. I felt assured Aspen and members of Robinia's group would find and rescue me. He understood the crucial reason for my survival, and through discreet exchanges, made certain everyone fully understood.

Among our core members were Astrid and Minx, formidable female freedom fighters who had shared the caves with Saxon before their capture. Cooper, Felix, and Zander were also with them, all seized in the same skirmish as Saxon while out scavenging. Together, we sought solace in our current shared struggle.

When we gathered to rest, we spent time plotting escapes and scheming to overthrow the tyrants who ruled our world. They shielded me, vowing to protect me from those who sought to drag me back into their grasp – promising that, if freedom ever came, I would remain beyond their reach.

'It's not glowed for a few days now. I guess I'm not as important as Aspen and Robinia made out,' I said, regretting the words as soon as I uttered them. Saxon's disappointment triggered an attack of guttural coughing.

'If what you say is true, they'll come for you. Just remember to free all of us too,' he said hoarsely, pausing to clear his throat. His hand swept around the mineshaft, gesturing towards his legion of walking corpses, nowhere near a match for Malus, his guards, or the one world army. 'We'll all fight with you. I'll make sure of that.'

I had withered as well. My skin felt tight, stretching across the bone, and with hands cracked and hardened with sores, they were hardly fit to wield a weapon. Rally a battle cry? I could barely stand at the end of each shift.

Saxon's face feigned a glimmer of hope. 'Once we escape, we'll tour the cave complex and assemble an army. My people distrust yours, but they'll place their faith in you. I sense it in these old bones of mine – your destiny is to save us all.'

The bark of the mine warden shattered the reprieve of our brief break. 'Back to work,' he yelled, stomping over in our direction.

Saxon's eyes rolled in his soot-filled face. As I helped him to his feet, a harsh fit of coughing wracked his frame once more. 'I'm fine,' he said, while he spluttered.

The mine warden's boots thudded heavily on the stone floor as he advanced, the leather of his whip cracking in the stagnant air. With a look of hatred, he raised it high above his head as Saxon's half-bent body braced itself for impact.

'Don't,' I said, stepping in front of Saxon and lifting my arm, palm open and facing outward, forming a barrier between the guard's whip and Saxon. I held my ground, meeting the warden's furious stare. Though my voice was soft, it carried an undertone of purpose. 'He'll be fine.'

With a guttural grunt, the guard nodded. I wrapped an arm around Saxon, feeling the sharp edges of his bones beneath his thin skin, guiding him back toward the coal face, where our tools lay scattered.

When I first arrived in the mines to serve my punishment, I was handed a pickaxe and swung it rhythmically alongside prisoners too beleaguered to speak. Weakened by a poor diet, deprived of sunlight and clean air, I eventually collapsed, yearning to end such a sorrowful existence.

Once revived, I was brought to this upper shaft, placed beside Saxon, and given a small hammer and chisel. In sharing our life story, his bony fingers clasped my hand, a gesture of solidarity; his eyes reflecting a shared understanding born from mutual struggles. At that moment, I knew I had found an ally in this desolate place.

I asked excitedly if he knew Mary. Though he had never met her, he was aware of who she was and expressed sorrow upon hearing of her passing.

Like Mary, he was born free and had never experienced the awful reality of growing up on Ruin, without the love of a family unit.

'It might be a full moon tonight,' Saxon said, wistfulness washing over his face. 'Make sure you get in line to haul coal up to the pit face. Get a bit o' fresh air in those dusty lungs.'

Our sole source of joy was volunteering for this task, hauling coal above ground during the hours of darkness. We prolonged this activity, seeking out stars and inhaling the refreshing dust-free air.

'Even if I need to carry you, you'll be coming too,' I said.

The ground quivered beneath my feet, and an earth-shattering roar erupted from the depths of the mine. I stumbled, the force of the explosion knocking me off balance, my ears ringing. The tunnel convulsed with shockwaves, launching me through the air. I slammed into the wall, my skull meeting it with a sickening thud. Darkness engulfed me, and I wasn't sure how long I was out.

* * *

I blinked, disoriented, trying to make sense of my surroundings. Slowly, I became aware of an intense burning sensation searing my skin. Hot thick air scorched the back of my throat as I inhaled, desperate for air.

Raising my hand to shield my eyes, I squinted through the swirling fog. The once familiar space now appeared a shadowy maze, its details obscured by thick billowing dust. 'Saxon,' I called, my voice distant and faint.

Every sound seemed muted, and a persistent ringing in my ears added a layer of pain, leaving me wondering if I would ever hear properly again.

A warden's torch sent a dazzling light ricocheting off the walls, its brightness wavering before settling into a subdued glow. The erratic interplay of light and shadow created an eerie spectacle within the cavern.

Figures stirred, wardens and prisoners alike, their bodies rising listlessly from the ground as if burdened by an invisible force, their faces streaked with blood and grime. 'Saxon,' I called again.

'Over here, Jasmine.' It was Cooper, one of my fellow prisoners. I couldn't hear him properly, but his raised hand indicated his location. 'Saxon's over here.'

Summoning every ounce of willpower, I fought through the blinding pain, forcing myself forward with trembling arms. I crawled inch by agonising inch, each movement a fresh wave of torment. 'Is he okay?' I gasped, my voice barely above a whisper.

Cooper pulled fallen debris off Saxon, his hands shaking as he worked. His voice sounded like rocks scraping together in a hessian sack. 'He's hardly breathing,
' he said, wiping beads of sweat from his face, smearing the dark dust clinging to his skin.

'What do you think happened?' I asked, as I helped Cooper pull fragments of stone and wood from Saxon's body.

'I'm not sure, but we'll need to find a way out quickly. Stay here and help free Saxon, and I'll go and assess the damage.'

Saxon looked ghastly. His face pale and slick with moisture. A deep, ragged gash on the side of his head oozed dark, sluggish streams of blood, staining his hair and trickling down his neck. His right leg, twisted out of place, lay at an unnatural angle, as though it had been shattered. Crimson stains soaked through his tattered clothes, but at least he was still in one piece.

I wiped his brow with the sleeve of my shirt. 'Hang in there,' I said, my voice choked. 'This could be our chance to escape.' I scanned the shaft again, happy to see many of our overseers were also victims. A sudden itch spread through my upper left arm, and as I peeled back the frayed cloth, my eyes widened at the sight of a soft red glow blinking under my skin. 'Wake up, Saxon,' I said, unable to contain the urgency from my voice. 'The blast has kick-started the glow on my implant.'

Astrid limped towards me. She fell to her knees and pulled me into her arms. 'Thank goodness you're okay. Cooper told me where to find you. Minx and Felix are looking for something to make a stretcher for Saxon. But, we can't find Zander.' Her eyes darted around the cavern, finally resting on Saxon. 'This could be our one chance to escape,' she said, her voice carrying a spark of hope amidst the chaos.

I glanced down at her thigh, frowning as I noticed blood leaking through the cloth she had used to bind it. 'What about you?'

'It's nothing. I'll be fine.'

'We need to help as many people as we can to safety,' I said, clasping Saxon's clammy hand, willing him to hold on to life. 'Saxon wouldn't want anyone left behind. Especially Zander.'

'We'll do our best,' Astrid said. 'But we need to hurry.'

Cooper made his way back towards us, small puffs of ash rising from each of his steps as he waded gingerly through the rubble. 'Here, Astrid,' he said, passing her a palm-sized stone. 'Keep this as a weapon, just in case. Follow my lead, and help me gather the robes, uniforms and whips from any mine wardens we come across. We'll use them to make bandages and a stretcher for Saxon.'

I lowered my gaze to Astrid's thigh. 'Let me go instead. Astrid's hurt.'

'No,' Astrid said, her voice firm. 'We can't risk anything happening to you. Stay here, and we'll be right back.'

Cooper nodded, taking her arm, and together they disappeared into the gloom. It didn't take long before Felix and Minx emerged from the shadows, their muscles taut as they dragged two sturdy wooden planks behind them.

I turned to Minx, my heart still pounding. 'I'm glad you're both okay. Any sign of Zander?'

Minx shook her head, her expression grave. 'I think he was digging in shaft three. It's completely blocked off, sealed tight like a tomb.'

Felix's voice cut through the tension. 'A wall of rubble won't stop Zander. If he survived the blast, he'll find a way out.'

Cooper and Astrid returned, each dumping bundles of clothing at our feet. Cooper sat on a boulder, knotting lines of whips together, and winding their leather around the two wooden planks, forming a makeshift stretcher.

Minx tied the clothing making a rope from the materials, her hands trembling as she spread them on the ground. 'Ready,' she said, her eyes darting anxiously to Cooper.

Cooper and Felix lifted the planks and placed them in the middle of the material. Gently, they lifted Saxon and laid him on top of them, using the remaining cloth from below to tie him firmly in place. Saxon groaned. It was the first noise he'd made since the explosion; his eyes briefly fluttered open.

Cooper's weary gaze swept the length of our ravaged mine shaft. 'The passageway to level six looks clear, and emergency lights are working. Let's head there and continue moving upwards,' he commanded. 'Minx and Astrid, can you lead the way while Felix and I carry Saxon? Hopefully, we'll find survivors on route. Look for something, a stone, a splinter of wood, anything you can use as a weapon. If there are mine wardens obstructing our way, take them out. Jasmine, you stay close behind me.'

Each step felt like an uphill struggle as we battled against the debris plodding forward, our movements weary from exhaustion. The path was horrific. The stench of burnt flesh hung in the air. Broken limbs littered our way, while the dead stared ahead with lifeless eyes.

Astrid and Minx screeched to a halt, fear flashing in Astrid's widened eyes as she turned to us. 'Do you hear that?'

The ground beneath us trembled, as a low rumble echoed through the narrow tunnel. Cooper and Felix laid Saxon carefully on the ground. Cooper touched the damp walls, feeling them shudder. 'I think it's shockwaves from a secondary explosion,' he said, as the tremors intensified, and the rumble grew louder. 'Everybody down,' he yelled, throwing himself on top of me as the ceiling gave way. Once again, we were plunged into darkness.

2

F ortune smiled upon us, sparing the ground beneath our feet, and preventing the roof from collapsing directly above us. Despite this stroke of luck, we found ourselves trapped, hemmed in by a wall of rubble both ahead and behind us. Cooper activated an emergency light beam he'd taken from a mine warden. Its initial brightness overwhelmed the darkness before gradually dimming.

Finding my voice, I asked, 'Is Saxon okay?'

Cooper pressed his fingers against Saxon's neck, his expression grim. 'His pulse is weak.' His gaze swept across our faces one by one. 'Is anybody hurt?'

'Just a bit shaken,' Astrid said, nursing her bleeding leg.

Minx placed her hand on Astrid's shoulder with a reassuring squeeze. 'We'll get through this. We've come too far to fail.'

Felix brushed the dirt off his knees, his legs straightening as he rose. With shaky hands, he inspected the rubble in front of us. 'How do we make our way through this?' he asked. 'There's hardly any space to move the stones and create an exit.'

A heaviness settled in my chest, its relentless grip blurring the edges of my vision. A pounding headache throbbed at my temples, and an unsettling sense of foreboding grew. 'I'm not feeling well,' I said.

Cooper took a deep breath. 'The oxygen is thinning. We need to find a way out quickly.' His brow furrowed as he explored every angle of our confined space, his fingers tracing the jagged rocks of the unstable walls. 'Felix, lend me a hand to move Saxon to the edge of the passageway.'

Saxon's head swayed from side to side as they lifted the stretcher, triggering a flashback of the moment Coral and I discovered Mary on the beach on Ruin. We had carried her together, each of us supporting her weight, all the way to the Black Cave.

Cooper wiped his dust-covered face. 'Let's form a chain, with me leading at the front. I'll dislodge smaller rubble from the top and pass it down to Felix. If we all relay it backwards, hopefully, we might create an opening or, at the very least, improve the airflow until we can think of a better plan.'

It felt unusual to witness Cooper taking charge, stepping into a role that typically belonged to Saxon. Nevertheless, he assumed the position confidently, and none of the crew seemed to question his newfound authority.

Placed at the tail end of the line, sweat dripped from my brow as my arms and legs strained under the weight of hauling and stacking rubble. My steps faltered, and I staggered back, clutching my chest. With a faint gasp, I slumped against the rock, my consciousness slipping away.

* * *

I woke to Cooper shaking me hard, his face hovering just inches from mine. His eyes gleamed with enthusiasm as his words rushed out. 'Jasmine, you did it. There are people on the other side – they're searching for you.' Cooper slid his arm under my back, hoisting me upright. 'You'll be fine. Everything is going to be okay.'

As my senses returned, I was aware of the suffocating heat and the cloying scent of dust. It filled my nostrils, coating the back of my throat. Claustrophobia gripped me, as I struggled to make sense of Cooper's excitement. I questioned if his news was simply a hallucination induced by our dire situation and my oxygen-starved state. Cooper's arm supported me, as he guided me towards the stone wall. I leaned in closer, pressing my ear against the rugged surface, straining to hear any sound filtering through.

With my senses sharpening, I picked up the frantic voices emanating through the rubble.

'Shout to them, Jasmine,' Cooper said, steadying me with both arms. 'Let them know you're safe.'

'Who sent you?' I called. My fingers pinched the skin around the glowing chip on my left arm. The realisation hit me; what if this was all a hoax? Malus would never allow me to escape from the grasp of his tyranny.

'Jasmine, is that you?' a voice reverberated from the other side. 'Robinia sent us. We've been tracing your microchip's signal on my tablet; and knew you were close by.'

As everything fell into place, a mix of emotions took over – joy, gratitude and an immense release of pent-up tension.

A tiny crack formed near the ceiling in the rubble, letting a spec of musty air into our stuffy space. Slowly, the gap expanded, some rocks falling inward, as the head of one of our rescuers emerged. 'We've formed a narrow channel with room for each of you to slither through one by one,' he stated, peering down at us. 'But you'll have to widen the opening at your end to squeeze your bodies inside,' he said, before disappearing from view.

I glanced down at Saxon lying on the stretcher. 'How do you think we'll get him through?' I asked Cooper.

Even though Cooper's hand on my shoulder fell light, it still offered reassurance. He raised his voice, calling out to the others beyond the debris. 'We've got an injured friend on a makeshift stretcher. If we lift him up and pass him through, do you reckon you can catch him at your end?'

'We'll do our best,' came the urgent reply. 'But time's against us. The soldiers will be closing in. You must move quickly, but be careful too, as this passage could crumble at any second.'

'We can do this,' Cooper said, easing the stretcher away from the wall. 'Let's gather around and spread ourselves out evenly.' Cooper positioned himself at Saxon's head, murmuring in his ear. 'You're going home, my friend, so hang in there.' Cooper's tense gaze connected with each of ours, one by one, the gravity of the situation reflecting in his eyes.

'I don't know if the robes will secure him tight enough to the planks. So, we'll lift him together as evenly as possible, on my count of three.'

As we all took a deep breath together, Cooper counted down. On his cue, we hoisted Saxon, our arms straining against the weight. Piloting the stretcher through the narrow opening was difficult. We braced ourselves, the air thick with anticipation as the makeshift contraption bumped and scraped against the precarious rock walls. The passage seemed endless, and just as Saxon was on the verge of disappearing, a voice echoed, breaking the tense silence. 'We've got sight of him. Easy. Keep him steady.' The minutes passed by like hours before the voice came again. 'Okay, send Jasmine next.'

Unease crept in, and doubt stirred inside me. The voice sounded familiar. As I focused on it, my wariness intensified. Leaning closer to Cooper, I kept my voice low. 'No, I'll be the last one to leave or I won't go at all.'

'Don't be foolish. They're here to help. You always wished for Robinia's people to rescue you. There's no need to be afraid.'

The doubts I harboured about Robinia and Aspen's

motives during my stay on Ruin resurfaced, refusing to fade away. I glanced at my friends who'd protected me through the darkest of times. 'I won't go ahead before of any of you. What if it's only me they're after and they leave you all behind? Cooper, you go first and check it's safe.

'You're not thinking straight,' Cooper replied.

Before I could respond, Felix grabbed hold of what appeared to be a solid chunk of rock and pulled himself up. His feet found footing where a few stones had tumbled. 'I'll lead the way. If there's any trouble, I'll call out.'

'Thank you,' I said, my voice a blend of relief and concern. 'Please be careful.'

It didn't take long before we heard Felix's muffled voice coming from the other side. 'Jasmine insisted we were all to come first, or she won't come at all.'

A burst of boisterous laughter erupted from the familiar voice. 'That's typical of her. The mines haven't changed her one bit.'

'Okay, we need to get moving,' Cooper said, gesturing to Astrid and Minx. 'Decide between you who goes next. I'll wait with Jasmine.'

'Off you go,' Minx said to Astrid with a grin. 'Hopefully, they've got a first aid kit and you'll get that leg looked at before it falls off.'

Astrid smirked. 'It's just a flesh wound,' she said, placing her feet and hands on outcrops of jagged rock, taking her upwards. 'The scar will be good for my hardball image.'

Astrid was no sooner through when Minx scaled to the top. Looking down, she flashed a cheeky smile. 'We live to fight another day, my friends.'

Alone with Cooper, I felt free to ask, 'Do you think Saxon will die?' It reminded me of how Coral must have felt when she repeatedly asked me the same question about Mary. Cooper was now my mentor, providing me with answers similar to what I had done for Coral.

'Saxon's a fighter. But, if death claims him, at least he'll die a free man.'

'Off you go,' I said, nodding towards the hole. 'Don't do something dodgy and bring the whole place down,' I teased.

Cooper bent down, placing a gentle peck on my cheek. 'I'll always protect you. You're like family to me.'

'Go,' I said, blinking back the tears stinging my eyes.

Alone in the darkness, the memories of Coral, Mary, Salix, Lily and Willow coursed through my mind – a torrent of their suffering and lost lives. The burden of guilt continued to stab at my heart, and if Saxon perished too, it would be unbearable. 'I'll avenge all of you, or die trying,' I whispered into the darkness as I climbed toward freedom. 'I'll hunt Malus down, along with every one of those who were complicit. They'll regret ever crossing my path.'

The narrow hole beckoned as I wriggled through on my front. The walls bore down oppressively as my skin grated against the scorching rock. It was a miracle we had delivered Saxon successfully. Each excruciating shuffle forward was a battle, my breaths growing shallow and constrained.

'Let me help you,' the voice from below offered, raising his hands to meet mine as they emerged through the hole.

His strong grip was a lifeline as he pulled me out and down, meeting his gaze eye-to-eye.

The air crackled with unspoken emotions as disbelief engulfed me. My pulse quickened, a mix of confusion and fear tightening my chest - leaving me feeling adrift and vulnerable. My saviour was Spindle – the boy who had despised me on Ruin.

3

As we emerged from the mine, the cool night air greeted us, offering a welcome relief to the heat on our skin. Spindle's team sprang into action, taking charge of Saxon on the stretcher, while Cooper and Felix worked out the kinks in their taut muscles.

Meanwhile, a figure hunched over Astrid's leg, skilfully stitching the wound with a needle and thread. Astrid grimaced, her teeth biting down on a rough leather strap to stifle her cries. Her fingers wrapped around Minx's hand in a vice-like grip, as waves of pain rolled through her. Once done, he saturated the wound with clear liquid from a small glass bottle.

Astrid's body convulsed with pain, her fist instinctively shooting towards his face. Before it could connect, Minx reacted with lightning speed, blocking the blow. Spindle exchanged glances with the man assisting Astrid, a silent communication that spoke volumes.

'We need to press forward,' Spindle called out. 'Three armoured vehicles are waiting for us at the base of the hill. They have orders to leave if we don't return to them soon.' He looked directly at me when he said, 'You'll have time to rest in a short while.'

As I closed the distance between us, I couldn't hide the shock stirred by his presence. 'Why would you risk your life to rescue me?'

His gaze bore into me with an intensity that bordered on patronising. 'I thought you would at least say thank you, but I'm not surprised. Perhaps Ash would have received a warmer welcome.' Swivelling on his heels, he called out to the other men, 'Remember to gather up all items, especially the first aid kits, or anything that could indicate our involvement in this mission.'

A wave of newfound guilt washed over me, stemming from my inability to express gratitude for his crucial role in my freedom. Perhaps the mere mention of Ash froze my mind, trapping the gratitude I owed Spindle inside.

Not only that, Spindle's hatred towards me was also deepseated, forming a formidable barrier to any friendship between us. He had instigated my demise in the mines. How could I express thankfulness without it sounding hollow or insincere? In a quest for peace of mind, I had to try to make things right. 'Spindle,' I called, catching up with him again. Once more, the words slipped through my grasp as I struggled to find something meaningful to say.

Shaking his head vigorously, he let out a long-drawn sigh. 'If the decision rested with me, I'd have willingly passed on this assignment. But, the leaders of the Resistance dispatched me to come for you. We follow orders, Jasmine, solely to bolster our cause. If you find fault in this, express your concerns to Robinia the next time you meet with her.'

It was obvious Robinia had enlisted Spindle into the Resistance at some stage, yet substantial gaps persisted in my understanding. 'How did you manage to smuggle yourself from Ruin?'

'Many changes have happened since your confinement. I'm now a guard on the mainland, strategically positioned in a role designed to execute any Resistance plans. As I mentioned, being here with you wasn't my choice.'

Spindle sidestepped around me. 'Let's get going,' he called out, spurring everyone into action.

Astrid limped beside me. 'Talk about tension. What's going on with that guy? He wasn't the friendliest but has soured more since you appeared.'

I shot Spindle a look of resentment before I answered. 'It was because of him I ended up in the mines.' As I recounted the events, my frustration simmered beneath the surface. 'I was supposed to have been cleansed in the firing chamber, but Spindle rallied the crowd behind him, orchestrating my exile here.' I paused, glancing away for a moment, collecting my thoughts. 'Malus had no choice but to comply because of the fervour Spindle whipped up.' My voice carried the unmistakable bitterness I felt. 'I guess Spindle's annoyed it was he who had to be the one to rescue me, especially when he can't stand the sight of me.'

As we descended the hill, a foul cloud of smouldering smoke cloaked our every step, clinging to us like a haunting spectre. My heart throbbed with anguish, echoing the unheard pleas of those still trapped inside the rubble.

There was little doubt in my mind the explosion resulted from Robinia's rescue plan. I prayed it was not deliberate, but rather a fatal glitch. How many more lives would be sacrificed because of me?

At the foot of the hill, a heap of black leather garments were folded neatly. Spindle and his men shed their clothes, donning the waiting attire, morphing back into the guise of government guards.

Three formidable vehicles waited. Spindle tapped the side of the first one. 'Put the injured man in here. We have a secluded base where a medic will attend to him.' His gaze turned to Astrid. 'We can provide you with antibiotics and a more potent pain relief when we get there.'

'Can I travel with Saxon?' I asked, my voice cracking. 'He looked after me in the mine, and I owe it to him to be by his side. We all should be with him, as we are his people.'

'Suit yourself,' Spindle said, his voice flat. 'But we need to get moving.'

Cooper and Felix raised the stretcher into the back of the vehicle, positioning it at the centre of the floor. Astrid, Minx and I climbed up beside them, settling into slim, lined benches, instantly catching a scent of oil. One of Spindle's men passed in a crate containing bottled water before closing the door with a clunk, plunging us into darkness.

As the vehicle lurched into motion, harsh fluorescent lights illuminated the space, casting a glaring glow. We rumbled along for a while, with Saxon moaning painfully.

Eventually, the vehicle halted, and the door smoothly slid ajar. The man who had initially locked us in now held out his hand, helping each of us down. 'Leave your injured friend there,' he said, nodding toward Saxon. 'It's warmer and will be easier for the medic to check him over.

The day was breaking, and a silver-grey light pierced through the dark sky. I could hear Coral's voice in my head. '*If we could unharness the Sun, would the Earth heal?*' She posed the question to Robinia and Aspen when we were held in the holding pen awaiting our fate. I pushed thoughts of Coral aside, determined not to let grief consume me.

'*Recall moments of joy and hold them close in your heart when the burden of sadness weighs you down,*' said the voice in my mind, speaking words Saxon had used to comfort me when I felt unable to carry on. I closed my eyes and tipped my chin upwards, relishing the sunlight caressing my face.

Inhaling deeply, I surveyed the expansive, flat terrain. It

wasn't as bleak as Ruin, with resilient tufts of grass poking through cracks in the barren terrain. The earth beneath my feet had a spongy texture, made from clusters of green moss.

Spindle appeared at my side, his eyes lingering on my head. 'You have hair.'

'They don't worry about such things in the mines,' I remarked, lifting my hand to run it through my short crop. 'They would douse us with chemicals to eradicate head or body lice at the end of each shift.'

'We've got a water tower equipped with makeshift showers. It'll allow you to wash off the coal dust. We lack purification facilities out here, hence the rainwater remains black. It's not contaminated and will help a little cleaning you up.'

'Thanks,' I said, aware of how tattered we all looked.

'We'll heat some soup, but you should keep hydrated. Even though we're off the main track, we're not out of danger yet. My orders are to transport you to a secret location a few days' drive from here. The sooner we get going, the better.'

The breath caught in the back of my throat. 'I'm not going anywhere with you. I'm staying with Saxon and my friends. We have plans, and are going to the caves.'

Spindle arched an eyebrow. 'I can't allow that. You must come with me and meet up with the Resistance. Progress has been made since your incarceration, and our movement is growing. You can engage with the cave people later, as that is a part of our plan, but you must come with me first.'

Cooper hurried over. 'The medic is assessing Saxon's condition. He's still unconscious, but I thought I should inform you.' He must have detected my unease. 'Is everything okay here?'

'I was telling Jasmine you can shower before you eat. We also have a box of uniforms which was supposed to be handed in to the salt factory in the capital. We'll say some went amiss, as you need fresh clothes. They might be over-sized but will do until you reach your home. One of the vehicles will drop you off along their route.But, Jasmine must come with me.'

Cooper's loud objection carved through the tension. 'If Jasmine's going anywhere, it will be by her choice, not yours.'

It drew the attention of Spindle's men, who formed a tight circle around us, ready to intervene if Spindle needed them. The entire episode made me realise that even though we were liberated, our challenges were far from over.

I rested my hand on Cooper's elbow. 'Let's wash, then eat. We can discuss the practicalities later.'

It was like meeting my friends all over again. Even with dust and soot ingrained in the lines on their faces, I saw them clearly for the first time.

Cooper's beard boasted a sandy brown colour with thick hair to match. His large hazel eyes held wrinkles at the side, which he jokingly called his laughter lines.

Felix possessed a mop of blond waves and captivating blue eyes. Though not as tall as Cooper, he still stood taller than Minx and Astrid. Speaking of Minx, her red hair and green eyes were complimented by a tiny black mole above her lip. Reluctantly, I acknowledged this might be what Rowan would look like, had we been allowed to grow our hair on Ruin.

But it was Astrid who captured and held my attention. Her skin reminded me of the night sky and her hair formed a majestic crown of tightly coiled curls. I had never seen anyone convey such striking beauty. Even Spindle glanced in her direction, more than a few times.

Their past suffering had affected them, visible from the wary glances from their hollowed faces. Nevertheless, their fighting spirit remained. As for myself, I was thrilled to reach up and brush my fingers through soft waves, a luxury previously denied to me. My objective was to allow my hair to grow as long as possible, or at the very least, enough to hide the pink scar tracing along my jawline.

We sat on the cold ground dipping chunks of hardened bread into piping-hot soup. Basic yet satisfying, it stood as the finest meal I had tasted since departing Ruin. In the mines, our meagre sustenance arrived randomly – mostly a mishmash of scraps and remnants sourced from the factories in the neighbouring settlements.

Spindle avoided eye contact. He and his guards maintained a reserved distance as we ate, offering no conversation. Afterwards, I balanced a stack of plastic bowls in my arms and wandered over to the trough, our makeshift sink brimming with black rainwater.

Spindle joined me, dumping his and his men's dirty bowls alongside mine. 'One of the men will wash these up. You're not here as our servant.'

Ignoring him, I rinsed the dishes, stacking them on a small table at the side to let them drip dry. 'You do realise we're utterly exposed here, in the event of Malus's soldiers discovering us. There's no shelter, only miles of open space,' I said, gazing across the vast, flat landscape.

'We're heading north. Hardly anyone ventures this far due to the harsh weather. There are no settlements, not even the people from the caves would try to establish homes here. Patrols do come by every so often, but only for routine, or military training.'

Incapable of concealing my scepticism, I turned to face him. 'The weather seems fine to me.'

'It's changeable, a lot like Ruin.' His words trailed off, and an awkward silence filled the space. It appeared his brain was working overtime, desperately searching for something to say. 'If a drone flies by, you and your friends must hide inside one of the vehicles. We'll look like a normal patrol without you. Malus will know you survived the blast because your microchip will show on their systems.' He looked down at my right wrist, where the implant sat beneath my skin. 'They'll know where you are and will come for you. That's why you need to come with me. If you go to the caves,' he said, nodding towards my friends. 'You'll endanger every one of them.'

'And will you take out the chip Aspen implanted in me too?' I asked, my fingers drumming against it.

'That's what led us to you and saved your life. I don't care if they take that one out or not. My orders are to get you to the Resistance outpost and return to my unit in the capital before suspicion of my duplicity is aroused.'

'Jasmine,' Minx interrupted, beckoning with a frantic wave. 'Come quick. It's Saxon. He's regained consciousness and is asking for you.'

My heart leapt in my chest as I sprinted towards her. 'Is he still inside the vehicle?' I asked, my voice mixed with hope and fear as I followed her hurried steps.

As we neared, I could see him, lying on the stretcher surrounded by my friends. They made room for me as I climbed aboard to sit by his side, grasping his hand. His eyes were half-open, and his forehead glistened with a sickly damp- ness. Short shallow breaths sounded, ragged and painful. The bloody clothing that had clung to him was now cut open. It exposed the raw red flesh across his arms and chest, stained with blood, sweat and dust.

My anxiety deepened, noticing the man attending to Saxon was dressed as a guard. 'You're not a medic,' I yelled, my fear for Saxon rising. 'He needs a proper professional who knows what to do.'

'I'm sorry,' the guard said. 'When out in operations, we are whatever any person needs us to be. I did my best.'

Before I could vent my anger further, Saxon's trembling fingers feebly squeezed mine. 'Bonnie lass,' he said, his voice barely a whisper. 'Don't fret.'

I placed his hand against my cheek. 'Saxon,' I said, my voice faltering as tears spilled down my face.

'Where's Zander?' he asked, his dimming eyes searching beyond me.

It was Cooper who answered. 'He's on his way home to inform our people of our escape.'

With a heart full of gratitude, I glanced at Cooper, recognising the comfort he provided to Saxon, shielding him from the the weight of worry in his final moments.

'Look after him, Cooper. Zander can be hot-headed, but he's a good lad. Tell him to make me proud,' he murmured, before shifting his focus back to me. 'They came for you. Just like you thought they would,' he s

aid, gasping in air. 'Now go and ignite a rebellion that will reshape our world. Be the heroine you were born to be.'

I rubbed my free hand through his wiry grey hair. 'Not without you. I need you by my side.'

'I'll be with you always, my presence lingering in your heart,' he whispered, his gaze heavy. A wistful smile touched his face. 'It's good to die a free man.' His chest heaved one final time, as his life slipped away.

I collapsed onto his chest, my fists pounding the vehicle floor. 'It isn't fair. I can't bear the thought of losing you,' I wailed.

Peering inside, Spindle stood frozen, speechless at the sight of my heartache. Cooper gently coaxed me away from Saxon's side, wrapping me in a warm embrace.

4

We buried Saxon in the frigid ground, Cooper stacking stones and piling them high to form a solemn mound over his grave. He picked up a piece of flint and scratched words in the old language on the a worn boulder placed at the bottom.

'What do they say?' I asked, still choked with grief.

'Saxon died a free man,' Cooper replied.

We all took turns sharing stories of Saxon, bidding heartfelt farewells while Spindle and his men loitered nearby. I could sense their growing restlessness.

Guiding Cooper away from the others, I explained, 'I'm going to go with Spindle. Malus knows I'm alive and will track me through my chip implant. The Resistance has medics who can remove it. It's the first step to being truly free.'

Cooper's brow furrowed. 'Do you trust him?'

'No more than I trust Robinia or Aspen, but what choice do I have? I can't go with you knowing I'll endanger your people.'

'Can Spindle guarantee your safety?'

'Can anyone? None of us know what's ahead. All I know is Robinia set this plan in motion. The Resistance appears more organised than I initially realised. She positioned Spindle here on the mainland with a plan to take me to an outpost. Spindle also mentioned I'd be returned to you in the caves, but I'm not sure of the details yet.'

Conflicting emotions danced across his face. 'Do you want me to come with you?'

'No, you need to get the others back to the caves. You've all been away from your families for far too long. Word of the explosion will spread, and they'll be worried.'

Cooper nodded. 'There's Zander too. I hope he made it out and is heading home now.'

Spindle approached, his expression hesitant. 'We need to get moving. The first vehicle heads back towards the capital and can take you and the others,' he said, addressing Cooper. 'There's no mountain range where we're going, so going back with them will take you closer to where you need to be.'

Cooper offered his hand to Spindle. 'I believe we're on the same side, and working together will create a bigger impact. Jasmine has coordinates, so she knows where to find us when you're ready to return her.'

Spindle hesitated, his blank gaze falling on Cooper's outstretched hand.

'He doesn't understand,' I explained to Cooper. 'On Ruin, there's no such thing as handshakes. Your gestures are as foreign to him as they were to me when I first met Mary.' I shifted my gaze to Spindle. 'Take his hand. It's an act of trust.'

Despite his cynical demeanour, Spindle did as he was told. Cooper drew Spindle in close, his lips against Spindle's ear. The words were said softly, but the meaning behind them was anything but. 'If you let anything happen to her,' he said, glancing at me. 'I'll hunt you down and kill you.'

Spindle maintained his hold on Cooper's grip, squeezing with force. 'You don't need to worry. My orders are to guard her with my life. Being a walking antidote for Control, she's too important to our cause. If we can at least release a percentage of the population from its spell, the government will crumble.' His tone hardened, as did his features as he faced me. 'You've five minutes to say your goodbyes, and then we leave.'

I clenched my fists, fighting to keep my emotions steady as I choked back tears. Memories flooded my mind, each one reminding me of the bond we shared throughout our hardship. How could I say goodbye to them? The weight of the moment pressed down on me, heavier than I had anticipated. Cooper, Felix, Astrid and Minx were now my family; they had taken care of me and helped me survive. I hadn't thought to ask Spindle how long I'd been locked away, as there was no such thing as time in the mines. But it felt as though I had been with them for an eternity.

'He appears rather young to command a group of men,' Felix said, eyeing Spindle as he gave orders.

'Spindle showed great potential back on Ruin.' I'm not sure why, but my voice took on a defensive tone. 'I'm surprised he was granted such a high-ranking position among the guards because of his standoff with Malus at my trial. There's so much that doesn't make sense.'

We joined together in a tight cluster, arms interlinked over shoulders, heads bowed and touching. The fragrance of carbolic soap wafted among us, a welcome difference from the mingling scent of dirt, sweat and dust.

'You know where to find us when you're ready,' Astrid said, a touch of sadness in her voice. 'Saxon was right, you were born to be a heroine.'

The desire to break down into floods of tears overwhelmed me, but I managed to control them, even as light sobs escaped. 'Please find Mary's family. Let them know I hope to meet them soon. Tell them how brave she was, and about my promise to avenge her death,' I said, between hiccups and gulped air.

A heavy silence settled over us, the impending reality of our parting striking a bitter blow. Cooper's eyes conveyed a depth of unexpressed thoughts, and none of us could voice the magnitude of the emotions we all felt.

'It's time,' Spindle called, jumping into the second vehicle.

As I hugged each of my friends for the final time, a lump formed in my throat. These moments, these connections forged in the fire of adversity, were all I had left. Each hug held a universe of unspoken words, a silent plea to freeze time and keep us together for a little longer. 'I'll keep you all in my heart,' I whispered, my voice barely audible. With a wavering smile, I turned away - forcing myself to walk forward, even though I longed to remain in the safety of their presence.

Spindle's jaw clenched as he banged on the wall that separated the passengers from the driver. His gaze flickered briefly towards me, a silent acknowledgement passing between us of the challenges we now faced together. The vehicle roared to life, and as the sliding door closed, my friends vanished from sight.

For much of the morning, we journeyed in subdued silence, each of us lost in our thoughts. Whenever our eyes met, they quickly flitted away, as if seeking refuge from the burden of hidden sorrows. The loneliness engulfing me felt familiar, reminiscent of the isolation I endured during my passage across the Pewter Sea to the mainland. The hum of the engine provided a steady backdrop to the silence surrounding us, broken only by the occasional creak of the seats or the soft shuffle of feet.

I twisted to face Spindle. 'You were at the pier to see me off when I left Ruin. I saw you stand on an outcrop of rock. Why?'

He sighed. 'Out of all the questions you should be asking, you think of the most feeble.'

'Well, I know it wasn't because you were sorry to see me go.'

My mind buzzed with countless questions, yet I grappled to find a starting point. An unsettling feeling seeped in, unsure if I

'What other reason could there be?'

'For the girl they claim to be unique, clever and brave, you sure are stupid,' he remarked, rising to his feet and pulling me up with him. 'Come on, if we don't go now, the others will devour Alder's efforts, and we'll starve for the rest of the journey.'

5

It wasn't long before we were back on the road again. Spindle remained tight-lipped, his gaze fixed on the space ahead. Eventually, I must have dozed off, only to awaken with my head cradled in the curve of his neck. His head rested on mine, his cheek cushioned by my hair. I stayed still, careful not to disturb his sleep.

We must have covered a significant distance, as the outside had plunged into darkness, with an inky sky devoid of stars when Taxus slid the door open. 'Time to medicate,' he declared. 'The air's beginning to thin.'

Spindle stirred, yawned, and stretched. A faint blush crept into his cheeks as our gazes met in the dim light. If I didn't know any better, I would swear there was a fleeting warmth in his eyes.

Taxus patted Thorn on the back as he jumped out and passed him. 'Can you take the wheel for a bit? I could use a short break.'

'I'll take over,' Spindle volunteered before Thorn had a chance to reply. It gave the impression he was trying to put some space between us.

The rest of the group followed Spindle out, casting off their leather jackets, and rolling up the sleeves of their cotton shirts. They lined up before Linden, who methodically jabbed their arms with the serum he'd prepared earlier.

Your turn,' Linden said, as I stepped out towards him, offering my arm. 'This will hurt for a few minutes, but when your lungs are struggling later, you'll be glad of it.'

'Is where we're going that unpleasant?' I asked, bracing myself for the sting of the needle.

'We're accustomed to it, having travelled this way many times before, but we still take precautions. You won't die without the medication, but the journey will be extremely difficult. This will hopefully prevent nausea, nose bleeds and a heavy lump weighing on your lungs and chest. The body takes time to adjust. This,' he paused, pricking my skin to let the serum enter, 'It will certainly help. If you still find it challenging, I've prepared some inhalers. It's important not to panic. Just keep reassuring yourself that you'll be all right.'

Linden wasn't joking – the pain was excruciating, and even after the sting subsided, my arm remained a dead weight.

Spindle thumped the side of the van. 'Let's get moving,' he shouted. 'Just one more pitstop before we reach our destination. Once we've delivered Jasmine, we'll double back and resume our posts alongside the government guards until the next call.'

Everyone piled back into the back of the vehicle, leaving me standing alone. Sensing a twinge of awkwardness, I stole a momentary look at Spindle before making my way towards the driver's cab.

He slouched in behind the wheel, roaring the engine to life with a heavy hand on the ignition. 'What do you think you're playing at?' he asked, a puzzled expression darkening his features. 'You belong in the back with the others.'

'I can't believe you're going to abandon me,' I said, brushing off his question. 'If I had known, I would've insisted on Cooper coming with us.'

'I'm not abandoning you, I'm handing you over. There's a significant difference. You have to grasp the danger we're all facing. If I'm absent from guard duty during my next shift, it could spell serious trouble and raise suspicion. Besides, when did you become so needy?'

His words hit me with the force of a lightning bolt. I had lost all confidence, felt submerged in unfamiliar territory, and was terrified at the prospect of being alone. 'I guess you'll be glad to see the back of me,' I said, feeling rattled. Spindle didn't answer, and I was anxious he was going to fall into silence again. 'How long has it been since I left Ruin?'

He sighed, 'Five months.'

'So much has happened. You've come of age and operate covertly for the Resistance.'

I hoped sparking a conversation would prompt him to open up, bridging the gaps I so desperately needed filled. His lips remained sealed as he kept his eyes on the road. I tried again. 'We haven't had a chance to talk about what happened back on Ruin.'

His knuckles whitened as he clenched his fingers around the steering wheel. 'And you choose to bring this up now?'

I bowed my head, uttering, 'I'm sorry for what happened to Salix.' I drew a deep breath, attempting to quell the tremor from my voice. 'He was your best friend. Not a day passes without me thinking of him or the others. So, I understand if you hate me more than ever because it was all my fault.'

His face softened as he stole a glance at me. 'I carry guilt too,' he confessed. 'If I hadn't been so bold during your trial, maybe Lily and Willow would still be alive.'

'You should've let Malus send me to the Cleansing Chambers.'

Spindle's jaw clenched. 'Your death was never an option. I

had orders to rally the crowds and prevent your cleansing at any cost. It was meant to be me who faced the Cleansing Chamber, as we ran so many scenarios, not thinking for one moment Lily or Willow would pay the price. Robinia assured me time and time again, that none of the others were at risk and Malus would demand for it to be me who'd swap places with you. If I had foreseen it otherwise, I'd never have agreed.'

My hand flew to my mouth to stifle a gasp. 'Hold on, you were prepared to give up your life for mine?'

His response came in the form of a curt nod, leaving me uneasy, and sensing hidden complexities behind his revelation. My mind churned, caught in a whirlwind of thoughts. Connecting the dots, I concluded, 'You were a member of the Resistance before my trial.'

His reply was simple. 'Long before. But I'm not willing to share that with you at the moment.'

Now, it was me who succumbed to silence, grappling with a tidal wave of disbelief. 'What about Rowan?' I finally managed to ask, her name sending involuntary shivers up my spine. 'Where is she now?'

'Rowan serves as a junior government official stationed in the capital's Midpoint. She travels around various smaller settlements, carrying out Malus's orders. It won't surprise you to learn that high expectations rest upon her shoulders.'

'Do you ever come across her?' I asked, curious about her movements. I had made a promise to avenge all those I'd lost, and finding Rowan would be a good starting point. 'How easy would it be to get to her?'

Spindle nodded. 'Yes, I see her often, as part of my duties as a Government Guard. Your access to her is out of the question. Each little town is a domed entity, and just like on Ruin, you need your microchip to gain access.'

My irritation flared hearing Rowan was beyond my grasp. 'You could get to her though? Do you still speak to her?'

'It's different now. She's on Control, and her memory of me is stilted. I only pretend to be medicated, and if I were to stop and spark a conversation, it would look suspicious. Anyway, Rowan's not your concern.'

His reasoning left me speechless. 'How can you say that? Of course, she's my concern. She needs to be held accountable for the part she played in all that happened.'

Spindle was adamant. 'No, Jasmine, your objective is to help find an antidote to Control, so we can put an end to the masses being enslaved. Only then will we have a fighting chance to get rid of the psychopaths who lead us.'

The thought of being hidden away and tested on didn't sit well with me, even though I knew the importance it would have.

A look of curiosity crossed Spindle's features. 'You haven't mentioned Ash, have you? I thought you'd be desperate to know all about *him*.'

I shuddered, the idea of Ash's head on a spike beside Rowan's consumed my thoughts too. But, I couldn't say that. 'It was his betrayal that put the whole saga in motion.'

'It wasn't. You sheltering the old woman in a cave instead of reporting her to Command started all of this.' He spoke through gritted teeth. 'Ash, sadly, was another victim.'

My nails dug into the edge of the seat, biting into the scuffed leather as I struggled to rein in my anger. Each muscle in my body tightened, a taut coil of frustration building inside me. Unable to hold back any longer, I spat the words out, 'He knew we were hiding Mary and told Aconite.'

His words carried a hint of reason, as if he were trying to mend the hatred I held for his friend. 'I managed to speak with Ash before he was arrested,' he said, in a soothing tone. 'He told me he sneaked into the holding pen to visit you and was devastated you thought he'd betrayed you. He could have been lying, but I honestly don't think so.'

'Ash was arrested,' I said, surprised. 'How did that happen?'

'Aconite and Malus saw the footage of his visit to the holding pen. Robinia claimed you set him up. She knew because you smiled at the hidden camera after Ash left.'

My mind was a storm of doubt and uncertainty. I was torn between anger and the possibility I had misunderstood Ash's involvement. 'But all those lies he concocted at my trial to save his skin . . .' I said, my voice trailing off.

Spindle's tone softened. 'What he did was unforgivable, and I told him so. Even me, who you thought hated you, would never have lied to that extent.'

I reflected on the trial, remembering the part Spindle played. He'd been honest, confessing his dislike for me, but had never fabricated lies about our encounters.

'Thank you,' I whispered, a sense of gratitude washing over me as I realised Spindle was the only one from my small group of friends who stood by me, even if he didn't intend to. Lily had sided with Rowan and backed up her lies, despite the evident discomfort it caused her. The question of whether Salix, had he not been medicated with Control, would have chosen to support me, weighed on my mind. The thought of him not having free will to do so was deeply distressing.

Spindle seemed to sense my gaze and turned toward me, his lips curling into a rare smile. In those passing seconds, there was a spark of camaraderie between us, bridging the gap of our differences and solidifying our deepening bond. 'For the record, I never hated you,' he said tactfully. 'It was complicated, and I still struggle with emotions. I guess being brought up in a society where feelings were suppressed affected me more than the rest of you.'

His words exuded an honest vulnerability, shedding light on the intricate web of our upbringing on Ruin. I thought back to the memory of the beating Robinia had given Spindle in our nursery years, where she thrashed him with a cane, and wondered if he remembered it too. I was going to ask when the microchip in my right wrist itched and began to glow. I rubbed it fiercely.

Spindle's gaze fixed on it too, his expression tightening with genuine concern. 'I had hoped for more time,' he said, chewing his bottom lip. 'But they now know you survived the blast. They'll attempt to track you down and will come for you. We need to reach the outpost immediately - our risk factor just skyrocketed.

6

I started to feel breathless, light-headed and tired. 'I think I'm going to be sick,' I said, placing my hand to my mouth. 'Can you please stop the vehicle.'

Spindle's voice remained calm and reassuring. 'There's a water flask under your seat. Take it and sip slowly. Concentrate on your breathing. If it worsens, we'll stop, and you can use one of the inhalers Linden prepared.'

After sipping water, I closed my eyes and focused on my breath, inhaling and exhaling slowly, trying to capture as much air in my lungs as possible. It was obvious Spindle was unaffected. I surmised he'd undertaken this journey a few times and had grown accustomed to the effects of thinning air. The rhythmic vibrations of the road beneath me lulled me into a drowsy state. My eyelids grew heavy and I drifted off to sleep. Suddenly, the vehicle lurched to a halt, jolting me awake. Blinking groggily, I glanced around, trying to orient myself.

'We'll stop here for ten minutes,' Spindle said, rubbing a hand over his head. 'There's some dense thicket nearby where you can relieve yourself, and Linden should have some wipes if you'd like to freshen up.'

The night sky dissolved into rich crimson and deep amethyst hues as I leapt down from the driver's cab. Beneath my feet, the ground was firm and gritty, coated with dust that stirred with each step. Despite the thin, oxygen-deprived air, it carried a faint scent of open space and liberation. It also served as a reminder of the vastness beyond the confines of our journey.

'How're you coping?' Linden asked, handing me an inhaler.

'Not great,' I admitted, taking the small tube. 'But I suppose without your potion earlier, I'd feel even worse.'

'It gets easier. The mines won't have helped your lungs. The medic will give you a thorough check-up once we reach the outpost.'

'No time for chit-chat,' Spindle said, his voice firm. 'We need to get moving. Jasmine's chip is active, meaning they'll pinpoint our location soon. We can't afford to be caught out here.'

'Can't Linden remove it?' I asked, my voice a little hesitant. 'If it stops them from tracking us and ensures your safe return, I'm happy to have him do it.'

Spindle and Linden exchanged glances. 'It's too dangerous,' Spindle said, after a few seconds. 'We don't have the proper medical equipment, and you could bleed to death.'

'Really?' I asked, glancing down at my wrist. 'It just sits below the surface. With a knife and some tweezers, I could pull it free myself.'

A chorus of laughter broke out, brightening their faces. Linden shook his head. 'If only it were that simple,' he said, patting my shoulder. 'The microchip has roots that latch onto nerve cells. It's a very technical procedure, and too much could go wrong.'

'Even reprogramming has an element of risk,' Spindle explained. 'Each of us who aligns with the resistance under-goes a procedure to add an extra transmitter. This allows our technical team to place us somewhere other than where we are currently.'

Linden must have noticed the confusion flit across my face. 'Right now, we're all on leave and resting until our next guard duty assignment is given in the coming week,' he said.

'Just five more minutes,' Spindle said, gulping back air and reaching for one of Linden's inhalers.

I left him in conversation with Taxus and ventured toward the thicket bushes to freshen up. They stood out, sturdy and prickly, unlike the saplings we struggled to cultivate back on Ruin. Once done, I noticed an odd, rounded stone protruding from the dusty ground. Bending down, I scraped away the loose earth around it unearthing a small human skull.

As I took in my surroundings, I noticed bone fragments scattered all over. Among them were skeletal fingers and sections of rib cage, some partially buried while others lay fully exposed.

'What's taking so long?' Spindle asked, appearing at my side, his eyes also taking in the worrying scene.

'What happened here?' I asked, gripped by a feeling of unease. 'It's as if we've stumbled upon a disturbed burial ground.'

'Come on,' Spindle said, taking me by the arm. 'We need to go.'

'But these poor people. Something awful must have happened.'

'Jasmine, we don't have time to figure it out now. Let's get you to the outpost first, or our bones will be scattered here too.'

Spindle was right, the longer I stalled, the greater the danger I brought to him and his men. 'Just so you know,' I remarked, following him back to the vehicle. 'I would go to great lengths to protect you and your team, even if it meant chopping off my arm at the elbow.'

Spindle chuckled, his smile reaching his blue eyes. 'There

will be no lost limbs on my watch,' he assured. 'Come on,' he said, helping me mount back into the rear of the vehicle. 'Taxus is taking over the driving again. Try to get some sleep, and when you wake up next, you'll be there.'

* * *

I rubbed away the remnants of sleep from my eyes as the door slid open, shivering as a frigid breeze snaked in. We stepped out into the underground tunnel. Our footsteps echoed off the cold, solid floor while the air hung heavy with the smell of ancient concrete and dust. Dulled lanterns on the walls cast long shadows and did little to hide the moss that crept over the aged bricks.

'What is this place?' I asked as we descended further underground.

'It's an old military bunker that was used before the End of Days,' Spindle said, his gaze settling briefly on Thorn. 'Given your expertise as our historian, you should tell Jasmine your theory.'

Thorn nodded, a grin breaking out on his face as he spoke. 'I'm not sure how much you know about weather manipulation. But, before the End of Days, weather was weaponised, and I believe this was a place where people gathered to hunker down to try and stay safe. There's a small museum with artefacts, so we've pieced together some of the happenings. But it was certainly a military compound. The area became toxic, and the outpost was abandoned and forgotten for generations. Rumours of its presence surfaced with the early Resistance, and it was found and brought it back to life.'

'So, our government isn't aware of its existence anymore?' A chilling realisation struck me. 'What if I've led them here? If they're tracking me, they could end up at this location.'

Spindle shook his head. 'They'll have a rough idea of where

we are, which makes our journey to and from here more dangerous. Now we're inside and underground, our transmitters block the signal. We need to get the chip out of your wrist so you can move forward positively.'

'And they have no clue that this bunker exists?' I asked, unable to hide the scepticism from my tone.

'None at all,' Thorn confirmed. 'Those in the Resistance who found it quickly removed any traces of a military compound or outpost from historical records.'

'How long has the Resistance been active?' I asked.

Thorn's smile was warm and friendly. 'The Resistance has been around before you or I were born. Take your friends in the caves as an example. Many defected over generations, creating a way of life as close to the old world as possible. Then there are those of us who stayed, working from the inside. We've never been able to unify both fighting platforms to make a real difference. The people from the caves are aloof and don't tend to trust our motives. The guerrilla warfare they adopt often sets us back, rather than push our freedom forward.'

I could understand their lack of trust, especially considering my reservations about Robinia and Aspen's theories. Recalling our conversation during my imprisonment and trial, I found the whole situation ludicrous. A sigh escaped me. 'Robinia and Aspen were vague with information, which made me think the Resistance was in its infancy. She mentioned they waited for signs and then knew what to do. Yet, being here with all of you, it's so much bigger.'

Spindle was quick to answer. 'That's what we're all told until trust is fully established. Brace yourself, because over the next few days, you'll receive an overwhelming amount of information.'

The tunnel narrowed and wound its way to a massive set of steel doors, towering above us like a fortress gate. To the side, there was a square panel decked with intricate mechanical symbols. One by one, the men entered a code and then positioned their right wrists on the scanner.

The doors parted with a faint mechanical sound. It was only then I saw how thick and reinforced they were. Layer upon layer of steel pressed together to withstand the most extreme warfare conditions. No wonder people had gathered here to make it their last stand.

We stepped inside the well lit and modern elevator, a stark contrast to the aging ruggedness of the tunnel we left behind. With a soft hum, we began our descent deeper into the belly of the earth. The elevator shuddered to a stop, opening up to a vast corridor. Its high ceilings and polished floors created the illusion of endless space while the faint whir of cameras stationed in every corner tracked our movement.

'I'll escort Jasmine to the medical bay,' Spindle said. 'If you could update Control and then get our supplies ready for our return trip. I'll meet up with you in ten minutes.'

Linden rubbed his hand through my short crop of hair. 'Don't let them shave this off, it suits you. You're in good hands, Jasmine, and have nothing to worry about.'

In a moment that took everyone by surprise, I hugged him tightly, gratitude flooding through me. 'Thank you,' I whispered in his ear. 'I know you did your best for Saxon, and I truly appreciate it.' I turned to face them all. 'Thank you for rescuing me, and for helping my friends escape back to the caves.'

'Come on,' Spindle said, pulling me in the opposite direction. 'It's not as if you'll never see them again. You're part of the Resistance now, and fighting on the same team. Your paths will cross sooner than you think.'

'Not if Malus has anything to do with it,' I said. The fact all of them could be found because of me weighed heavy on my conscience. 'Would you be able to stay with me, Spindle? I've lost so many friends, and having you near makes me feel safe?

'Friends come and go around here.'

As he led me to the entrance of the medical bay, Spindle took hold of my hand. A comforting warmth spread through me as our fingers intertwined, and my heart also beat a little faster. His piercing blue eyes met mine, and I could hear the sincerity in his voice. 'You'll be fine. I'm leaving you in good hands.'

My stomach flipped unexpectedly. I longed to caress the side of his face, trace my fingers across his lips and draw his head closer; yearning for his mouth to meet mine.

The doors to the medical bay slid open with an inflated hiss, shattering the fragile bubble of intimacy we shared. My gaze snapped away from Spindle's, only to freeze in shock at the unexpected sight awaiting me.

With my heart racing and mouth suddenly dry, I confronted my newfound companion. Their presence electrified the air, thick with confusion and outrage. Spindle's offhand suggestion to leave me in capable hands now felt like a stab in the back. The desire to kiss him faded, replaced by a primal instinct to punch him square in his gut.

7

Memories flooded back – betrayal, deception, and heartbreak. My heart thumped erratically, while a storm of emotions churned within me. 'What's he doing here?' I asked Spindle, my voice trembling with a mixture of anger and pain, as my gaze remained fixed on Ash.

'I'll leave you two to it,' Spindle said, releasing my hand and taking a step back. 'You've much to catch up on, and I need to get going.'

'Wait,' I said, my fingers wrapping around Spindle's arm and pulling him back. 'Where's Aspen? I thought you said I needed my microchip removed urgently?' The high pitch in my voice mirrored my escalating concern. 'Don't tell me Ash is now a medic? Seriously, you can't leave me with *him*. And going by the past, Malus will know exactly where I am.'

Spindle shook me off as if my fingers were burning his skin. 'Don't be silly. Ash is our friend. He's part of the Resistance, or he wouldn't be here.'

My heart thudded against my chest, each beat pulsing loudly in my ears. 'No way, I won't stay here. It's far too dangerous. I have scars on my back because of him,' I said, pointing my finger at Ash. 'Coral and all our friends are dead too.'

'I've already explained, Ash didn't betray you,' Spindle said, and turned to Ash. 'Go and fetch Aspen, he should have been here to meet her, not you.'

A heightened sense of fear took over and before Spindle or Ash could act, I squeezed past Spindle and sprinted down the corridor, making my way back to the lift. Acting on pure adrenalin and fear, I wasn't sure what I hoped to accomplish.

'Jasmine,' Spindle called, catching up with me and yanking me back. 'What's gotten into you?'

Pivoting without a second thought, I delivered a hefty blow to his nose with my fist.

The sound of the smack echoed through the corridor, and I watched in slow motion as a dam of blood burst forth, splattering his face. Spindle swiftly pulled the taser attached to his belt and delivered a shock to my neck, and then the world faded into darkness.

* * *

When my eyes blinked open, it was as if I were peering through frosted glass. Blurred shapes, both distant and near, appeared with softened edges, while an unbearable thirst parched my throat.

'Water,' I croaked to the silhouette sitting beside my bed. Gentle hands lifted my head and guided a cup to my lips. Afterwards, as my head touched the pillow, I drifted off into a light sleep. Though hazy, I picked up on the subtle beeping of machines, the soft rustle of movement and the hum of a fan circulating cool air. Voices, their names eluding me, drifted in and out.

'How's she doing,' one said, their hand resting on my brow.

'She sipped some water, and her eyes keep flickering. Spindle said she saw the graveyard on the way here.'

'Spindle wasn't supposed to stop there. What was he thinking?'

'He said he had no choice. Jasmine asked about it, but he didn't offer her any explanation. He implied that was your job.'

'Call me when she's fully conscious.'

* * *

I woke with a blinding headache as if a sledgehammer were pounding against the walls of my skull.

'Welcome back. How're you feeling?' Ash asked.

'Like Spindle ran over me with his armed vehicle,' I said, too groggy to fight. There was no point, I was stuck in a situation where Ash was here and I would have to find a way to work around my hate for him. 'When did Spindle learn to drive anyway?'

'He knew how to drive before leaving Ruin. Most of us did as we learned inside the illusion dome in the gym.'

'I was never good enough to be allowed inside,' I said, now cursing myself for not having tried harder.

'I'm sure you'll get a chance to learn, and I bet you'll be good at it too,' Ash said.

There was so much I wanted to ask. Yet my distrust of him prevented me from doing so. An awkward silence hung between us.

'Let me go and fetch Aspen. You'll be desperate to connect with him again,' Ash said, standing to leave. 'We can catch up properly when you feel up to it.'

I breathed a huge sigh of relief when he left, trying to reconcile my emotions. Now, fully aware of my surroundings, I reasoned the voices I heard while recovering belonged to Ash and Aspen. They had mentioned the skeletons I found in the graveyard Spindle wasn't supposed to stop at. Had Spindle taken me there on purpose and was warning of future deceptions? My head hurt too much to keep contemplating reasons why.

'How's my patient?' Aspen said, strolling into the room and straight to my side, wrapping his arms around me. 'I've missed you.'

I couldn't hold back my tears any longer. 'Aspen, it's so good to see you.'

He gently picked up my bandaged arm. 'The operation was successful and we'll remove the bandage tomorrow. For now, you need plenty of rest and nourishment before we can start running tests and working on finding an antidote to Control.'

'Has Spindle left?' I asked, hoping for some reason he was allowed to stay, but realising the chances were slim.

Aspen chuckled. 'No, he had to go, but your parting gift will have a lasting impression. That punch you threw broke his nose. It's good to see the mines didn't extinguish your fighting spirit.'

My face must have paled. 'Are you okay?' Aspen asked.

'Gosh, I didn't mean to hit him so hard. There's so much I don't understand. Spindle told me Ash was imprisoned, yet he's here, working with the Resistance. I was sure it was him who found Mary and revealed her hiding place. If he didn't betray me, then who did? There's also the explosion in the mines, and all those who lost their lives because of my rescue,' I said, my voice on the verge of breaking again. 'And, I can't stop thinking about Coral. Do you have any contacts on the Island of Mortem who could confirm if she was sacrificed to Pax?'

'Aspen laid a hand on my shoulder and spoke in a solemn tone. 'We don't know what happened to Coral. Robinia reached out, but after hearing she arrived on Mortem, nothing of her death was ever confirmed.'

'Then she could still be alive,' I said, a glimmer of hope

lifting my spirits. I pulled the covers down and swung my legs out of the bed.

Aspen quickly halted my escape. 'Where do you think you're going?' he said, pushing me back and righting the covers. 'You need to give yourself time to heal.'

'I have to find her,' I said, my voice firm despite it's quiver. 'Even if it means facing Pax herself.'

'The likelihood of Coral being alive is exceedingly low, and even if we were to discover evidence suggesting her survival, it would require meticulous planning before embarking on a rescue mission. With you, we had signals from your chip, from Coral, there's been nothing.'

This news weighed down on me, crushed my heart and had me in floods of tears again. Aspen didn't comfort me, he simply allowed my grief to flow. I guess he felt I needed to let the pain of it out, in order for me to come to terms with it - to help me move on.

'Where's Robinia now?' I asked, pulling myself together.

'She's still on Ruin, and still on the Council of Twelve. She works diligently behind the scenes. Right now, I'm going to arrange for some soup to be brought to you - you need to eat. Afterwards, try and get some sleep. You'll be fully briefed tomorrow on all that's happened since you've been gone.'

Wincing, I placed my hand on my head. 'Can you give me something for a headache, it's been throbbing since I woke up.'

'It's probably from all the stress and tiredness,' Aspen said, not sounding too concerned. 'I'll give you a painkiller to take once you've eaten.'

Aspen rose from the chair, his eyes lingering on mine for a few moments as he reached the door. His voice was warm and reassuring. 'There's a buzzer beside your bed. Just press it if you need anything, but someone will be along with some dinner soon.'

My eyes welled up with gratitude. 'Thank you, I appreciate

all you've done. But please, don't send Ash, and keep him away from me as much as possible.'

After Aspen left, I lay contemplating the skeletal graveyard and wondered why I hadn't mentioned it to him. Maybe I was still wary. I held on to the belief that the only person I could truly rely on was Spindle, of all people. I closed my eyes tightly, willing in my mind's eye we'd be reunited soon.

* * *

I stirred to a reality steeped in pain, the constant throbbing in my head blurring the passage of time. A knot of nausea rose in my stomach as I groped blindly for the buzzer at my bedside.

Footsteps echoed from the hallway, growing louder. When the door opened, a harsh light spilled into the room flooding my vision. The glare stabbed at my eyes, forcing them shut, as a woman in a medic's uniform stepped inside.

'How can I help?' she asked, her voice full of concern.

'It's far too bright,' I said, shielding my eyes. 'I can't bear the pain in my head, it's awful.' Groaning, I attempted to sit up, but a wave of dizziness crashed over me sending the room spinning. As my head swam, I felt a warm, sticky sensation in my nose. Crimson droplets fell onto the pristine white sheet, and as I coughed violently, blood splattered from my mouth in short bursts.

The medic produced a small black gadget from her lab coat pocket. 'We have respiratory failure in station two,' she said, her fingers pressing the side of my neck. 'I need a medical team right now!'

It happened quickly. Four hands lowered me onto a gurney. With a soft click, the wheels began to turn, and I was propelled down a corridor. The harsh glare of the fluorescent lights overhead blurred into streaks of brightness as we sped past.

The faces of the medical team hovered above me, their

expressions a shifting kaleidoscope of concern. I struggled to keep them in focus, my vision swimming in and out of focus. I caught a glimpse of Aspen, his presence a reassuring anchor in the sea of uncertainty. His voice reached me through the haze, a lifeline of comfort as I clung desperately to consciousness.

Panic clawed at the fringes of my mind as I sensed the shift from the gurney to the operating table. Every beep of a monitor, every distant voice, every touch of my body - I tried to keep hold of. Yet, in my vulnerable state, I couldn't grasp the full extent of what was happening. The reality of it all slipped away like grains of sand through trembling fingers.

8

After the surgery, the post-operative period felt longer. My recovery seemed slower in comparison to when the microchip implant was removed. As I lay on the sterile bed, an intricate web of wires and sensors covered me. Their cold metal prongs pressed against my skin like unwelcome intruders. With each shallow breath, I felt the faint hum of machines monitoring my heartbeat. The beeping a reminder of my vulnerability. The sharp, sterile scent of antiseptic invaded my senses adding to my discomfort.

I tried shifting into different positions, but the wires tethered me to the bed leaving me trapped and exposed. Each movement sent a jolt of pain through my limbs. I felt more alone and helpless than ever before, surrounded by the cold, impersonal machinery of modern medicine.

Each time I stirred, my eyes met Ash's steady gaze, his presence a constant reminder of the emotions churning within me. His vigilance felt suffocating, like a weight pressing down on my chest. Eventually, as I began to feel better, I turned towards him. 'This feels like déjà vu,' I rasped.

Ash rushed to his feet. 'Aspen, come quick.' His voice rang

out. 'Thank goodness. We didn't know if you'd pull through,' he said, his voice heavy with worry.

Aspen appeared, waving a small torch in front of my eyes. 'You gave us quite a fright,' he said, his voice tinged with relief. 'Take some time to gather yourself, and when you feel up to it, we can discuss what happened.'

Despite Aspen's cautious advice to take it slow, I ignored the warning and forced myself upright. 'What's happening to me?' I asked, pressing my hand to my forehead as a dull throb pulsed behind my eyes.

Aspen pulled a chair across and sat on the opposite side of me from Ash. 'I want to run some tests. It's nothing to worry about, but there's a few matters giving cause for concern.'

'Like what?' I asked, feeling my heart dip.

Aspen stole a glance at Ash before giving me his full attention. 'Remember back on Ruin, we discussed the symptoms of being on Control over a long time if given too young.'

I nodded, thinking back to our conversation. As much as I had been on Control since an early age, I had never shown any symptoms.

'I believe what occurred may be a side effect. The stress from your experiences, including the escape from the mines and your current situation, might have triggered something in your system.'

Ash leaned closer to me, his face a mask of concern. 'Have you experienced any kind of memory loss? Robinia explained everything about Control when she helped wean me off it. I can't believe you were on it for so long without it affecting you.'

I still clung to the anger from the argument we had on Ruin, its bitterness entering my thoughts. 'My memory's fine. I remember every word we said to each other in the holding pen.' His face flushed.

Aspen broke the awkwardness. 'If you feel up to it, I'm going to organise a brain scan. What happened was probably a one-off episode, but we need to take a look to make sure nothing more sinister is going on. Are you okay with that?'

I sighed. 'If you feel it's necessary. But I don't want to be stuck here in bed. I want to know what's going on and play a part in the Resistance. Surely, I didn't come through everything I have to end up hospitalised?'

Aspen took my hand and began to unpack the bandage on my right wrist. 'If you'd like, after we do the brain scan, Ash can give you a wheelchair tour. I'm sure he'll do a quick stop by the Operations room, and you'll see how impressive our organisation is.'

'I'd love to show you around,' Ash said, cheerfully. 'I can brief you on all that happened after you left Ruin.'

I ignored Ash's enthusiasm, focusing my attention on my wrist. Now free from the bandage, it felt surprisingly light. A new pink scar sat atop the brand on my skin that I carried since birth, and I gently probed the area with my fingertip. A sharp pain shot through my arm, but the relief of the chip's removal outweighed it. 'You should've taken out the one you put in my left arm too,' I said, turning to Aspen.

'We can't,' he replied, his tone serious. 'We can never afford to lose you. You're too vital to our movement.'

The weight of his words bore down on me. 'Okay, let's proceed with the brain scan, but I'm only going to be wheeled around if it's necessary for my recovery.'

* * *

As I lay inside the narrow confines of the MRI machine, the walls seemed to close in around me. The rhythmic whirring and clanking echoed in the chamber, drowning out my thoughts and amplifying my anxiety. Each moment passed as an eternity as I struggled to suppress the rising tide of fear.

Sweat prickled at my temples as I fought to keep my breath steady against the suffocating pressure.

I let memories from my time on Ruin rush in, hoping they'd distract me from the task at hand. Ash came to mind, and how he revealed Aconite's plans to tap into our dreams to decode their meanings. I couldn't help but wonder if further advancements had been made to this technology. If we managed to overthrow the government, my first act would be to destroy all such records.

As suddenly as it had begun, the noise ceased, and the walls of the machine receded, releasing me from their grip. Swamped with relief, I gave a shaky exhale, as I emerged from its suffocating confines.

'That wasn't too bad, was it?' Aspen asked.

'It was awful,' I said, feeling light-headed. 'I'm glad it's over with. When will you know the results?'

'Go and enjoy the next few hours. I'll call you when I know what we're dealing with,' he said, helping me into a wheelchair. He pushed me out of the room, guiding me towards Ash who waited patiently.

'She's all yours,' Aspen said, as Ash looked up and smiled.

'I suggest we start with the museum,' Ash said, his tone carrying a cheerful lilt. 'We share our historical discoveries in the Resistance and try learn from them to avoid repeating past mistakes. Not like on Ruin, where anything uncovered was concealed from us to obscure the truth,' he said, as he wheeled me down the corridor.

We stopped beside the elevator, which I presumed to be the same one Spindle and his team had used to reach the bunker when we first arrived. 'Are we heading above ground?' I asked, feeling a little startled.

Ash coded in some symbols on the keypad on the wall. 'No, further down. The first floor is the Medical Bay. It makes sense, as any of our injured operators would want this as a first stop.'

Ash's words were unsettling, forcing the realisation he was an active part of the Resistance, no matter how much I found it difficult to believe. 'How did you become involved with all this?' I asked as the lift doors closed.

'Spindle recruited me. He knew how much I was in love with you, and knew I'd do anything to save you.'

Sarcasm crept into my voice. 'You don't have a clue what love is, Ash. If you had truly loved me, you wouldn't have stood in the Justice of Pax and told all those lies.'

'The guards came for me because I snuck into the holding pen to see you, and I was locked away. If I didn't have feelings for you, I would never have dared to make that visit,' he said, as if it would dismiss my doubts. 'I was given a prescription for Control, and it took effect rapidly. It's still hard for me to believe it had no impact on you whatsoever, especially given the years they fed it to you.'

As we proceeded, we descended into a lower-level corridor where the air grew cooler. The passage branched off into several directions, each pathway disappearing into unknown territories. Ash pushed me down a corridor marked by a sign reading "Lost World."

'Malus decided to forgive my mistakes, drawing comparisons to everything I did right.' Ash said, his tone laced with a hint of pride. 'Robinia was given the task of figuring out the best job for me on the mainland. With all my skills, it made sense to place me right at the heart of government.'

This was the Ash I remembered, smug and self-assured. 'Where did they send you?' I interrupted, more out of curiosity than genuine interest.

'I'd prefer to be a medic if I had the choice. That's why I spend most of my time with Aspen when I'm not on duty, learning to help injured comrades. I'm serving as an administrator in the government offices in the capital, under Rowan's command.'

Laughter bubbled up inside me, spilling from my lips in an uncontrollable rush. 'That must please her,' I said, once I regained my composure.

He engaged the wheelchair's brakes beside a door showing the symbol for classroom, then sidestepped around to face me with a puzzled expression. 'No, not really. She's under the influence of Control, so she doesn't have any feelings on the matter. I thought you would have realised this.'

'I guess so,' I said, stifling my laughter, and finding the irony funny as well as the fact he couldn't see it.

'I don't know why you think it's odd. Robinia was responsible for overseeing my evaluation, and assessing my potential. She was the one who believed my talents would be best utilised by keeping a close watch on Rowan, all while serving under the guise of working for the government. That's all there is to it.'

I could sense his growing irritation by the sharp edge in his tone. Not wanting to provoke him further, I simply nodded in response.

'Are you ready?' Ash asked, pushing the classroom door open wide revealing a scene from the past. Rows of wooden desks and chairs stood in perfect alignment, each one a relic from a bygone era. At the front of the room, a larger desk commanded attention, and behind it, a blackboard was fixed to the wall. Every word chalked on it was scribbled in the old language.

'What do they say?' I asked, pointing to them as he pushed me into the heart of the room.

'We were lied to, and will never let it happen again,' he replied, parking my wheelchair beside the end desk in one of the rows. I ran my finger over the rough wood, feeling the carvings left by generations who had once sat at it. There was a small heart shape, the writing inside probably the name of someone's sweetheart.

There were numbers too, perhaps they were dates - a birthday, or a celebration of sorts. Scribbles were etched beside doodles that fired my imagination. If our life had been normal, and I had sat at this desk, I might have engraved Ash's name inside that heart. But our life was anything but normal, and Ash had no claim on me whatsoever.

'You'll enjoy the next room' he said. 'It's designed to resemble a household, where they lived together as a family unit.'

I thought of Ash's family, the one he was unaware of, living in the caves. Mary had been his grandmother, and Laura had died giving birth to him. Perhaps Larch was still alive, hoping against all odds his son would return to him one day.

But I could never tell Ash, as part of me still believed it was he who had betrayed me. How could I tell him when he was the cause of his grandmother's death? 'No,' I replied, concealing my nostalgia. 'I want to see the Operations room, and to understand how it all works. I want to hear the plan in place to defeat the One World Order.'

I rose from the wheelchair and strode briskly towards the door. 'It doesn't matter how ill Aspen believes I am, it's time to do something, Ash. We need to prepare for battle and bring the government down.'

9

Deep within the bunker, the Operations room hummed with activity. Computers buzzed, casting a bluish-white glow of an otherworldly feel. Diligent operators, sat focused, their fingers dancing over the symbols on keyboards, creating a steady beat of clicks. They were made up of men and women, around forty of them, sitting at scattered workstations.

Some were bald, while others boasted a full head of hair.

'Where do those with the hair come from?' I whispered to Ash, not wanting my ignorance to be heard. 'I wasn't aware we had established a working contact with those from the caves.'

Ash's smile widened in response to my question. 'They're our people who've been burned.'

'Burned?'

'The government's aware of their affiliation with the Resistance, so they live and operate from here as it's too dangerous for them to return to their Midpoint or settlement. Then there are others like me and Spindle, who still work in secret when given leave from our government postings.'

His gaze followed my fingers as they brushed through the short crop of growth on my head. 'Those who've been burned can choose how they want to look, but if we are part of ongoing missions, we need to blend in.'

'Nobody cared in the mines. We were never made to shave because they knew it was only a matter of time before we'd die.'

'It must have been awful,' he said, unable to hide the sadness in his voice.

'We had a cavern for sleeping, catching a few hours and a bite to eat if there was food. We slept on the floor wherever we could find room, often sharing a blanket if we could find one.'

A tall, slender man approached us, his face brightening as he introduced himself. 'Pleased to meet you, Jasmine,' he said, offering his hand. 'I'm Spruce, and I help command operations. I've heard a lot about you.'

'I wish I could say I'd heard of you, and all of this,' I replied, feeling the firm grip of his hand. I looked around the room. 'Robinia and Aspen hinted at a movement, but I never expected this.'

'All our newcomers feel overwhelmed, but keeping secrecy is key to our survival.' He patted Ash on the back. 'I'll never forget the look on this one's face when he arrived.'

'What was Spindle like?' I asked, wanting to know more about his journey with the Resistance.

'Spindle was more aware. Robinia had him prepared for his transition long before he came of age. He's perfect and has earned the respect of men twice his age in such a short time.'

'Jasmine and Spindle never really got along back on Ruin,' Ash said, his gaze flitting between Spruce and me. 'I wonder if you'll be able to work together. Usually, Spindle sticks around to chat, but this time he seemed desperate to leave.'

The warm feeling I had disappeared, and despite feeling my jaw clench, I willed my face into a natural guise. 'And when do you need to return to your administration duties, Ash?' He missed the note of sarcasm that came with my question.

'Not for another three days. Rowan is touring all the small

Midpoints and outlets. I was rewarded with a week's leave due to hard work and commitment.'

Spruce picked up on my pessimism. 'Ash's role is of huge importance. He's an operative with eyes and ears inside the heart of the government. We have a few, but none of them have been able to supply vital information the way Ash can.'

I glanced around the room, trying to distract myself from the praise Spruce gushed about Ash. My eyes landed on a peculiar machine in the corner, churning out what looked like sheets of paper. Paper was a rare luxury in our world, so the sight caught me off guard.

'What's that machine over there,' I asked.

Ash followed my gaze, his expression shifting from self-satisfaction to curiosity.

'That's a fax machine,' Spruce said as we approached the bulky-looking box on the nearby desk. He rubbed his fingers over the outer plastic casing. 'We resurrected it because it's great for communications, and so antiquated that government technicians would never expect to find messages coming from it.'

My lips parted slightly as I leaned towards the mystery object. 'How does it work?'

Spruce picked up one of the sheets of paper the machine had spat out and handed it to me. 'This is a message from another one of our secret outposts. You can see it's written in the old language. The operative would have placed into the feeder,' he said, pointing to the slit at the top. Then the number to this machine is inputted on the number pad here, and when both machines connect, the message is received.'

I was more curious now than ever. 'How many secret outposts does the Resistance have?'

Spruce chuckled. 'That's information I can't share with you now.

Disappointed, I pressed on. 'But how do you find the

paper?' I asked, rubbing the sheet I held between my finger and thumb.'

'Now, that I can do better than tell you. Ash will take you down a few levels and you'll be able to see for yourself. As well as food, we've cloned plants and made paper from their fibres. Nothing is wasted, as once used, it goes into a recycle bin, pulped down, bleached, and new sheets are then made.'

'So, I could send a message to Spindle,' I asked, already planning in my head what I'd say. More than anything, I wanted to know why Robinia chose him early on and prepared him for the Resistance. She must have seen something great in him.

Ash furrowed his brow. 'Why would you want to send a message to Spindle?'

'Because if I'm to be working with him in operations, I want to know how it's done, without putting his life in danger,' I said.

'Easy now,' Spruce said, his dark eyes widening. 'You need to be able to speak and write in the old language first. Even Spindle hasn't mastered that. Anyway, you're on Aspen's detail, and under his charge. We need to find an antidote for Control before you go trigger-happy with messages of any kind.'

Noticing my disappointment, he suggested, 'Let's check if one of our drones is near Spindle's location. We can trace him through his microchip. Would you be interested in that?'

'Wow,' I gasped. 'You can do that?'

Spruce led me towards a huge plasma screen, its expansive surface dominating the room. Ash followed closely behind. Nearby, an operative sat engrossed in her task at her workstation. Spruce tapped her on the shoulder, imparting instructions on the information he sought.

Ash's jaw tightened. 'Why're you wasting time wanting to know what Spindle's up to? He's doing the job appointed to him by the government.'

I ignored him, my attention captivated by the plasma

screen's awakening. It crackled to life, emitting static that gradually faded, unveiling a landscape that puzzled me. It felt as though we were looking down from a great height, gazing upon a vast expanse of nothing but orange clay, stretching out for miles below.

Spruce was back at my side, but called over to the operative, 'Hone in on the microchip number I gave you.'

It took a few minutes for the picture to focus, but as the camera fixed itself, the person I stared at could have been anyone. Donned in the black leather of a guard's uniform, the dark visor of the helmet concealed his identity. I had to take them at their word, and believe it was Spindle.

'What's that he's sitting on,' I asked, curious at the two-wheeled contraption.

'It's a motorcycle,' Spruce said. It's easy on fuel and moves like the wind. All the guards on the mainland have them, for security purposes in guarding the vehicles our leaders travel in from the capital midpoint to all the other settlements. With the amount of guards we have here, it looks as if there is some sort of procession underway. Someone important must be visiting.'

I felt a growing sense of bewilderment as I grappled with the intricacies of the mainland. Their compact indoor Midpoints known as settlements, secret outposts belonging to the Resistance, vehicles, motorcycles, and cameras that gave a lofty view of the ground below. I lifted my chin towards Spruce. 'What's a procession?'

'All will become clear as you watch,' Spruce said, pointing at the screen. 'You can see all the guards are lined up at the entrance of the Midpoint. It's a settlement called Celestial, where certain individuals are taken to be indoctrinated into Pax's holy order.'

'I thought they were taken to the Island of Mortem,' I said, feeling a pang of guilt as I said it. It was Coral's last known destination.

Spruce's focus remained solely on the plasma. 'They eventually move on to Mortem from this settlement.' He paused before snapping his fingers and addressing everyone in the room. 'Do we have any coded messages about what's happening here today from any of our operatives working in the field?' he asked. 'It must be someone highly important as the guard detail is extremely heavy.'

His question echoed through the room, stirring a flurry of activity as papers rustled and murmurs rose, each operative frantically scouring their notes for clues. In a matter of minutes, a hush fell as the entire room converged around the screen to watch the events unravel.

Nothing happened. Suddenly, the stillness shattered as a convoy of five sleek vehicles emerged from the gateway of the settlement, and although we had no sound, I imagined their engines rumbling like distant thunder. Each bore the emblem of authority with the government crest painted on the bonnet while purple and red flags fluttered boldly from their hoods. Against the backdrop of the clay desert, Spindle and the other guards waited to protect them.

'Who could it be?' Spruce asked, more to himself than to anyone else. He snapped his fingers at the operative in charge of working the drone. 'See if you can get a fix on the first vehicle and find out how many are inside.' He turned to Ash. 'Were you aware of anything significant happening today?'

Ash's eyes were glued to the screen, his face growing pale. 'No, nothing at all, and certainly nothing on record for something this size.'

'Wait, this is unusual,' Ash said, pointing at the first vehicle, 'It's stopping. Why would they stop outside of the settlement where there's more risk of an attack.'

The driver exited the vehicle and walked its entire length to reach the rear door. He extended his hand, and a long sleek arm emerged to accept it, aiding her as she elegantly stepped out.

'What on Earth is she doing?' Ash exclaimed, his wide eyes fixed on Rowan.

I stood frozen, my mouth parched and my heart pounding in my chest. If only I could plunge into the screen, I'd seize her with my bare hands and extinguish her existence on the spot.

Malus emerged from the other side of the vehicle and walked around to stand with Rowan. Both looked up into the unblinking eye of the drone. Rowan's expression remained emotionless while Malus wore his trademark, a yellow twisted grin. It was a sight that churned my stomach. With a chilling wave, he acknowledged us. Then, the screen erupted into a chaotic frenzy of static.

Spruce's tone grew grave. 'They were aware of our surveillance and shot down the drone.' His gaze shifted to Ash. 'You should return to your post immediately. Uncover why this visit escaped our detection and what its purpose was.'

'Wait,' I said, holding out my hand, stealing Spruce's attention. 'Will it be safe for Ash to return? If he was unaware of this going on, could it mean they suspect he's working with the Resistance?'

Although his face remained pale, Ash didn't sound fazed at all. 'I guess we'll soon find out,' he said, his tone unruffled.

As I teetered on the edge of voicing my concerns about the peril Ash could be walking into, a woman darted towards him. His body coiled like a spring, as she whispered in his ear.

Turning to me, his face was solemn. 'Aspen needs to see you immediately. Come on, I'll take you to the medical bay.'

10

My mind was a storm-tossed sea with waves of confusion crashing endlessly. I prowled the clinical confines of the Medical Bay. Air snagged in my throat while my heart hammered fiercely against my ribs. 'Where is he?' I asked, my gaze darting down the empty corridors. 'He said to come at once, but he's nowhere to be found.'

Ash patted the seat next to him. 'Come and sit down. He's probably being updated on the situation at the Celestial settlement.'

I stopped pacing and faced him. 'Are you sure heading back to the capital is the right thing for you to do? I'm worried they know about your involvement with the Resistance. What if they've deliberately kept you out of the loop on what they were up to today?'

His eyes sparkled with determination. 'I don't have a choice. These things happen, and we have to continue for the good of us all.'

'I'm not so sure,' I said, shaking my head. 'You could be walking into a situation where they'll torture you to extract information.'

He fixed his gaze on the floor. 'If I'm caught, I'll swallow the cyanide capsule I carry. It's quick, painless, and ensures the Resistance's safety.'

A swell of emotions swept through me, each brief pang leaving its mark. The conclusion I reached with was that, despite my distrust of him, I didn't want him to come to any harm.

Ash must have noticed, offering the familiar lopsided grin that once stole my heart. 'Correct me if I'm wrong, but it seems like you may still have feelings for me. Perhaps there's still hope for us after all.'

A door to the left slid open, providing an escape from having to answer. Aspen loomed in its threshold. 'Sorry for the delay, Jasmine. Care to step inside?' He swivelled toward Ash. 'Spruce updated me on matters. I assumed you'd be gone by now.'

'I wanted to wait, to make sure Jasmine was okay,' he said, glancing at me.

Despite all that had happened between us, his concern appeared genuine. 'If you need to go, don't let me hold you back. I'm sure I can handle whatever's coming my way,' I said, masking my fear with false bravery.

It was as if a silent connection flowed between them as Aspen suggested, 'Let's wrap this up quickly so Ash can get on his way.'

We followed Aspen into the room and took our seats on a stiff vinyl couch facing a huge wall screen. The screen sputtered to life, revealing a cascade of X-ray images and brain scans.

Aspen didn't hesitate. 'Let's cut to the chase. This anomaly here,' he pointed, his finger tracing the white spongy-looking abnormality. 'Indicates irregular white matter. It's linked to memory loss, concentration issues, and diminished problem-solving skills.' He paused, studying my expression. 'Have you experienced any of these symptoms?'

I shook my head. 'Not that I'm aware of. The throbbing headache is the first sign that something's not right.'

'What about any trouble with muscle movements, balance or coordination?'

Biting my lip between my teeth, I let out a deep breath. 'Are you saying this is what I should expect to happen to me?'

'We can't say for certain,' Aspen admitted, sounding defeated. 'But we can't dismiss the possibility that Control may have affected you more than our understanding of it. Remember, there has never been a case like you before.'

Ash rested a reassuring hand on my shoulder, his voice trembling a little. 'Is there any hope of reversing or halting the damage?'

Aspen took a moment before responding. 'We do have an option, but it will affect our primary objective. Reintroducing you to Control is a possibility, but this will hinder our quest to find an antidote. Doing nothing will only lead to a worsening of the condition.'

'There's no doubt about it,' Ash said, without hesitation. 'Jasmine's wellbeing is our top priority, and we must prescribe Control at once.'

I pushed Ash's hand from my shoulder. 'The antidote supersedes everything. Without it, humanity will continue to be enslaved.'

Ash was about to argue, but I silenced him by pressing my fingers against his lips. His eyes brimmed with sadness as they met mine. 'It's okay, Ash. I've been walking a tightrope for some time now.' Releasing his mouth, I clenched my fingers tightly in my lap. 'How much time do I have, and what's our next move?'

A frown crossed Aspen's face. 'It's challenging to pinpoint an exact timeline, but we'll closely monitor your condition. You'll need to inform me of any numbness, tingling or changes in perception you notice, and I can prescribe painkillers for the headaches.'

'And what do you need from me concerning the antidote for Control?'

I could tell by his expression I might not be receptive to his suggestion. 'You'll remain in the lab, where we'll perform multiple blood tests. You'll also undergo routine medical evaluations so we're prepared for when your health deteriorates.'

My stomach lurched, and a feeling of dread settled in my gut realising the gravity of the situation. I yearned to be a warrior, to fight for our freedom. I wanted to avenge those who had brought about the loss of my loved ones. There was also the need to ensure that those who toppled our government would uphold fairness and justice, untainted by corruption. 'This isn't what I signed up for,' I whispered, the frustration sending tremors through my body.

Aspen closed the distance between us in just a few strides. Kneeling in front of me, he took hold of my hands. 'I understand. This condition is not what you wanted. Nor did we. Now, more than ever, you need to find your courage.'

I'm not sure if it was courage, but I realised if I were to meet death, it would be on my terms. 'No, there must be another solution.' My voice rang out loud and clear. 'I refuse to spend my remaining days confined to a lab. Take whatever you need from me when I'm dead. But while I'm here, I'll stand with cave dwellers, fighting every step towards freedom.'

Aspen's eyes narrowed 'That's not a wise decision to make. What if you become seriously ill?'

'Am I your prisoner?' I asked, my tone edged with defiance.

'Of course not,' Aspen said. 'I'm just pointing out the tough road of chasing what you want instead of doing what's best for your health.'

'What if Jasmine stays here and collaborates with our operations team? This way, she can be available for clinical testing while contributing to our cause,' Ash asked. 'We were going to find a part for her to do before this diagnosis. Why should it change?'

'It's a possibility,' Aspen replied. 'I'd rather that than have Jasmine head off to live with the people from the caves.'

I wrestled with my growing frustration. 'None of you seem to grasp the urgency of our situation,' I said, no longer hiding my exasperation. 'Today, we witnessed a drone flying over a procession from the Celestial settlement with a high-ranking government official, Malus, in attendance. If we had people on the ground, we could have taken him hostage or eliminated him. Tell me, what progress have you achieved with all your technology and covert agents?' I paused to give them a chance to respond. Neither of them did. 'The cave dwellers are known for their resilience, but they lack the resources at your disposal. Once our forces join together, just imagine the progress we'll achieve. It has to be me who sees to this.'

Aspen and Ash shot each other a glance, but it was Aspen who offered insight. 'The people from the caves are like ghosts - nomads living in caverns connected by a network of tunnels. Their way of life is sometimes tribal, sparring with each other due to a lack of collaborative structure. Mary told me this herself when I tended to her on Ruin. Working with them won't be as easy as you think, especially if your health begins to fail.'

'They trust me. That's why I have to go with them.' I said, with full conviction. 'It's the only viable option.'

Ash crossed his arms over his chest. 'I don't like it, Jasmine. It would be different if you didn't have this health issue. You said yourself, finding an antidote for Control should come above all else planned.'

My eyes widened as I silently pleaded with Aspen. 'Can we not try to work something out? Take enough blood in the meantime, and we can figure out how to get more to you when needed?'

He paused and rubbed his chin. 'We have a means to freeze

blood in our haemo-frost chamber. I suppose I could take some samples over five days which would give me enough to go on with,' Aspen said.

Ash slammed his fist on the arm of the couch. 'I don't understand how you can consider letting Jasmine leave?' What if something goes wrong and she's captured?'

'It's not your decision to make,' I snapped. 'And you should be on your way too. If you want me to ever look at you kindly again, start demonstrating you're capable of the tasks assigned to you. Don't let events like today slip under the radar.'

My words stung. He rose to his feet. 'Very well,' he said, walking towards the door. Glancing back, he took a deep breath. 'I wish you good health, Jasmine, for as long as possible. You'll always be in my heart, and no matter what you think, I never betrayed you.'

Aspen waited until the sound of Ash's footsteps faded away. 'That was rather harsh,' he remarked. 'I don't think Ash deserved that. He's provided valuable information to the Resistance since his government appointment.'

I couldn't find it in me to feel any remorse. 'It was Ash who reported Mary to Aconite,' I claimed, my voice firm. 'Even though he denies it, who else could it have been? It was also his actions which led to me and Coral being whipped. You've seen the scars on my back.'

With a heavy sigh, Aspen looked directly at me, saying, 'Ash was crushed after he visited you in the holding pen. He told me you accused him. It could have been any number of people who reported you. What makes you so certain it was him?'

Spruce barged into the room, his face a mask of tension. 'Sorry to interrupt, Aspen, but do you have a moment?' he asked, his eyes skimming over me. 'I won't keep him long.'

With a quick nod to Spruce, Aspen redirected his gaze to me. 'Give me five minutes, and if you're okay with it, we can begin to draw blood.'

The faint whispers of their conversation outside the room piqued my curiosity. Creeping closer, I nudged the door slightly ajar.

'And you're sure the message came directly from Robinia?' Aspen's voice was just audible - enough for me to register the wariness concealed within his words.

'As sure as we can be,' Spruce replied, his tone reflecting a shared concern.

Aspen's eyes narrowed. 'This is all we need. Whatever happens, Jasmine must never find out.'

I sank back into my seat, seething at the shroud of their secrecy. If their commitment to me and our cause was sincere, why keep me in the shadows? It further fuelled my desire to reunite with my friends from the caves. First, I would uncover their hidden secrets; then I would leave.

11

I lay on the operation table, all sensation drifting away as the anaesthesia took hold. My gaze remained fixed on Aspen, who returned, this time with a specialised high-tech needle to extract bone marrow from my hipbone.

'I promise you won't feel a thing,' he assured me, his gloved hand plunging the needle deep into my skin.

'Don't make promises you can't keep,' I replied, with a hint of scepticism, feeling a slight discomfort. 'Do you have all the samples you need to get started?'

Aspen settled on the chair beside me and spoke in a reassuring tone. 'Hopefully, we should be good for a while. You'll feel like a warrior with battle-worn bones for a few days. You can embrace the pain as a trophy, or I can give you something to help.'

'If it becomes unbearable, I'll let you know,' I replied, flinching as a throbbing tenderness spread over the area.

'Any more headaches, or tingling sensations in your hands?'

'No, everything feels fine.'

Aspen's expression turned serious. 'Remember, the minute you feel unwell, or something out of the ordinary affects you,

you must let me know. The sooner we find an antidote, the sooner we can put you back on Control.'

It was all a mess. The very drug I sought to free humanity from, now held me captive, ensuring my survival. 'What if I don't ever take it again?' I asked.

His brow creased, the worry lines stretching across his forehead. 'You do understand the consequences. The longer you go without Control, the more your health will deteriorate.'

'Aspen,' I said, my voice wavering. I took a deep breath before continuing. 'I feel my place is with the people from the caves. I'd rather work with the Resistance from their surroundings. I'm sure we could set up communications between us.'

He rolled his eyes. 'I've told you before, you're not our prisoner and the original plan was to have you unite our forces. If you go now, we can't guarantee your well-being, not to mention your safety. We also need to consider the logistics of getting you there. These things take time.'

'Would it be Spindle who'd take me?' The thought of seeing him again filled me with anticipation.

'This would depend on Spindle's shifts, and we also have his safety to think about too. Before you decide anything, give yourself a few days to gather your strength.'

'Am I fit enough to go and visit Spruce in Operations?' I asked, sensing this was the best starting point in my quest to uncover the information Spruce and Aspen were hiding.

Aspen nodded. 'All I ask is that you don't overdo things, and make sure you take time to rest.'

* * *

I was grateful for the two painkillers Aspen provided, as they dulled the tightness spreading through my hip area. Bathed in an unsettling light, the Operations room looked different, maybe because of the medication I'd taken. Spruce stood before the large plasma, which displayed a barren landscape of orange clay. Wisps of grey smoke rose from the fractured ground, and a haunting familiarity crept over me.

'Is that Ruin?' I asked. 'What happened to the mountain scene we couldn't get rid of?'

He raised an eyebrow. 'We managed to remove the hold Malus had on our systems. Do you recognise Ruin?'

'Coral and I trekked that terrain countless times,' I recalled, a twinge of sadness tugging at my heart. 'I didn't realise your drones could fly that far,' I said, my curiosity heightened. 'Are you looking for anything in particular?'

'Our drones function like digital teammates, creating a tight-knit network that enables them to connect though each other's signals,' he said, gesturing toward the screen. 'The image you see here is being relayed from a drone stationed on Ruin. It communicates with another drone positioned at the dock on the mainland, which then transmits the data to us here at the outpost.'

'But who is manning it?' I asked, amazed I had never noticed them in the sky watching. 'Does Aconite or Malus know about them?'

Spruce nodded. 'The government has long been aware of the Resistance lurking within their ranks. They're slowly coming to realise our organisation is more formidable than they imagined. Malus possesses technology that detects our drones and shoots them down.' He paused as an operative tapped his shoulder, handing him a note from the fax machine. He glanced at it quickly before passing it to a woman at a nearby desk. 'The drone on Ruin is manned by one of the Elders working at the port, and we're transmitting information to him as we speak. When it comes to Ruin, and many of the other islands, Aconite and the government remain unaware of any threat and feel secure. It's only here on the mainland they fear an uprising,' he said with an air of confidence. 'Robinia is our master recruiter. Take Ash and Spindle, for example. With the authority vested in her by Aconite, she strategically placed them with roles on the mainland to help advance our cause.'

'Have you ever struck back at them?' I asked, feeling hopeful.

'We are in the process of positioning ourselves strategically, coordinating our efforts, and methodically expanding our movement.' Spruce said, his voice faltering. 'We've been hampered many times by the people in the caves carrying out surprise and unorganised attacks. That's where your influence will help.'

'But if you've been in place for a long time, why are you hesitating? The longer you wait, the more difficult it will be to overthrow them.'

Spruce narrowed his gaze, weighing up my impatience. 'You don't fully understand what we're dealing with,' he said, his tone serious. 'We'll only ever have one real chance to strike, as they will annihilate us if we fail. So, we can only do so when we are one hundred per cent sure we'll succeed.' His words were laden with caution. 'We know time is against us, as there is a scientific programme looming to decode our thoughts and dreams. If they succeed, our entire movement will crumble. We can mask being on Control, but we can't hide or block our thoughts from them.'

'Ash told me about this a while back,' I said. 'Do we know how close they are to achieving this capability?'

'It's new to us all, so we're unsure. Thankfully we've people on the inside to keep an eye on matters. They keep us informed as much as they can.'

Two cloaked officials materialised on the plasma screen, strolling toward a waiting watercraft. Unlike the basic model I had travelled in, this vessel exuded opulence, boasting an interior cabin designed to shield its passengers from the harsh elements while crossing the Pewter Sea.

The drone zoomed in on the figures boarding, capturing the moment when one of them tossed back their hood and stared at the sky.

'Robinia,' I gasped, recognising her immediately. I grabbed Spruce's arm. 'Is that what the note was about, the one slipped to you earlier? Where's she going?'

'We presume she's coming here, to the capital,' Spruce said, his eyes never leaving the screen. 'The note I received alerted me of last-minute travel arrangements being made to transport an Elder of importance from Ruin. Robinia hasn't been able to make contact directly, so we're hoping to hear from her as soon as she can establish a safe connection.'

'Do you think she'll come here?' I asked, mesmerised by her image, feeling an irresistible need to connect with her.

Spruce's expression morphed into one of bewilderment. 'Goodness, no. Robinia doesn't have the same freedom of movement we have. Take my schedule for example – it's divided between my duties for the government and the responsibilities here. I'll depart shortly and another will take over till I return. Robinia isn't afforded the luxury of deviating from her designated itinerary.'

I shot him an inquisitive glance. 'So, if I understand correctly,' I began, crossing my arms, 'Notes are passed from operatives via fax, and the drones serve as our eyes in the sky.'

Spruce smiled. 'Just like the government, we have eyes and ears everywhere.'

As I looked around the room, I found solace in the rhythmic clatter of keyboards and the vibrant energy of the operators. Everyone was fully immersed in their assigned tasks, unwavering in their dedication to the Resistance.

It also brought a wave of frustration, realising my own limitations would hamper any chance I had of uncovering the secrets I so desired.

My eyelids grew heavy, and I couldn't suppress a yawn. 'I

think I'll go and lie down. I can barely keep my eyes open,' I said, rubbing my sore hip.'Thanks for showing me all of this. I've so much to learn.'

'That's a good idea. Why don't you head to the Be Thankful Hall before you sleep? The chicken broth will give you some sustenance,' he said, with a grin. 'It was the last thing Spindle mentioned before he left. He asked me to make sure you were eating and not skipping meals. He remembered it was a habit you had back on Ruin.'

I felt blood rush to my cheeks. 'Spindle said that?'

His eyes skimmed my slender from. 'He worried you were too thin.'

A seasoned Elder dressed in a camouflage uniform marched in, surveying his surroundings before catching Spruce's eye.

'Excuse me, Jasmine,' Spruce said, his tone shifting to a more serious note. 'Duty calls. You're welcome back anytime, but make sure you're fed and rested first,' he said, emphasising the word fed.

I couldn't tell if it was the mention of soup, the atmosphere, or Spindle's lingering influence making my stomach grumble. Glancing down at my loose-fitting clothes, I had to admit Spindle was right – I needed to fill them out.

* * *

The Be Thankful Hall was a blend of cosy charm set against a clinical, cool backdrop. Brilliant lights bathed the space with an organic feel by mimicking daylight in the underground expanse. Seating arrangements featured polished metal and high-quality synthetics, with sleek modular designs, making cleaning a much easier task. Touchscreen displays decked every table, showcasing a modest menu. Taking a seat, I tapped the chicken broth icon.

The room was large and buzzed with life, a chaotic chorus of movement and sound. People scuttled past, their voices merging with the clatter of dishes and the lively hum of conversation. Laughter rippled around, mixing with the sharp clink of cutlery against plates.

I noticed Aspen perched at a table next to a sturdy pillar. He exchanged words with a man dressed similarly to the one who had drawn Spruce's attention earlier. Curiosity eclipsed my appetite, so I drifted closer, slipping behind the pillar to eavesdrop on their conversation. I'm glad I did.

Aspen's tone carried an air of urgency. 'Can you confirm without a doubt the microchip activated on the Island of Mortem belongs to the girl?

'The chip has indeed been activated.' The man sounded composed and unwavering in his reply. 'It's emitting a clear and precise signal from Mortem. We cannot determine which girl. You know what Malus did, so it could be any one of them.'

A wide grin broke across my face as the pieces fell into place. Robinia was coming to the mainland, and the mysterious messengers had arrived with news of a microchip activation on Mortem. A thrilling tingling shot up my spine - Coral was alive. The resistance was mobilising, prepared to bring her back at any cost.

12

As I paced my cramped quarters, anticipation coursed through me, the possibility of Coral's survival sinking in with each step. Despite my exhilaration, a nagging doubt crept in. Why would Aspen and Spruce want to withhold such vital information?

A million thoughts ran through my mind as I yearned for her return. Coral must have escaped her captors and found refuge. She must have found a way to switch her microchip off or hide its signal. It was the only conclusion I could come to. I couldn't remain still. If Coral was being rescued, Spindle would be there, and I had to be there too.

My hurried footsteps echoed down the hallway like a drumbeat, making a direct path toward the Medical Bay. Arriving at Aspen's office, I hammered the door with my fist. 'Are you in there?' I bellowed. 'I need to speak with you right away.'

Without waiting for an answer, I flung the door wide and marched into the room.

'What's going on, Aspen?' I demanded, leaning against his polished desk.

He sat at a high table, looking down through a microscope.

'Ah, that's the Jasmine I remember from Ruin,' he remarked without looking up. 'Have you lost your manners again?'

'Why didn't you tell me Coral was alive?'

Aspen abandoned his work, his eyes narrowing as he pushed the microscope aside. 'Where did you hear such nonsense?'

'From you, Spruce, and your new friend in the Be Thankful Hall. I can't believe after everything we've been through, you would choose to keep this information from me.'

His expression grew solemn as he dismounted his stool, circled the table, and finally came to a stop in front of me. 'You must have misunderstood.'

'Enough,' I snapped, cutting him off sharply. 'If Coral's being rescued, I need to be there. She'll be traumatised and will need me to take care of her.'

His gaze bore into mine, and he must have realised I wouldn't be swayed by any narrative he tried to spin. 'There won't be a rescue attempt. It's too dangerous,' he murmured, sadness colouring his voice.

'What do you mean?' I stammered. 'You're joking, right?'

'No, I'm not,' he replied, his tone adamant. 'And if you want to be part of the Resistance, you must be ready to follow orders, no matter how difficult. We can't risk our resources for Coral,' he explained. 'We don't even have confirmation it's her.'

'But it's her microchip?'

'We don't know for sure if it's Coral. It could be a trap.'

Fury bubbled up inside me, but I fought to keep my cool. 'You were willing to risk lives to save me in the mines,' I said. 'But now you won't lift a finger to rescue Coral. And don't you dare deny it's her. It's her microchip – who else could it be?

He spoke with a heavy tone, ladened with regret. 'Please believe me, this hurts me too. Sometimes microchips are recycled.'

'Stop pretending to be sorry,' I said, wrenching my hands

from his grip. 'How could you do this to Coral . . . to me? Especially after everything I've done – giving blood, and bone marrow. I've followed every rule without complaint since I got here. Can't you do this one thing I ask?'

He sighed. 'Jasmine, this is exactly why we kept it from you. We knew you'd react irrationally.'

Instinct guided my actions and the desk lamp felt weightless in my hand. I swung it through the air, the metal connecting with a thud against the side of Aspen's head. His eyes widened in shock. Then, like a puppet with its strings severed, he crumpled to the floor.

'Aspen,' I muttered, dropping to my knees beside him, my heart pounding against my ribs. 'Get up,' I pleaded, shaking his shoulder with trembling hands. 'I'm sorry, I didn't mean it. Please get up.' I brushed his forehead, the warm stickiness of his blood staining my fingers.

Gripped by panic, I scanned Aspen's motionless form. No subtle rise and fall of his chest . . . no faint breath escaping his lips. 'What do I do?' I whispered. The voice I hadn't heard in ages resurfaced, clear and insistent through the fog swirling in my mind. *'Run.'*

Obeying without hesitation, I bolted out of the room and into the corridor. I sprinted its length with every ounce of energy, my heart pounding in my ears. Reaching the lift, I hurled myself inside, fingers pressing buttons in a frenzy. I had no idea where it would take me or where I would run to once the doors opened, but I couldn't stay here.

An ear-splitting alarm pierced the air, its blaring sound echoing through the corridor like a relentless assault. A crimson light flashed in time with the noise, casting eerie shadows that danced before my eyes. My vision blurred, and a searing pain lanced through my skull, as if a thousand needles were driving into my brain. I fell to my knees, hands clutching at my temples in a futile attempt to quell the agony.

The thud of boots thumped ominously along the hallway. In a haze of pain and confusion, I barely registered the approach of camouflaged figures. A strong arm wrapped around me, lifting me from the ground. I may have screamed but I couldn't be sure - as they carried me back to the Medical Bay. The world spun in a chaotic blur of agony and alarm.

* * *

I drifted in and out of consciousness, each time greeted by the feel of restraints binding my limbs to a rigid bed. My eyes fluttered open, feeling a prick in my arm, and I was relieved to see Aspen looming over me, drawing blood.

'You're alive,' I whispered. 'I thought I'd killed you.'

His voice remained soft and calm, a stark contrast to the turbulence my mind conjured. 'Don't worry, everything's fine,' he said. 'You only gave me a mild concussion.'

'I'm so glad you're okay,' I said. 'I panicked. Didn't know what to do.'

His fingers grazed my cheek. 'Rest for now. You've been through so much. It will all be over soon.'

Trapped in an endless mist, time blurred in a relentless cycle. Each day merged into the next, interrupted only by Aspen's regular visits; the sting of needles piercing my skin.

'Why am I tied down?' I managed to ask, my mind focusing in a rare moment of clarity.

He wiped the sweat from my brow before firing another injection into my arm. 'It's for your safety,' he explained, his stroke on my face soothing. 'Don't worry, everything is under control.'

Exhaustion stole any fleeting moments of consciousness, pulling me back into a cocooned stupor. Aspen's voice occasionally penetrated the haze, jolting me from my surreal state. But try as I might, I could never fully emerge from the fog.

It was Aspen's voice I heard, laced with concern. 'Are you sure the orders were clear?' he pressed. 'Why deviate from our original plan? Losing Jasmine will be a devastating blow to the Resistance.'

'As sure as the paper it's faxed on.' Came a new voice. It took a few confusing moments before I recognised it as Spruce's. 'She's too much of a risk. Take as much blood as possible, and anything else you need. Once you're finished, she's to be transported to the Cinder Scape outpost. There your superiors will carry out an autopsy and freeze her body. If none of you can find an antidote with all of her organs at your disposal, our Commander believes none of you ever will.'

'You're going to have a multitude of disgruntled people within our ranks, not to mention those from the caves,' Aspen said, his voice grim. 'How do you think we'll unite them without her?'

'You know the score. Orders are orders.'

Although I was engulfed in a swirling cloud of mist, my mind was acutely aware of the approaching danger. Strangely enough, I didn't feel fear. I was resigned to the inevitable, wrestling only with the bitter regret of never having played a significant role in our struggle for freedom – unlike Spindle.

I couldn't shake the thought he might find relief in my absence. The vengeance I had sworn to carry out would remain unfulfilled, and my mind drifted back to those I had cherished and lost. Lying still on the bed, I felt a single tear slide down my face.

Ghostly images of Coral haunted my thoughts, her sky-blue eyes begging for rescue. 'I'm not dead, Jasmine,' she said reaching out her hand. 'So, why don't you come?'

My heart ached with helplessness, a bitter irony in the face of Coral's strength. She would have moved mountains to come to my aid, while I remained trapped on a bed, a pawn in the Resistance's pursuit of their own agenda.

I couldn't be certain, but I had a strong sense of being transported on a gurney down the corridor, into the elevator, and back through the tunnel to a waiting vehicle. The frigid air whipped against my face, jolting my eyes open. This sensation breathed life into half of my brain.

Spruce strode alongside, his hand gripping the edge of the gurney as he barked orders. My body tensed as it was bumped up into the back of a vehicle, the tight restraints holding me in place. I strained to shift my head, but a sturdy cushioned neck brace held me in place.

The vehicle trundled along, its hum lulling me into a daze, a sense of calm settling over me. Suddenly, chaos erupted, shattering the tranquillity. It started with a thunderclap sound, loud and alarming. Metal shrieked against rock and earth as the vehicle flipped, hurling me and others into a tumultuous whirlwind of horror and agony.

We tumbled and spun, disoriented and helpless, the scent of thick burning rubber filling the vehicle. The bedlam stretched for what felt like forever, until the motion ceased abruptly - leaving the vehicle overturned and silent.

A sharp object jabbed into my ribs, sending a shiver of pain through my body. Beside me, twisted metal littered the space, while bodies stirred, shaking off the shock of the impact. Time had warped, hurtling from breakneck speed to a surreal crawl.

Even though my head was set at an awkward angle, I caught sight of Spruce hauling himself up, one hand clutching the gash on his brow while the other reached for the weapon strapped to his side.

'Don't let them take her,' he called, as he climbed out of the wreckage.

Short, sharp bursts of laser gunfire shot through the air, casting angry flashes of light across the wreckage. Those tasked with protecting me unleashed their weapons in a desperate attempt to fend off our attackers. Yet, there was a strange absence of any retaliatory shots fired back towards us.

Spruce continued to call above the noise. 'We can't let her fall into our enemy's hands.'

As my muddled thoughts struggled with the identity of our enemy, a warm glow of hope spread through me. If those attacking couldn't fight back with lasers, it had to be Cooper and my friends. Somehow, they had learned of my predicament and found their way here. Yet, another chilling possibility lurked in the recesses of my mind. It could be Malus and his army, biding their time until all the lasers lost charge. Regardless of who they were, one thing remained certain; Spruce would sooner end my life than let anyone take me.

The panic was almost palpable, not solely due to my predicament, but also because of the grave implications it held for the Resistance. If Spruce or his men fell into the clutches of Malus's army, it would signal the death knell for any hope of toppling our totalitarian regime. They would crumble under torture, divulging all they knew. Despite the Resistance potentially sealing my fate, I still had a desire for an end to Malus's tyranny.

I strained my neck, managing to twist it just enough to peer through a gaping hole in the floor of the vehicle. It was stark proof of our collision. The bluish-white flashes streaking from lasers carried an acrid smell. If only I could free myself to catch a glimpse of the target we shot at.

I lost track of what unfolded next, but a sudden hush descended, replaced by a swarm of bodies converging around the wrecked vehicle. A somewhat familiar face appeared, just beyond my recognition, peering down through the hole. 'She's here,' he shouted. 'She's alive, but we need to extract her fast.'

More footsteps echoed, more hurried figures rushed by. Spindle materialised at my side. 'Saving you seems to be a recurring theme,' he said, unfastening the straps holding me down.

As Spindle lifted me from the gurney, the sharp pain in my ribs stole my ability to respond. I was barely conscious when he cradled me across his arms. For the first time since he had left me at the outpost, I felt completely safe.

13

My head rested upon the curve of Spindle's firm thighs, his lap providing a cushion as I drifted back to consciousness. His eyes brimmed with tenderness, smoothing away the creases on his brow. 'Let me help you up,' he murmured, shifting to allow me to sit on my own. 'Take as much time as you need. That's it.' His supportive hands lingered on me for a moment, ensuring my steadiness before letting go. A shy smile played on his lips as he shifted away, creating a small space between us.

'What's happening?' I asked, glancing around the cramped interior of the vehicle I now found myself in. I was surrounded by Spindle's men, and there was a sense of excitement, their faces lighting up with joy at my presence.

The familiar face from earlier turned out to be Linden, whose grin was infections. 'I checked you over, and other than bruised ribs you seem fine,' he said, putting me at ease. 'With some food and a good night's rest, you'll be feeling more like yourself. It's a stroke of luck you were strapped to that gurney.'

The engine roared as we sped along, and I presumed Taxus would be at the wheel. Spindle rummaged beneath his seat, producing a plastic bottle of water. He handed one to me. 'Aspen got word to Ash about the decision our leaders made to end your life. You were becoming too difficult for them to deal with. So, Ash got in touch with me, and together, we orchestrated this mission.'

I rubbed at my forehead. 'I thought Aspen was involved in this. It's all a bit hazy as I could only make out snippets of conversations.'

Spindle's jaw dropped. 'Aspen was trying to save your life. You're too fiery, Jasmine, and incapable of thinking strategically. Aspen had no option but to keep you drugged until we could carry this off.'

Once again, I was struck by guilt, feeling the grim toll of another rescue gone awry. 'Are Spruce and his men . . . are they dead?' I forced the words out, dreading the reply.

'No one back there sustained any injuries. We stunned them with flash-bang grenades,' Spindle said meeting my gaze with a firm look, the corners of his mouth lifting slightly as if to reinforce his words. 'Aspen's medication shielded your nervous system from the blast. Spruce and his men will awaken under the impression you're in government custody. It was a textbook tactic.'

The tension in my shoulders eased. 'So, what happens now?' I asked, realising as a fugitive of the Resistance, it limited my options.

'You'll head for the caves,' Spindle said. His lips pressed into a tight line and a hint of apprehension clouded his face. 'It's sooner than planned, but we have no option now.'

'Cooper gave me coordinates, but to be honest, I'm not sure if I could find them on my own,' I said, annoyed at my lack of ability in fending for myself. 'It's not like Ruin. I'm a stranger here, without any knowledge on how to survive. It's all so different.'

Spindle nodded, and I sensed his understanding of my

predicament was genuine. There was no malice in his tone. 'It must be difficult, but you'll adapt. You don't need to worry about heading off on your own as we sort of have it in order, but it all depends on you.'

'What's that supposed to mean?' I asked.

Spindle's face didn't give anything away. 'You'll see. Learn to observe, wait, and assess situations before jumping in. It will serve you well in the future, especially as you become the leader of the Resistance.'

My eyes widened. 'Me … lead the Resistance?'

'Your friends from the caves have placed their trust in you, and you've no choice but to trust me. On hearing the decision to eliminate you, we decided to restructure our organisation. Those who sought your demise have been removed, and we aim to move forward positively. Time is running out, and if we don't make progress, we're doomed.'

His suggestion startled me, probably more so because I was still groggy from the medication given to me. Spindle's proposal meant taking the lead, which would empower me to rescue Coral and confront Malus's regime head-on.

Despite my burning desire for revenge, Spindle's insight ran true – I had to cultivate patience and juggle responsibilities for two distinct factions - the emerging Resistance and the cave dwellers.

'What will happen to Spruce and his group?' I asked, glancing around at Spindle's men. 'Will they be okay?'

Their laughter flowed freely. It was Linden who explained. 'Spruce and the others will have a long trek back to the outpost. Upon their arrival, they'll be briefed on our new leadership. Any resistance to our terms will have been dealt with by then, ensuring Spruce and his group have no choice but to align themselves with our plans.'

I thought this was the right time to talk about Coral, aware of the burden we both carried from losing friends. 'Spindle, did you know Coral is alive? We must use all your contacts and resources to find her.'

Exhaling a heavy sigh, Spindle raised a hand. 'At this moment, it's impossible, and I beg you to accept this reality. If there existed even the faintest possibility of reaching her, I'd hijack a watercraft and embark tomorrow. Our focus must remain on one battle at a time, and that is toppling the government,' he said, his voice stern. 'This is partly what compelled the former leaders of the Resistance to want rid of you.'

The vehicle lurched to a sudden stop, bringing our conversation about Coral to an end. As I suspected, Taxus was the man who got us here. 'We meet again, Jasmine,' he said, sliding the door open and extending his hand to help me out. 'I was concerned when your vehicle tipped over, so I'm glad you're okay. You missed some wild driving while you were drugged.'

I stumbled forward, my legs betraying me. 'Sorry.' I gasped, feeling grateful for Taxus's strong hands steadying me.

He guided me towards a circularly laid-out camp, where five canvas tents stood. Each one bore the marks of time and weather, their surfaces etched with wrinkles and wear. Some stood taller, while others appeared more compact. We headed to the smallest tent in the cluster.

'Is this a safe place,' I asked, my anxiety seeping through.

'This is one of the remote stations we patrol for the government, and very little happens way out here,' Taxus said, giving my elbow a reassuring squeeze as we entered through the flap. A faint scent of campfire smoke mingled with a subtle mustiness. In the dim light of a lantern, I noticed a figure bound to a sturdy chair beside a wooden table, a hessian sack shrouding their head.

A shiver of unease rippled through me as I shifted my gaze to Spindle. 'What's going on?'

Spindle casually strolled over to the hooded man. 'And here, Jasmine,' he declared, his voice dripping with dramatic flair. 'Is precisely why we need your assistance.' With a swift motion, he pulled the hood from the man's head.

'Zander,' I shouted, my heart racing with relief at the sight of him. He was alive.

His mouth was muffled by a cloth gag, and the left side of his face and neck bore the cruel scars of a significant burn. Traces of soothing potions covered his skin hinting at an ongoing battle with pain, but at least Linden had tried to alleviate his suffering.

'You made it out,' I exclaimed, breaking free from Taxus and staggering towards him. Collapsing onto my knees, I threw my arms around his middle. His head bowed, finding a resting place atop mine. As I broke into sobs, I felt the wetness of his tears seeping through my hair. 'I'm so glad you're alive. The others said you'd find a way out.'

As I turned to confront Spindle, my gaze pierced his, my voice slicing through the air. 'Why on earth is he bound like this?'

Spindle sighed. 'Because he's as stubborn as you are. We've been trying to help him, but he's convinced we're the enemy.'

I cradled Zander's face in my trembling hands. 'It's okay, Zander,' I said, assuring him. 'I'm here now. Everything will turn out fine.' My fingers moved quickly to loosen the knots on the ropes. I was unable to look at Spindle as I spat out the words. 'Why was his face covered?'

'Because until he can cooperate with us, he's considered an enemy,' he said, with a cold edge to his voice. 'We found him wandering in the outer zones, observing our station. There's a risk he might lead others back and stage an attack.' He eyed me while pointing at Zander. 'Your task is to bring him up to speed and ensure his loyalty because he's going to be responsible for getting you safely back to the caves.'

Linden handed me some ointment and a cloth. 'You can

clean his wounds tonight because he acts feral when I try to help him.'

'Come on, let's allow them some space,' Spindle said, gesturing for the others to follow him. He paused at the flap door, his eyes narrowing. 'Alder is preparing some soup and will bring two bowls when ready. There's also a temporary toilet and shower facility in the tent next door. I'll make sure you have some privacy. You'll find a towel and clean clothes for both of you. But,' he said, nodding in Zander's direction 'He must remain here. I'll arrange for a basin of hot water and a sponge for him to wash himself down.'

Spindle stormed off without so much as a passing glance, and it upset me to see us falling back into our previous pattern. Still, I had a right to be angry with Zander's mistreatment, and Spindle's indifference disappointed me.

'How did you manage to get out of the mine?' I asked, dabbing Zander's injured face with lotion. 'Cooper and Felix attempted to reach you, but every route was blocked.'

Zander grabbed my wrist, his damaged vocal cords punctuating the words in a strained rasp as he insisted. 'You can't place your trust in these men.'

I reassured him in a soothing tone. 'It's okay. Honestly, Spindle wants a collaboration between our two groups. By working together, we can make a more significant impact in bringing down the government.'

'No, you don't understand. I'm telling you. You can't trust them.'

Alder appeared at that exact moment. 'Is everything okay?' he asked, picking up on the tension. He set two steaming hot bowls filled with a light brown liquid on the table.

'It's all fine,' I replied, plastering a false smile on my face. 'The soup smells good. We'll eat it once I've finished cleaning Zander's wounds.'

Alder no sooner left when Zander started again. 'It's not

okay. Look at what he did to you back on Ruin. He's the one who got you carted off to the mines in the first place. Have you gone soft?'

'No,' I replied with a deep sigh and handed him a spoon. 'But I can grasp the bigger picture now. He was ordered to orchestrate the whole saga. The Resistance could save me from the mines, but not from the Cleansing Chamber.'

Zander thumped the spoon on the table. 'Let's get away now, there's no one guarding the door. We could make a run for it.'

'Don't be naive. They'd find me in no time,' I said, my hand absentmindedly rubbing my left arm.

Worry masked his face. 'If you truly believe in their sincerity,' he whispered, 'Ask about the graveyard you stumbled upon. See what tale he spins. I caught wind of their conversations.' He paused, stealing a glance toward the tent flap, then leaned in closer. 'Jasmine, they're plotting genocide against everyone from the caves.'

14

As I marched through the camp my voice bounced off the canvas walls. 'Spindle,' I yelled over and over. He emerged from a tent, the smell of simmering soup wafting after him.

'Where's the fire?' he asked, his puzzled eyes locking onto my icy stare. 'If you're still hungry, you're welcome to come and join us?'

I had no patience for banter. 'Cut the pleasantries,' I snapped. 'I need the truth about the burial ground. Trust starts with honesty. Now.'

A multitude of emotions flickered across his face, each one a conundrum I struggled to decipher. His lips remained sealed, his gaze intense.

'Well,' I said, my patience wearing thin.

Half turning, he reached for the flap of the tent, pulling it open just enough to allow entry. 'Come in,' he said. 'We can have some hot mead. Better to discuss it over a drink. You're right, you deserve to know the truth.'

Despite its simplicity, the canvas tent contained all the essentials for Spindle and his crew. A portable grill and stove

occupied one corner, where Alder scrubbed a black pot in a
basin of soapy water. A metal shelf propped up by brick legs
hosted an array of dull pots and utensils.

Spindle led me towards a shabby table where Thorn,
Linden and Taxus sat. The mismatched chairs groaned as they
rose from them, welcoming me with warm smiles. Alder gave
the shelf a final wipe. 'We'll leave you two to it,' he said, ringing
out the cloth before setting it aside. 'I'm sure you don't want us
hanging around.'

They all filed past, offering curt nods before disappearing,
leaving Spindle and me alone in the tent.

Spindle motioned towards one of the empty chairs. 'Take a
seat.'

'What, no ropes to tie me down?' I asked. 'Or is that just
reserved for special guests?'

I saw him flinch for a split second, and a small feeling of
satisfaction stirred within me. Without a word, he busied
himself by placing a pot of water on to boil.

'The ingredients I need are in here,' he said, pulling a tin
from the metal shelf, and prising the lid open. As he worked,
his words began to flow. 'It happened a long time ago, but its
memory still hangs heavy, casting a shadow over the early
Resistance and those who found refuge in the caves. It shattered trust, making an alliance seem impossible.' He paused,
adding dried herbs and a thick golden liquid to the pot, then
blended them with a wooden spoon.

'Did the Resistance kill them?' I asked, a growing sense of
unease knotting my stomach.

Instead of answering, he reached for a large glass bottle
resting beside the utensils. He pulled out the cork and brought
it to his nose, inhaling deeply. Satisfied, he poured a generous
drop of the clear liquid into the mixture. 'A small group of men,
calling themselves Pioneers, weaned themselves off Control
and sought refuge with the people from the caves. They were

made welcome and spent months learning the old language and embracing their freedom.'

After giving the mixture a final stir, he poured the boiling concoction into two flasks, passing one to me. 'Be cautious,' he warned, 'It's still warm and packs quite a punch on the first sip.'

'So, what went wrong?' I asked, smelling a sweet earthy fragrance as I held the flask to my nose.'

Spindle pulled out a chair, settling beside me, resting his elbows on the table and clasping his hands. 'They realised that while the people in the caves possessed a strong spirit, they lacked the endurance, organisational skills, and weaponry necessary to overthrow the government. The Pioneers sought high-tech lasers, stun grenades, and tasers.'

Growing up, we honed our skills with bows, arrows, and spears – weapons vastly different from the advanced lasers wielded by Malus's army and guards on the mainland. Those from the caves would have been just as unprepared as we were on Ruin.

Spindle's tone shifted, his hesitant manner suggesting a reluctance to admit what he was about to say. 'Not only that, the Pioneers saw themselves as superior to the people who sheltered, fed, and cared for them. Despite their desire for change, they found much to dislike about the cave people's way of life.'

I took a sip from the flask, expecting a warm, comforting sensation, but instead, a fiery liquid burned my throat. Coughing and sputtering, I barely managed to choke out, 'Are you trying to poison me?' I set the flask back on the table, my throat ablaze with the unexpected taste. 'What's in this?' I asked.

Spindle chuckled, 'It's a concoction of water, herbs, and honey, but it's the moonshine that adds the kick.'

My nose wrinkled as I sucked my cheeks together. 'What's moonshine?'

'It's alcohol, which isn't allowed, so we produce our own,' he said, with a sense of pride. 'Alder has a makeshift distillery he rigs up whenever we can get our hands on some honey, and we brew our own batch.'

'What's honey?'

'An insect called a bee used to make it by gathering nectar from flowers before the End of Days.' Spindle said. 'Nowadays, we use bioreactors to synthesize a honey-like substance using plant-based ingredients grown in a lab.'

The second sip I took proved just as horrible as the first. This time I detected a faint warmth spreading across my chest. Cursing my distraction, I pressed on, 'Why did the Pioneers think they were superior, and what didn't they like about life in the caves?'

Spindle traced the rim of his flask with his fingertip, a pensive expression crossing his face, as if he were selecting his words with care. 'They harboured prejudice and bias against individuals from different racial backgrounds, favouring a society of a specific skin colour, like what we had on Ruin.'

The realisation struck me like a physical blow. Faces of those whose appearance differed from mine flashed through my mind, including Astrid's. Until now, I had never truly acknowledged our differences; had only seen the beauty in them. Shock and disgust overwhelmed me as I thought of the breeders. They weren't just tasked with birthing healthy infants for the state – they were systematically chosen to shape society according to the preferences of the elite who ruled over us.

Spindle's words echoed my thoughts. 'Without the strength of those in the caves over generations, countless ethnic groups would have vanished.'

A chill crept down my spine at the thought. 'It's awful,' I said, angry at the extent of their injustice to humanity.

Spindle continued his story. 'The Pioneers had stumbled upon an abandoned outpost, nestled in a remote region with air so thin it seemed forgotten by time itself. One brave soul emerged from their ranks, embarking on a perilous journey back to the capital, wielding his influence to purge any trace of its existence from historical records.'

I shifted uneasily in my chair. 'And that is the outpost you took me to.'

Spindle nodded. 'There were a few other outposts too, but the Pioneers needed labour to bring them into repair and make them fit for purpose. They carefully selected individuals they saw as most fitting, with a workforce they believed was disposable. To lure those in the caves to their cause, they spun deceitful tales, painting the outposts as havens for all, promising a new start to anyone who would join them in their mission.'

It felt as though a switch had been flipped inside my head. Answers flooded my mind before I had the chance to form the questions. 'So, the ones selected to help were from ethnic groups the Pioneers had animosity towards?'

His expression hardened. 'While the outposts underwent preparations, more and more citizens managed to wean themselves from Control. Dissent brewed within the government's ranks, boosting the Resistance's numbers. Instead of outright defection, they were instructed to remain within their roles, operating in secrecy – a tactic we still employ today. We only seek refuge in the outposts once our positions are compromised.'

Spindle paused, as if weighing the gravity of his revelations and what still needed to be disclosed. 'It's crucial to understand this happened over a long time,' he began again. 'Impatience festered with the cave dwellers, especially among those burdened with the most gruelling demands of rebuilding the outposts. They were also prime targets for passing patrols; constantly living on the edge of fear.'

He drained the last remnants of mead in a single gulp then

wiped his mouth with the back of his hand. 'Frustrated and desperate, the workers began to devise a plan for a daring uprising. Whispers reached the ears of the Pioneers. Any attempt would have been doomed from the start as their primitive weapons would have been no match for the arsenal the Pioneers were accumulating.'

I let out a slow, heavy breath. 'Tell me how they met their end?' Did a barrage of lasers mow them down?'

'No, they didn't want to waste their supplies, wanting to save them for when they would eventually take on the government.'

'Then how?'

Spindle's gaze drifted downward, unable to meet mine. 'In the depths of the outpost's basement, the Pioneers stumbled upon a vault holding canisters safeguarding ancient chemical gases. They decided to experiment with a compound labelled Entropy or EN-7. After a brief visit to reunite with their loved ones, the returning workers – mostly men and young boys – were met with Pioneers dressed in hazmat suits. They unleashed the gas and recorded the chilling results.'

A wave of revulsion swept through me. Though decades had passed, the shadows of such a heinous act still tainted the Resistance. The depths of Zander's mistrust were understandable. It struck me that Cooper and the others had remained silent on the matter, their minds perhaps clouded by the intoxicating allure of their newfound freedom from the mines.

'What was the effect of the gases on them?'

'Do you really want to know?'

The answer to his question reflected in my expression, a silent demand Spindle could not evade.

'I was told the gas spread out like a cold fog, blistering the skin of those it touched - as if they burned alive from invisible flames. It was an agonising death.'

Tears welled in my eyes. 'Why were they abandoned and left to rot?'

Spindle's gaze was heavy with remorse. 'The bodies were piled in a mass grave, but an earthquake unearthed them some time back,' he explained. 'Doing anything about it then or now would draw too much unwanted attention.'

I found comfort in his honesty. 'If this happened so long ago, why was I to be kept in the dark?'

'Because of your love for Mary. Aspen and Robinia feared if you knew the truth, you'd distance yourself from the Resistance and want nothing to do with us.'

'So, why did you disobey their orders and make the stop?' I asked, my confusion evident. 'You took me to the graveyard on purpose.'

He hesitated, his lip caught between his teeth as his fingers trailed along the table's edge. 'It wasn't easy opposing their orders,' he said. 'Taking you there was my attempt to demonstrate my commitment to honesty, even though I struggled to find the words to tell you. I knew the truth would surface eventually, and I didn't want any secrets between us. Despite my reservations about those from the caves, their trust is essential for uniting our forces.'

'And there's nothing more you're keeping from me?' I asked. 'Because if I discover later you're plotting a genocide, I won't hesitate to kill you.'

'Don't listen to the mad ramblings of your friend,' he said, placing a hand over his heart. 'I promise, I've shared everything I know. If there's more, I'm not aware of it,' he declared. 'You must persuade Zander to cooperate with us, to ensure the past remains in the past. Above all, he must take you to the caves and allow you to build a collaboration.'

My fingers brushed the microchip in my left arm. 'He knows you're tracking me, so he may not be as amenable as you think. Perhaps if you . . .'

He interrupted. 'Before you ask, it stays in for two crucial reasons. Firstly, you know it's too dangerous to remove without proper medical procedures. Secondly, we need to keep track of your whereabouts. I won't risk losing you again.' He blushed. 'I meant the Resistance can't afford to lose you again.'

Disappointment settled heavily in my heart hearing Spindle correct himself. I did my best not to show it. 'What if I can't convince Zander?'

'You can and you will. You managed to manipulate Ash and Salix.' He paused, cringing as soon as Salix's name slipped from his lips. 'Sorry, I shouldn't have brought him up like that,' he added. 'You're a leader, Jasmine. You need to find a way to embrace and master it.'

'There's so much I don't know.'

'Finish your drink,' he said, his tone soft. 'Have a shower, get some sleep, and think about how you'll convince Zander that we're not his enemy.'

* * *

As I entered the tent, the scent of wood smoke mixed nicely with the earthy aroma of burning peat. It came from a crackling fire surrounded by a circle of stones. A large pan of murky rain-water bubbled over the flames. Beside it sat a basin of icy dark water to help regulate the temperature - with the help of a pouring jug. This was the shower.

Privacy came in the form of a large sheet hanging from a sturdy pole, swaying gently in the cool breeze. The canvas walls of the tent glowed with the warm light of a hanging lantern, casting dancing shadows across the worn fabric.

I slipped off the medical gown, standing bare as I savoured the hot water rolling over my skin. The mead had taken hold, blurring the world into a soft golden haze, and I drifted on a cloud of pure happiness. A towel emblazoned with the government crest hung from a stand, and grabbing it, I wrapped it around myself.

As I searched for something to wear, my gaze landed on a glinting object on top of a stack of boxes. I crept over to find a small bristle brush with a sturdy wooden handle, a razor, and a mirror. Raising the mirror to my face, I swept my hand through my dark hair, loving how it complemented the deep brown of my eyes.

As I studied my reflection, Spindle stepped into the tent, holding a bundle of clothes. Our eyes connected in the mirror before his gaze shifted to the scars visible on my upper back. I remained motionless, allowing him to feast his eyes on me.

He placed the clothes on a chair and within a few strides he was beside. His fingers tenderly explored my blemished skin. 'Do they still cause you pain?' he asked, his voice deep and husky.

At his touch, a pleasant shiver ran through me. 'No, not anymore.'

'I knew you and Coral were hiding the fox, trying to help the poor animal.' His words came out in short, tender bursts. 'It never crossed my mind to report you. Perhaps I was too afraid you'd seek revenge. Even back then, I recognised you were a force to be reckoned with. Ash was a fool, Jasmine.'

I turned to face him, his head dipping towards mine, his warm breath brushing against my cheek. A flurry of nerves danced in the pit of my stomach, quickening my heartbeat. Our lips met in a tender, lingering kiss, igniting a deep longing for him that defied explanation.

15

He pulled away from me, and in that moment, it felt as if the world had ended. 'What's wrong?' I asked, my voice trembling. Reaching out for him, I sought reassurance, but he stepped back, widening the gap between us. An icy air settled, resistant to any flame's attempt to thaw its grip. 'What did I do wrong?' My words hung in a taut silence, filled with confusion and desperation.

'I'm sorry, I can't,' he said, his gaze dropping to the floor. 'It wouldn't be right.'

'Why not?'

His solemn blue eyes met mine again. 'It's the moonshine,' he said. 'It's affecting your judgement. It wouldn't be fair to take advantage of you.'

I closed the distance between us, craving the feel of his skin against mine. 'I don't care,' I murmured, grasping his hands and pulling him nearer.

'Don't do this, Jasmine,' he pleaded, his voice a mere whisper. 'It's not fair to Ash.'

The mention of Ash's name sparked a flicker of resentment, as if he were forcing his way back into my life without permission. My anger flared. 'Ash has nothing to do with this.'

Spindle pivoted, heading towards the tent flap. As he reached it, he halted, his voice returning to its usual tone. 'Ash is in love with you. Since losing Salix, he's been my closest friend. Whatever this is that I feel for you, I can't betray him.' He left without looking back.

* * *

In the cramped quarters of the tent, our bodies pressed close together on the coarse sleeping mats, the fabric rough against our skin. The space was thick with the sound of snores and occasional grunts, as well as the smell of sweat and body heat. Zander remained apart, banished to a tent of his own, awaiting confirmation of his loyalty to our cause.

Before retiring for the night, I did my best to persuade Zander, assuring him Spindle had divulged all he knew about the graveyard to the north. I implored him to work with us, clinging to the hope he would do so by morning.

The relentless wind howled outside, its mournful wail penetrating the thin canvas walls. With each gust, the canvas shuddered and strained against its tethers, sending ripples and billows through the fabric like waves on a storm-tossed sea.

Lying beside Spindle, I felt a pang of sadness as he silently refused to acknowledge my presence. Despite the magnetic pull between us, I summoned all my willpower to resist tracing my finger over his face.

I woke with a weariness that clung to me like a heavy cloak, my mouth parched and my head throbbing with each pulse. As I blinked away the last traces of sleep, I noticed Spindle's absence. The tent felt empty without his presence. Nearby, Alder was busy rolling up his sleeping mat.

Despite the queasiness in my stomach at the thought of

food, I forced myself to ask. 'Do you need any help making breakfast?' My voice came out rough, almost gritty.

'I think you'll have your hands full as it is,' Alder replied, a trace of concern in his tone. 'You and Zander need to leave within the next few hours. Our plan is to return to the capital to avoid arousing suspicion with our government superiors, but Spindle won't budge until he knows you'll be escorted to the caves.'

'Where's Spindle now?' I asked, trying to mask my eagerness.

'He's keeping our secrets safe, ensuring the passing patrol remains unaware of our activities,' Alder said.

I raised an eyebrow and pressed, 'Secrets?'

'We need to bury the moonshine kit, for starters. Can't risk the next patrol finding out about our distillery,' he said, acknowledging my less-than-ideal state. 'Perhaps Spindle gave you too much.'

The thought of the alcohol sent a shiver down my spine. 'Next time, I'll stick to water,' I muttered as I exited the tent.

My steps were muffled by the soft shoes I wore as I approached the tent where Zander was being held. Spindle glanced over as I passed, offering a curt nod before returning to packing crates into the armoured vehicle. I was desperate to approach him, to inquire about our kiss. But, I dismissed the idea after a few seconds. It was obvious he had closed the matter, moving on without a second thought. I wish I could have done the same, but the memory of his fingers on my back sent a shiver of delight up my spine. And the recollection of his lips meeting mine left me breathless.

It was a stark contrast to the kiss Rowan had given me back on Ruin. Hers had caught me off guard, leaving me bewildered. But with Spindle, it was different. I felt warmth, passion and a tingling sensation – craving more of him.

Why did he have to mention Ash's name? How could I make

it clear Ash was nothing but a distant memory, extinguished from my heart? This left me pondering a crucial question – was I falling in love with Spindle?

Zander sat at the table, unbound, staring at an empty bowl.

'I see you've already eaten,' I said, entering the tent.

'They didn't tie me up last night, so I managed to get a better sleep. I guess they were testing to see if I'd leave without you.'

'Will you take me back to the caves?' I asked, hope stirring deep within. 'If I can't rally your people to join forces with the Resistance, then I'll abandon my position as well. My allegiance lies with all of you in the caves, so I'll abide by your decision. I'll even cut my left arm off, freeing myself from their chip forever.'

Zander sighed. 'My father saw your strength and believed you'd lead us to victory. If he remains convinced, there will be no need for you to sacrifice any part of yourself.'

A chill swept through me with the realisation I hadn't shared the news of his father's passing. So much had been discussed in the short time we had been reunited, and we had both been lost in our own concerns. He must have presumed Saxon made it home unscathed when I hadn't mentioned him.

'Zander,' I began, my voice betraying a tremor I couldn't suppress. Reaching out, I laid my hand on top of his and took a deep breath. 'I wish I didn't have to be the one to tell you this, but your father . . . .' I faltered, the words heavy on my tongue. 'He didn't make it back. Saxon passed away shortly after the explosion.'

As this news sank in, Zander's eyes glazed over, his expression blank. Then, as if struck by a sudden revelation, anguish flooded his features. He buried his face in his hands, his frame trembling with overwhelming sorrow. Without a second thought, I rose from my seat and held him in a tight embrace. My tears mingled with his, a shared heartache.

Pulling away, he offered a faint, wistful smile, but his eyes betrayed the deep well of grief that lay beneath the surface. 'He'll be looking down, cursing me for not holding it together,' he murmured, his voice crushed by remorse.

'I made sure he had a marked grave,' I said, hoping it would bring Zander some comfort. 'If it's along our path, I'll take you there so you can say a proper goodbye.'

His eyes glistened from a thousand tears, as he reached out, tenderly wiping away mine. Then, he pressed a soft kiss to my forehead, his lips lingering as if finding solace in its touch.

Spindle marched into the tent at that moment, his demeanour tense and wary. Catching sight of Zander and me, a brief flicker of surprise crossed his face, quickly replaced by indifference. 'I'm sorry,' he said, averting his gaze. 'I didn't mean to intrude. I'll leave you two alone for a bit.'

I gave Zander's shoulder a gentle squeeze. 'I need to go and speak with him,' I said, feeling bad I was leaving while he still needed comfort. 'But I'll be right back. Will you be okay?'

'I'm fine. Go and do what you need to do.'

'Spindle.' I called out, catching up with him by the side of the vehicle. His head turned, and I approached, explaining, 'I just wanted to let you know - I was consoling Zander. Saxon, his father, was my friend who passed away. It's hit him hard.'

Spindle shuffled awkwardly, but his expression softened. 'It's alright. You don't owe me an explanation. Is Zander okay?' he asked.

'I should've told him about his father as soon as I saw him. So much has been going on, I wasn't thinking.'

Spindle's voice took on a hardened edge. 'Right now, we don't have time for him to mourn. Is he going to cooperate and take you back to the caves? Because if he doesn't, I've been ordered to eliminate him before we leave - only if he fails to comply. We then need to look at how to transport you, which further complicates matters for me and my men.'

His words slammed into me. I could feel the tension coiling in my muscles, my breath catching in my throat. 'How could you contemplate such a thing? I said, my voice barely above a whisper. 'You promised there would be no more killing?'

Though his response carried solemnity, he shifted uncomfortably. 'I promised there would never be another genocide,' he said, his voice low and grave. 'But this is different. For all we know, the government is just a frequency away from tapping into our thoughts. We can't have strays wandering around ready to be captured. Zander must commit to working with us, escort you safely back to the caves, or face death.'

'He'll take me,' I snapped, cutting him off. 'But what about others who'll resist? Will you kill them too?'

'If you do the job tasked to you, there will be no need for killing. Can you convince those in the caves to work with us?'

'Yes, as you implied before, I'm Jasmine the manipulator,' I said. 'Unlike some, I don't murder to get what I want. You said I would be in charge of the Resistance,' I added, flexing my fingers. 'Take this message back to whoever gave you yours. Any decisions in the future need to be run past me. I will decide who lives and dies.'

I smashed my fist against the vehicle, regretting it immediately. Pain shot through my hand, pulsating up my arm. Swearing under my breath, the curse words sat hot and bitter on my tongue. I stormed off towards Zander's tent.

'Count yourself lucky it wasn't my nose you punched,' Spindle called out, his voice tinged with amusement and warning. 'You only get one shot at breaking it. When you've rallied your cave comrades to the Resistance, then you can start calling the shots.'

A seething rage boiled in my gut. Instead of turning away, I shot my middle finger skyward with a flick of my wrist, silently daring him to challenge me. Secretly, I hoped he'd follow at my heels and make things right. It was only when I opened the tent flap, I cast a swift glance back, but he was gone.

Our argument had reached Zander's ears, escalating his already heightened unease. He sat at the table, his face in his hands. When he looked up, his complexion was drained of all colour. 'We can't place our trust in them.' The strain on his already damaged vocal cords turned his words into a whine. 'They'll kill anyone who doesn't agree to do things their way.'

I hoped the smile I gave was reassuring as I returned to the seat beside him. 'I understand your concern. But I don't think they're out to betray us the way the Pioneers did in the past. They're scared, like all of us.' I reached across the table and placed my hand on his arm. 'They're afraid you'll be picked up by the government guards and tell them of the Resistance plans. But we're in this together, and we'll find a way to keep each other safe. Trust me.'

Taxus poked his head through the flap.' Spindle wants you both to come right away to the cook tent.'

With a wry smirk, Zander pondered aloud, 'Is he offering us a last meal before he digs our grave?'

'No, we're too valuable. He needs us for the rebellion,' I said, linking my arm through his as we followed Taxus.

The camp began to adopt a sparse appearance as boxes and crates were packed away, preparing for the next government patrol. Supplies were stowed, signalling our immediate departure. The once lively sounds of camp life faded, replaced by a quiet anticipation. Even the cook tent, once filled with aromatic scents, now projected a hollow emptiness.

Spindle stood, hunched over the table, its surface cluttered with maps and scattered parchments. With a weary sigh, he straightened, glancing up to meet Zander's gaze. 'I'd be grateful if you could come and have a look,' he said, beckoning Zander closer with a silent plea in his eyes. 'Let me show you where we are.'

As Spindle explained the contours of the map, I stood transfixed, never having seen such a detailed sketch before. The lines etched upon its surface showed rugged elevations, the rolling terrain, and many settlements marked by distinctive milestones.

My eyes traced the winding paths through valleys and across plateaus, leading to a formidable range of mountains where the cave dwellers sought refuge, and had made their home. No wonder the government found it challenging to track their whereabouts.

Spindle pointed at a cluster of tents on the worn paper. 'This is our current position,' he announced, his voice carrying authority. 'Your father's grave is here. If you wish to visit to bid farewell, please be careful. Other patrols may veer off their course and find you,' he paused, allowing Zander a few respectful moments. 'Steer clear of these markers,' he cautioned, indicating other government camps along our route. 'And remember your coordinates. I figure it will take three days to reach the mountain range.'

Zander's brow knitted as he scrutinised the map, his eyes plotting out the various paths and hurdles each presented. 'You certainly took me far from my intended course when you picked me up,' he said, unable to hide his disdain. 'I was on the verge of reaching home.'

Spindle avoided meeting my gaze when he spoke my name. 'You must convince me now you can guarantee Jasmine's safety, and take her to the caves. Otherwise, we can end this right here,' he said, his grip tightening around the laser gun nestled in his holster.

'My father held an unwavering belief that Jasmine was a beacon of hope, destined to guide us to freedom,' Zander said. 'He trusted her implicitly, and I do too. If the Resistance ever betrays my people again, mere threats or laser guns won't deter me from coming for you.'

'We need to make a fresh start,' I said, my hands resting heavily on each of their shoulders. 'How can I unite two formidable forces without cooperation? There will be no further talk of violence among us, unless it is directed against our mutual enemy. Is that understood?'

Spindle rummaged in his pocket, retrieving a small plastic box. 'There's one more request I must make, one I'd rather not, but it's essential.' His expression darkened as he passed it to me. 'These are cyanide tablets. They're to be taken in the event of capture. Our ultimate goal is more important than any person. You can never allow yourself to be taken alive.'

A deafening rumble shattered the already tense atmosphere, as the ground beneath our feet shook violently. The sudden quake jolted Spindle's men into a flurry of motion.

'What's happening?' I asked, my eyes fixed on Spindle.

'It's an earth tremor,' Spindle said, a slight sheen of sweat forming on his forehead. 'We have to move - now!'

16

I was unfamiliar with the concept of an earth tremor, but the frantic movements of Spindle and his men indicated this was something dangerous.

Spindle must have sensed the bewilderment on my face. 'The ground might split open any moment and swallow us whole,' he said, snatching the map from the table and thrusting it into Zander's hands. 'You're on your own now, and will need to get moving quickly. The tremor will register on weather instruments, and soldiers will be here soon to map it out and assess any damage.'

Pivoting, he gripped my elbow, his piercing blue eyes locking onto mine. 'Stay vigilant and safe. You'll know when I'm coming as you'll see a sign, and it won't be long. Believe me, it will be huge and you won't miss it. Make sure those in the caves are ready and committed to our cause. The revolution begins the instant you step beyond this tent.'

A shiver raced down my spine as the gravity of our preparations for war settled upon me. I was burdened by the weight of the Resistance's covert plans, which I had yet to grasp. How could I convey them to the cave dwellers? Moreover, I was further weighed down by the uncertainty of Spindle's arrival.

His cryptic instructions offered little reassurance, having me question the readiness of our rebellion. It seemed evident the uprising was in its budding stages – being built on a rebellion within a rebellion – with the previous leaders overthrown. As I fretted over the imminent internal conflict, I couldn't shake the nagging question of Robinia's loyalties. Was she even aware of the brewing turmoil?

'Jasmine,' Linden called, as he approached. He handed me another small box. 'You have to take these if the headaches return. Or if you feel any of the symptoms of Control taking hold.'

Spindle stared at the box, then met my gaze. 'You've got this,' he said, before ordering the men to hurry their pace.

With the last crates stowed away, the men piled into the back of the vehicle while Taxus took to the driver's cab. Spindle lingered behind, his eyes scanning the camp with a sense of foreboding. They finally rested on Zander. 'Alder's left some supplies in the cook tent. Take what you need and head off. But be as quick as you can,' he said, his tone tense. 'Remember,' he added, 'If anything bad happens to Jasmine, the consequences will be dire.'

I thought he was going to head off without saying goodbye, but he suddenly turned and marched toward me. In one swift motion, he grasped both my hands, his eyes locking onto mine. 'No matter what happens, know I never hated you. It was anything but that. I just didn't know how to express it . . . I still don't. Whatever this thing is between us.'

* * *

In morbid silence, we stood rooted to the spot, our attention fixed on the departing vehicle. Its metallic frame kicked up a cloud of orange dust that hung in the air like a sinister omen. As it vanished into the horizon, a deep sense of isolation settled over me, suffocating and relentless. Despite Zander's presence, I couldn't shake the feeling of loneliness gripping my heart like a vice.

Zander nudged my arm. 'Come on, let's get moving. The government guards will swarm this place like ants on a crumb.'

Alder had left behind two tightly rolled-up sleeping bags, securely fastened to a backpack brimming with water flasks and powder for making soup. Near to the provisions, lay neatly stacked piles of fresh clothes, camouflage jackets, sturdy hiking boots and night vision goggles.

Making my way to the tent with the makeshift shower, I found the mirror left behind, its surface reflecting my apprehensive gaze. As I studied my reflection, Spindle's words resounded in my mind like a mantra. *'You've got this.'*

Zander's voice pierced through from the cook tent. 'Jasmine, what's the hold-up?'

'Coming,' I called back, securing the laces of the boots with a double knot, relieved they fitted snugly. The weight of them served as a reminder that my legs were still in the process of regaining their strength after periods of disuse. The thought of the upcoming trek seemed daunting, to say the least.

'I can't wait for a decent meal,' Zander remarked, lifting the backpack and wrinkling his nose. 'Alder only knew how to make that awful powdered tasteless soup.'

I chose not to mention the moonshine, which, to be honest, wasn't much better. 'Thanks for doing as they ask.' I said, changing the subject.

'I didn't have a choice,' Zander replied. He gave the map one last glance before folding it up and tucking it into his jacket pocket. 'Okay, let's go,' he said, as we set off, heading east.

Our journey had barely begun when we came across a network of fissures on the earth's surface. We followed the jagged cracks towards a gaping chasm that yawned before us, its depths unfathomable. Zander approached the edge with caution, his gaze fixed on the abyss below. 'This isn't good,' he muttered, his jaw clenched, as he surveyed the perilous drop.

'What was this?' I asked, joining Zander at the edge. We peered down at the chaotic assortment of shattered brick, and splintered wood strewn on the rocks below. Among the debris were what seemed to be fragments of broken lanterns, their shattered glass gleaming amidst the debris. A faint smell of upturned earth and charred wood wafted from the disturbed ground, mingling with the faint scent of burnt oil, probably coming from the broken lanterns.

A look of worry crossed Zander's face. 'This is a vital part of our underground tunnels. I hope none of our people were passing through when this happened.' He chewed the skin around his thumb nail as he surveyed the damage below.

I felt a knot form in the pit of my stomach, as his concern pressed down on both of us. 'Is this how you manage to move around undetected?

A deep furrow etched in his brow as his gaze swept the fracture. 'Yes. Nobody knew they existed, not even your friends in the Resistance,' Zander said. 'Spindle estimated it would take us three days to reach the caves, but with our underground network, I could have had us there in two. I hope only a small section is damaged.'

His tone was heavy with foreboding as he continued. 'Something like this could lead to the government soldiers figuring out where we are.'

My heart skipped a beat at the thought of our vulnerability, exposed by this unexpected disaster. 'How did Spindle and his men manage to catch you?' I asked, suddenly realising I hadn't heard Zander's account of his escape from the mines.

'I was heading to one of the tunnel entry points when Spindle's vehicle appeared out of nowhere,' Zander said, his expression grave. 'With them driving straight toward me, there was no chance of slipping underground without risking the tunnel's exposure. So, I surrendered thinking they'd take me back to another mine. And now, here I am with you,' he said, patting me on the back. 'And together, if we survive, we'll free our world from tyranny.'

Much like the shifting earth beneath our feet, everything seemed to be collapsing. The Resistance was in the throes of upheaval, and the intricate tunnel system crucial to the cave dwellers' survival might have sustained irreversible damage. The responsibility to restore order rested on my shoulders, yet I felt utterly lost, unsure of where to even start. 'What do we do now?' I asked, hoping Zander had a plan in mind.

'We'll navigate around this fissure and aim for another tunnel entry before nightfall. With luck, it'll still be intact. Our immediate priority is to alert my people about the risk to our sanctuary and ensure the safety of the women and children. We must also inform the neighbouring tribes of the impending danger to their homes.'

'I thought you all lived in one big cavern,' I said, intrigued by their living arrangements, realising how much I had to learn. Not only with the Resistance, but with the cave dwellers too. 'How many tribes and caves are there?'

'Quite a few. Initially, when people started defecting they probably settled in one place. But, over the generations, as resources dwindled or new ones were discovered people branched out, forming new habitats or tribes, as we call them.'

I did my best to take in every piece of information Zander offered as the landscape stretched before us. It was a vast expanse of flat, bleak earth extending endlessly into the distance. The ground beneath our feet was uneven, littered with rocks and the usual layer of orange dust, kicked up by the wind and clinging to our clothes.

It felt as though we had been walking for days. My legs

ached, each step a struggle. We were driven by our mission and the knowledge time was not on our side.

As daylight ebbed, we found ourselves approaching an outcrop of jagged rocks. They jutted up from the barren landscape like the teeth of some ancient, long-forgotten beast. The fading light cast spooky shadows across the rugged terrain.

'We'll make camp here for the night,' Zander said, shrugging off the heavy backpack. He began unfurling the sleeping bags, laying them out on the ground. 'If you could gather some of those and arrange them in a circle,' he instructed, gesturing towards the scattered stones. 'I'll see if I can scrounge up some tumbleweed to start a fire.' His gaze swept over the desolate landscape. 'The rocks will hide us from any passing patrols.'

There were plenty of small stones to be found, but our hopes of a cosy campfire dwindled as tumbleweed or any form of sticks were nowhere to be found. With the chill of the night air seeping into our bones, we eventually gave up, retreating to our sleeping bags instead.

Zander's voice cut through the stillness of the night. 'Come close and lie together,' he said. 'Combining our body heat will help.'

As I shuffled closer to him, we lay side by side, our faces inches apart. Studying the contours of Zander's face, I searched for any resemblance to his father. My efforts were thwarted by the burn scar marring his features. His eyes held a familiar gentleness to Saxons – pools of warmth amidst the darkness, offering comfort and solace even in the bleakest of moments.

'I loved Saxon,' I whispered. 'During the brief time I knew him, he became like a father to me.'

Zander's tone was also hushed. 'He loved you like a daughter too, and I swear on my life I'll protect you as fiercely as he would have.'

'We'll visit his grave, and you can give him a proper goodbye,' I said, feeling the weight of his sorrow.

'We can't afford to hang about. He would want us to press on and warn our people. I'll get a chance to visit and say my goodbyes when this is all over.' He closed his eyes. 'We'll sleep for a few hours, then rise early to make a good start.'

My thoughts raced with visions of Spindle, anticipation stealing any chance of sleep. Eventually, I succumbed to exhaustion, but it felt like mere moments passed before Zander's urgent shake jolted me awake. He crouched beside me, his finger pressed firmly to his lips, his free hand pointing beyond our rocky outcrop. Slipping from the sleeping bag, I donned the night goggles, pressing myself against the rocks.

Six large vehicles had arranged themselves in a tight group near our camp. 'What do you suppose is happening?' I asked, squinting to get a better view.

They've likely come to measure the tremor and assess the land damage. If they discover the hole back there,' he said, gesturing in the direction we came from, 'More of them will come with equipment, slowing our progress.'

I watched the soldiers, as they erected canvas tents and kindled fires, intensifying my shivering. I yearned for the comforting warmth emanating from the flames dancing inside the iron baskets.

'The soldiers don't appear much different from the government guards in their black leathers,' I said, unable to hide my surprise.

'Trust me, they're every bit as deadly,' Zander said.

'I don't believe it,' I whispered, seizing Zander's arm, the hairs on the back of my neck standing. My gaze locked onto them as they emerged from one of the vehicles, gathering around the fire, the glow illuminating their features. 'What are they doing here, and why are they together?'

Zander's eyebrows shot up, his mouth slightly agape. 'Who are they?'

My heart pounded as more soldiers emerged from their

vehicles, standing guard over them. Uncertainty gnawed at my insides and I found it difficult to tear my gaze away from them. 'The older of the two is Robinia,' I murmured. 'A member of our Resistance.' I paused, doubt colouring my words. 'I'm not sure of her allegiance as I don't know if she still stands with the former leader - or Spindle.'

Zander nodded, sensing my apprehension. 'Who is the other girl?' he asked, his gaze flitting back to the figures by the fire.

'Rowan,' I seethed, each syllable dripping with venom as her name escaped through clenched teeth. My whole body trembled with rage as I thought of the part she had played brining us to this point. 'Before dawn breaks,' I said, my voice low and charged with hate. 'I'll have my revenge at last.'

17

I couldn't tear my gaze away from them. My heart thudded at an accelerated pace, a drumbeat of uncertainty echoing in my chest. Each breath felt like a struggle as I fought to regulate my breathing. They occupied camp chairs by the fire, their silhouettes stark against the flames in the eerie twilight. Shadows flickered across their faces, obscuring their features and adding to the sense of foreboding I couldn't shake.

Robinia's gaze held a distant expression as it swept past our rocky outcrop. My insecurity about her loyalty transported my thoughts back to Ruin, where I continually questioned her motives. A tsunami of emotions slammed into me alongside memories of Rowan. Each recollection interweaved with the web of lies she had spun. Her betrayal bore heavily on me.

'I'm going to sneak into her tent while she sleeps and choke the life out of her,' I muttered, my voice barely audible.

Zander leaned in, his expression grave. 'If you're going to lead us, you need to think strategically. What good is she to us dead?'

Taken aback, I asked, 'What do you suggest we do?'

His eyes twinkled with mischief, and a tight smile tugged at the corners of his mouth. 'We capture her, break her reliance on Control, and extract as much intel about our enemy as we can. Jasmine, consider the possibilities. We've never pulled off a stunt of this magnitude. Their defences are always formidable. Imagine the rapport this would give you in your quest to rally all those from the caves to your cause.'

The idea was brilliant, but how were Zander and I supposed to pull it off? With just the two of us and no knowledge of their numbers, the task seemed utterly impossible.

With a defeated sigh, I voiced my doubts. 'We don't have any weapons, not to mention her microchip that would lead the army straight to us.'

Zander chuckled. 'I managed to swipe Spindle's stun gun, the one he used to coerce me into compliance. After you showed up, he seemed to rein himself in a bit, so he didn't miss it. As for her chip, we'll cut off her hand, cauterize the wound and bandage it up.'

This revelation startled me – the realisation Spindle was capable of torture and Zander could chop off a limb without blinking. As for the act of stealing, it was a skill necessary for survival in the caves.

'So, with one stun gun between us, how exactly do you propose we go about it?' I asked, my doubt undeniable. As I weighed the options, the practicality of having her eliminated became increasingly apparent.

Zander surveyed the dimly lit camp, his eyes tracing the orderly rows of crates and trollies scattered among the tents and campfires. 'Each step needs precision, and every move must be tactical.' He plotted, his mind racing through the approach. 'They'll probably station a few guards on watch while the rest settle in. Our priority should be neutralising them first.'

'Do you truly believe we can pull this off?' I asked, still believing the task impossible.

'It's an opportunity we can't afford to miss,' he remarked, adjusting his angle for a clearer view. 'Once they realise she's missing, they'll escalate their efforts to find her. That's why we need to be clever and quick.'

While Zander exuded enthusiasm, a persistent dread clung to me. I couldn't dispel the fear our attempts would lead to capture, hurling me back into the unforgiving grasp of Malus. 'What if we fail?'

'My father always supposed nothing was impossible if you truly believed. He never once doubted he'd break free from the mines,' Zander said, his eyes shimmering with emotion. 'Where's your sense of adventure, Jasmine? We also have the cyanide pills. If the worst happens, we'll take them together.'

Saxon's words had resonated with me throughout our time in the mines, and I embraced his belief that anything was possible with unwavering faith. So why did I struggle to place the same trust in Zander, his son?

Fearful of the consequences, I murmured, 'It's an enormous risk.' Yet, I couldn't help but envision the rewarding outcome if we succeeded. 'We can't outrun them on land. You mentioned there may be a tunnel further along, but how confident are you it will be passable?'

Zander smiled, approval dawning his face. 'Now you're starting to think like a leader.' If we can't navigate through the tunnel, we'll end her life there and hide her. Then we carry on. It's as simple as that.'

* * *

Time stretched as we crouched in the shadows, every passing minute seeming interminable. We waited with bated breath for the fading crackle of embers and the gradual hush of voices. Eventually, the camp fell into a quiet lull, disturbed only by the watchful presence of two vigilant lookouts. It was time to make our move.

Adrenaline rushed through me, as Zander tapped me on the shoulder. Without hesitation, we dropped to the ground, our bodies melding with the earth beneath us. The staccato rhythm of our breath matched the frantic beat of our hearts as we snaked forward toward the enemy camp.

The harsh terrain clawed at my skin, its ruggedness leaving a trail of stinging scratches along my hands, neck, and face. Every inch forward was a battle against the brutal landscape, the scent of dry earth finding its way into my nose and mouth. We crawled as quickly and quietly as we could, keeping low for as long as possible to evade the watchful eyes of the guards patrolling the perimeter.

As we reached the edge of the camp, we exchanged a silent nod before lifting ourselves to the cover of nearby crates. From our vantage point, we better assessed the layout.

'Are you okay?' Zander mouthed.

Nodding, I offered two thumbs up.

As one of the guards approached our position, Zander sprang into action. Seizing him from behind, he entangled him in a chokehold before lowering him gently to the ground. We took hold of an arm each, pulling the body behind the crates. Using the toe of my boot, I swept away all signs of a scuffle on the loose dirt.

After subduing the second guard, Zander pointed towards the tent where we last saw Rowan enter. His hand gestured toward the ground, a silent reminder for me to stay low as we advanced.

On our approach, I noticed Zander's fingers clenching around the stolen stun gun, a soft flick bringing it to life. He glanced in my direction, nodded, then parted the door flap and disappeared into the dimly lit space.

Rowan lay sprawled on her travel mat, her features softened

by slumber. Robinia slept nearby with her back turned to us. As the stun gun cackled against Rowan's skin, a fleeting spark outlined her now unconscious figure. Zander handed me the gun before lifting her into his arms.

'What do you think you're doing?' Robinia's voice sliced through the silence. She sat up, her startled eyes meeting mine. 'Don't even think about using that weapon on me. I'll scream before you can blink, and the soldiers will be here in seconds.'

Sweat prickled on my brow as I pointed the muzzle of the stun gun towards her. My hands trembled, the cold metal slipping slightly in my grasp. 'Robinia,' I begged. 'Please, I don't want to hurt you. Just let us go.'

'Jasmine!' she exclaimed, her voice filled with genuine surprise and warmth. 'I didn't recognise you.' She jumped from her mat, held me at arm's length and scrutinised my appearance with a look of concern. 'You're so thin, and you've grown your hair out.' Her fingers traced the contour of my face before pulling me into a tight hug. 'What brings you here? You should be heading to the caves.'

'So, you're familiar with the latest plans?' I inquired, a wave of relief flooding through me.

'Yes, Ash informed me of your escape from the outpost, and our new leadership. But you should be much closer to the caves by now.' She glanced past me to Zander, then to Rowan in his arms. 'What's happening?' Her voice carried a note of concern, her eyes darting between all of us.

'This is Zander. He's part of the rebel faction from the caves. Your camp blocked our path, and when I spotted Rowan, I considered taking her life.' My eyes dropped to the ground briefly. 'But Zander proposed capturing her instead, believing it could be more to our advantage.'

'What about her microchip, it will lead the soldiers straight to you,' Robinia said.

'I'm prepared to handle the microchip,' Zander said. 'Do

you have a sharp knife or axe, as well as some bandages? It will make the process easier. Also, can you give me a long length of rope – enough to cover a twelve-foot drop.'

'It's a daring plan,' Robinia said, mulling it over 'One that's never been attempted before. It'll also grant you credibility among those from the caves who might question your leadership. Let me find a sharp knife, some painkillers and a blowtorch too.' She rubbed her chin, contemplating how she could help further. 'I'll come with you, but will linger behind, allowing them to discover me. I'll claim I escaped but couldn't rescue Rowan, and divert their attention from your trail.'

Zander's face betrayed his confusion, a flicker of surprise crossing his features. 'You'd do that for us?'

Robinia crossed her arms, her gaze fixed on Zander before she spoke. 'I don't know who you are, or if I can even trust you. I would go to any lengths for Jasmine, to ensure her safety and the success of her mission. We need to unite your fighting forces with ours. It's the only way we can accomplish our goal.'

'We should start moving,' Zander said, nodding towards the tent flap. 'I can't stand here all night with this weight in my arms. Do you happen to have a trolley we could use to transport her until she's able to walk?'

Robinia put on her socks and shoes. 'Let's go. I'll find you something, but let's keep it quiet. The last thing we need is for someone to hear us.'

We crept through the camp, every footfall made with the dread of discovery. Robinia signalled for us to wait as she melted into the shadows. After a while, she returned, pushing a trolley with a coiled rope inside. Zander gently lowered Rowan, who lay sprawled across the rope.

Robinia handed me a cloth bag. 'Handle this with care. Inside, there's a sharp blade along with all the tools needed for a safe operation. I've included painkillers for her and something to prevent infection as well.'

As Zander guided the trolly through the camp, the wheels released a soft, protesting squeak. Our departure seemed endless, with each moment teetering on the knife-edge between freedom and discovery. We quickened our strides, unable to spare even a moment for a backward glance.

The first light of dawn stretched across the horizon, casting a golden hue over the landscape. In the growing brightness, the imposing enemy camp diminished. It shrank into a distant speck against the backdrop of the awakening sky.

We were weary beyond measure, our bodies desperate for rest, but our determination kept us moving forward.

Robinia's gaze drifted to Rowan in the trolley. 'I should leave you here. It's probably best if I'm not with you when she wakes.' She sank to the floor and peeled off her socks and shoes. 'It'll seem more authentic if you took me without these,' she explained, handing them to me. 'Tell Rowan you stole them. Having footwear will be less of a hindrance for her.'

'Thank you,' I said, with a lump in my throat.

She pulled me into a final hug. 'Be safe,' then turned to Zander. 'Perhaps I'll trust you more the next time we meet. Please, make the amputation as quick and painless as possible. You might not think it, but Rowan is just another victim in this cruel, sad world.'

As she turned and left, I couldn't help but watch her retreating figure. She didn't get far before I called out, 'Wait,' and ran to catch her. 'Did you know Coral was alive?' Her delayed response served as confirmation. 'We must find a way to reach Mortem. I have to save her.'

She avoided my gaze. 'We can't be certain it's Coral.'

'But it's her microchip,' I said. 'It must be her.'

Nervously, Robinia's fingers traced the curve from her neck to her ear. 'Do you recall the time on Ruin when you saw those four children tethered to a machine behind the blue curtain in Aspen's office?'

'How could I forget?' Aspen led me to believe they were conjured from hallucination, induced by the sedative he'd administered. Their haunting figures still stalked my dreams, their tiny bodies looking as if they'd been brushed in oil. 'What connection do those children have with Coral?'

'Only one of the four was the original child from the breeder. The other three had been cloned.'

My brow furrowed. 'But why? Why do this with children, and what does it have to do with Coral?'

'As you know, cloning creates a replica of a living organism. Before Coral left for Mortem, Malus had her cloned.'

'Why would he do that?' I asked, feeling sick at the thought. 'And for what purpose?'

'Unfortunately, I don't have the answer. You would need to ask Malus himself.'

18

Z ander grunted, the strain evident in the tightness of his muscles as he pushed the trolley over the rugged terrain. The wheels struggled against the uneven ground, occasionally catching on stones and dead roots, sending jolts through Rowan's limp body. Each bump elicited a faint shiver from her.

He came to a stop, wiping the sweat pooled at his brow.

Retrieving the map from his back pocket, he unfolded it, meticulously verifying the coordinates. 'Not far now,' he muttered, shielding his eyes with his hand as he scanned the distance.

'There's not a hill in sight, let alone a mountain range,' I remarked, squinting into the distance.

Rowan stirred, a moan escaping her lips.

'Do you still have the stun gun?' Zander asked.

'Yes,' I said, pulling it from my jacket pocket, the weight of it now familiar in my hands.

'Zap her again,' he instructed, glancing down at Rowan. We don't have time to deal with her right now.'

'Gladly,' I said, and watched as the electric current surged through her. Rowan's limbs spasmed briefly before she slumped back into oblivion.

After another ten minutes of trekking, we arrived at a cluster of thicket bushes. To their right stood a small rocky formation. Zander pushed the trolley towards the rocks, then crouched down. With his bare hands, he cleared away the dirt on the ground, gradually revealing a small wooden trap door. 'Can you give me a hand to open it?' he asked, making room beside him so I could help.

We heaved on the knotted cord, and with a groaning creak, the door finally gave way, swinging open to expose a solid metal ladder that plunged into the yawning darkness below.

Once again, the idea of bringing Rowan with us seemed impossible. 'How do you propose we lower Rowan down?' I asked.

'Let's dismantle the trolley first, and then we'll worry about her.' He scanned the landscape. 'There's a light wind. It should disperse the dust, masking the tracks we've left behind. We can't risk them discovering this entrance.'

'Painting the wood and cord a similar colour to the orange dust was a smart move,' I said, marvelling at how something so simple was highly effective. 'It certainly makes it less notice-able, especially from a distance.'

'While we may lack advanced weapons, our camouflage tactics have served us well over the years,' Zander said. 'Let's pray Robinia's diversion works and they look for us in a different direction – we can never be too careful.'

Zander lifted Rowan from the trolley and set her on the ground. Upon landing, she lost control, and urine seeped through her night clothes, pooling beneath her. 'That's all we need,' he said, wrinkling his nose at the sour smell.

'I'll check how much water's left and tear a piece of my shirt to clean her,' I replied, though compassion wasn't what fuelled my actions. The truth was, I needed a reason to stay busy, to keep my mind from spiralling into the harrowing reality of our situation. Tending to her gave me something to focus on, a distraction from the constant feeling of dread.

'Forget it. Our water's too valuable. She'll be dry by the time we're done here, and I'm sure the smell down there will be equally unpleasant.' He began unscrewing the bolts on the trolley. 'We can lower this down piece by piece.'

As Zander handed me each section, I hurled them into the abyss below, where they struck ground with a deep clunk, the noise swallowed by the oppressive darkness. 'At least it doesn't sound as if it goes down too far,' I muttered, the words doing little to alleviate my growing sense of unease.

'Our tunnels are as intricate as the caves, with some delving deeper than others,' Zander explained, the trolley now stripped to its wheels and all parts safely stashed away. 'I'm going to go down. Are you happy to stay here with Rowan for a few minutes on your own?'

'Of course,' I replied, watching Zander as he placed his foot on the first rung. 'If there's any sign of it not being safe, you come straight back up,' I said, biting my top lip.

He offered a feeble smile in response before disappearing into the dark hole. As he descended, time stretched out. The minutes felt like hours. I peered down into the darkness to listen, but there was no trace of his presence.

'How's it going down there?' I called out, my patience wearing thin, my anxiety intensifying by the second as I waited for his response.

'I'm fine. You concentrate on staying alert up there,' he hollered, his voice ringing from the depths below. 'I'll need some time to figure this out. There's an underground lighting system, and I need to find the source of its power. It's not easy fumbling about in the dark.'

Even though he couldn't see me, I nodded in acknowledgement. His progress was marked by the sound of his hurried footsteps echoing up from the tunnel. They were accompanied by metallic clicks as if some sort of tool was striking a dull surface. Then came the heavy scrape of something being dragged across the floor.

'What're you doing?' I called down.

'Clearing a path to the electrics,' he called back, his voice bouncing off the tunnel walls. A faint glimmer of light expanded, casting a dim unearthly glow. He climbed back up and out. 'It's your turn to go down,' he said. 'Take your time, and wait at the bottom while I secure the rope around Rowan. Once I lower her, you'll need to catch her – make sure you're ready.'

As I placed my foot on the first rung and began my descent, the cold metal of the ladder felt slick with moisture from the damp air. The walls shimmered dimly in the poor light, their rough, craggy surfaces coated with a thin layer of grime and mould. With each step, I ventured deeper into the tunnel, and the musty scent of damp earth, with a sharp tang of rust, grew stronger and more oppressive.

As my feet touched solid ground, I tilted my chin and shouted, 'I've arrived.'

Zander dropped Rowan into the opening as if he delivered something fragile. She dangled above me, suspended like a puppet with limp limbs caught in mid-fall. The rope slid through Zander's hands as she slowly descended, her body swaying a little and casting shadows on the walls.

Reaching up, I caught hold of her legs, helping Zander with her weight. As her feet finally met the ground, I braced myself, taking her full weight. 'Okay, I've got her,' I called out, feeling the soft thud of her body against mine.

'So far so good,' Zander said, closing the trap door behind him.

'Let's hope it only gets easier from here.' I replied, my gaze searching the depths of the tunnel. It stretched long and narrow before us, its low ceilings supported by thick wooden beams straining under the weight of the earth above. Cracks spiderwebbed across the walls, with the occasional pebble dislodging itself, tumbling down with a faint thud. 'It looks as if it could fall any minute,' I said, the fear of being trapped under the earth again causing my heart to race.

Zander did his best to bolster my confidence. 'If we managed to find our way out of the mines, getting out of here will be a breeze if anything goes wrong.'

'There's no space in the passage to push the trolley,' I pointed out, eyeing the scattered parts, picking up one of the wheels.

'Don't worry about it,' Zander said. He crouched down next to Rowan, rolling up her sleeve. Beneath the skin on her right wrist, a faint red light blinked intermittently. 'What does its flashing mean?'

'They could be looking for her. To be honest, I don't know. Mine flashed for a while, and then it stopped. I don't know how their technology works.'

Zander straightened her arm, securing it with a tourniquet just below the elbow. Raising the knife, he began to carve through her flesh, the metallic tang of blood filling the air as her arm was cut from her body.

My nerves jangled as the blowtorch hissed to life. Its shimmering flame hosting a hypnotic spell with its raw, untamed energy. Zander positioned it against Rowan's severed stump. The stench of blood dissipated, overpowered by the acrid odour of searing flesh as he cauterised the wound.

Zander wrapped a clean bandage around her arm, layering it in overlapping folds until it reached its end, securing it with a firm knot. Rolling down her sleeve, he twisted the now lengthy material to provide an extra layer of protection for the bandaged area.

I glanced at Rowan's lower right arm, now discarded on the

cold ground. The once almighty microchip, helping to imprison her existence, lay dead beneath its skin.

'I'll bury it before she wakes,' Zander said, following my stare. 'We should rest for now and once she regains consciousness we'll give her some painkillers. If she can't walk, we'll have to take turns carrying her.'

My whole body felt like a block of lead as I sank onto the hard floor opposite Rowan. 'A break would be nice,' I murmured, giving into the weight of fatigue settling on my shoulders. Even my eyelids felt heavy.

'Try to rest, even for a few hours. I'll keep watch,' Zander said. 'Once she wakes up, we'll share some of the rations we've saved before continuing our journey.'

I was uncertain of how long I slept, but I stirred to the soft sound of Zander's snoring. Exhaustion was finally catching up with him too.

Glancing over at Rowan, her complexion was a ghastly grey with droplets of sweat glistening on her forehead like minuscule diamonds. Despite her weakened state, her eyes held a fierce intensity, staring past me with a distant hollow gaze - until, slowly, they sharpened, locking onto mine, and the sudden clarity sent a chill through my bones.

'Who are you?' she croaked, her voice strained with confusion rather than fear. 'What have you done to me?' Her bewildered gaze shifted to her stump and with that, the realisation half of her right arm was no longer there.

Perhaps she remained composed due to the Control still in her system, dulling the horror of her situation. It was the only explanation I could think of for her calm demeanour amidst the chaos – as if a protective fog shielded her from the panic that would have overwhelmed anyone else.

'You know who I am,' I replied, trying to keep my voice steady despite my racing heart.

The sound of our voices roused Zander. Shifting, he rubbed

sleep from his eyes, his gaze flickering between us as he regained awareness.

Her gaze lingered on the ladder, soft and distant, with the realisation any hope of escape was out of her grasp. 'I'm sorry. I don't.'

'Look at me,' I demanded, my voice spiked with hate. I leaned closer to her. 'Look closely. Don't you recognise me at all?'

Rowan searched my face for recognition. 'Other than you being my enemy - vermin from the caves.'

'Perhaps it's the hair,' I said, recalling Robinia's failure to recognise me too 'My name is Jasmine. Does that ring any bells?'

Her expression remained blank. 'You're the escaped prisoner from the mines Malus is after, aren't you?' she said, matter-of-factly.

Zander took a loaf of bread from our dwindling supplies, dividing it into three small portions. 'Here,' he offered, handing a piece to both Rowan and me. He placed two pills on her lap. 'Take these too,' he said. 'They'll help with the pain and infection.'

As we chewed the bread in silence, our eyes remained locked on each other, Rowan's stare remained wary, as if trying to decipher our intentions.

Zander passed me a flask of water. 'Don't drink it all at once. We'll have to ration everything we have. Stretch each drop and crumb to last as long as possible.'

The water tasted stale, like it had been sitting too long, and each sip only amplified the thirst clawing at my throat. It did nothing to ease the gritty dryness lodged deep inside, leaving my mouth parched and raw.

Rowan's voice was hoarse from her ordeal. 'May I have some, please?' Her eyes fixed greedily on the flask.

'Only if you admit your role in my downfall - spinning

those deceitful lies,' I said, licking my lips slowly, hoping to make it seem as though the water tasted wonderful and refreshing.

Rowan shook her head, her brow furrowing. 'I'm sorry, I don't know what you're talking about,' she said. 'I barely know anything about you.'

Shrugging slightly, I handed the flask back to Zander. 'Looks like you'll have to go without.'

Zander shot me an irritable look as he leaned toward Rowan. 'Open your mouth,' he said, holing the flask above her and spilled droplets on her dry tongue.

'What happened to your face,' she asked, her gaze fixing on the burns scarring his cheek and neck. 'We can perform skin grafts, and if you take me back, you'll be rewarded. I'm confident our medics will be able to make you look as good as new.' Her words held a note of earnestness, offering the promise of healing - an allure for Zander's cooperation.

'You should've seen me before the explosion,' he said, then chuckled. 'I was much uglier back then. This,' he rubbed a hand over his face. 'Is an improvement.'

My patience was wearing thin. 'If you don't start remembering what you did, Rowan, you'll need a medical team to reconstruct your face as you'll be unrecognisable by the time I'm finished with you.'

Zander rose from the ground. 'She's under the effects of Control, so her memory will be hazy. Once she's weaned off it, she'll recognise you and remember everything.' With a firm grip, he grasped her shoulders, pulling her to her feet. 'Are you able to walk?'

Snatching the socks and shoes Robinia had provided, I tossed them over to her. 'Put these on. They'll save your feet from hurting.'

She leaned on Zander for support as she wobbled into

them, allowing him to tie the laces for her. 'Thank you,' she said. 'You're very kind.'

Her legs gave way as she attempted her first faltering steps. Zander intercepted her fall, his arms wrapping around her to prevent her from hitting the ground. He guided her arm over his shoulder, supporting her.

'I suppose you'll have to help me till I fully recover. You must have zapped me more than once,' she muttered, her voice trembling. 'Not to mention you cut off my arm too.' With a soft gasp, her eyes rolled upwards and she crumpled against Zander.

She drifted in and out of consciousness as we moved along, her presence both fragile and haunting. When she was aware, her movements were unsteady and laboured, as if each step demanded immense effort, dragging us down and slowing our progress to a crawl. After a while, Zander asked, 'Can you help her for a bit? My shoulder's cramping.'

'Sure,' I replied, stepping closer and slipping my hand under Rowan's arm taking the weight from him.

As she shifted positions, her eyes fluttered open, locking onto mine. Her brow furrowed, and for a moment I thought I saw a flicker of recognition cross her face. 'Thank you, Jasmine,' she murmured, her voice barely above a whisper. 'Ash didn't tell Aconite about the old woman. It was Lily who betrayed you.'

Once again, her eyes rolled up to reveal white orbs. The little colour she had left on her pale face drained away, leaving her features ashen and lifeless. Her body fell limp against mine.

I stood still as I held her, my anger and confusing rising. Lily would never have betrayed me; the thought felt like a knife twisting in my gut.

19

Her words landed like a deadly blow, stealing my breath and constricting my throat. As my grip slackened, Rowan crumpled into a heap on the ground. 'What did you say?' I asked, fury boiling over as I delivered a hard kick to her side.

Zander intervened, pulling me back. 'Hey, calm down. She's out cold.' He crouched down, feeling for the pulse in her neck. Looking up through narrowed eyelids, he said, 'She'll be fine, but you've got to keep your cool.'

Despite my anger, I couldn't help but feel relieved she was still alive. I needed to know why she blamed Lily. 'She's brought this on herself,' I murmured.

Eventually, her eyelids fluttered open, confusion masking her face. 'What happened?' She winced as she raised a hand to her brow.

Zander placed a supportive arm around her back helping her sit. 'Take a sip,' he said, offering her the water flask. 'You can have some more painkillers soon. Hopefully they will help.'

I found the stun gun and held it out toward her. 'Zander won't always be around to protect you. If you don't start being honest about what you know, expect more of this. ' I pressed the trigger switch and watched the electric lines fizzle together in a display of crackling blue and white sparks.

'Please don't.' Her voice quivered, as she pressed herself against the damp walls, fear pooling in her green eyes. 'I swear, I have no idea what you're talking about.'

The words left my mouth in a venomous hiss. 'How dare you accuse Lily. What proof do you have? She was our friend, kind and caring. I don't believe she'd do such a thing.'

I was poised to strike, prepared to deliver a jolt straight to her heart. But before I could, Zander seized my arm, pulling the weapon free of my fist.

'Stop,' he yelled. 'If you keep this going you'll seriously hurt her. The shocks messed her up. She might be having flashbacks or something.'

Together, we watched her trembling figure, her gaze unfocused and disjointed. 'She's clearly not herself,' Zander concluded.

With a sudden, violent movement, my foot connected with her ribs once again. The force of the blow knocked the wind from her. Her scream rang out like a haunting melody, a satisfying harmony playing in my ears.

'Drag her back by the ankles, for all I care,' I said, my tone cold. 'If she doesn't snap out of it soon . . .' I let the implication hang, the decision to end her life at the forefront of my wishes.

Turning my back on them, I marched onward through the tunnel. 'If you expect me to lead you to freedom, Zander, never disarm or obstruct me from doing what needs to be done again.'

We pressed forward, the underpass closing in around. Lacking any conversation, it was as if the dank walls conspired to suffocate our words. Zander lagged a few paces behind, lending his support to Rowan. Despite her fatigue, I was restless and moved on, refusing to stop for us all to rest.

The absence of conversation allowed contemplation of the turmoil Spindle brewed within the Resistance. I wondered how many of the steadfast allies would rally behind his new direction.

Irrespective of their intentions, understanding the impact on those from the caves remained a top priority. Despite my growing feelings for Spindle, a persistent suspicion remained. I couldn't shake off misgivings about the Resistance's motives for uniting the rebels from the caves with our forces. Perhaps my doubts stemmed from the inherent lack of trust between both factions. To be candid, Zander's mistrust exacerbated my concerns.

Adding to the complexity was Rowan's revelation, implicating Lily as the one who betrayed me on Ruin. As I reflected on the situation, I remember Lily being confused and lost. Could she have ended up on the beach and stumbled upon Mary hiding in the Black Cave? Despite this, something about Rowan's claim didn't feel right. The desire to extract answers from her was overpowering.

Our footsteps no longer crunched, swallowed by the squelch of the soggy path beneath us. Sporadic drips from above gave birth to puddles below. The atmosphere thickened, saturated with a salty dampness that clung to the back of my throat.

My fingers trailed along the cold, wet walls as I rounded a narrow bend, entering into an expansive open space. 'What is this place?' I whispered to myself in the stillness, waiting for Zander and Rowan to catch up.

I was mesmerised by the intricate patterns adorning the ancient rock formations as I gazed around this large, rounded chamber. Each etching held elaborate designs, suggestive of a time when skilled craftsmen painted them in vivid hues. These patterns, inscribed in the cryptic script of the old language, appeared to weave tales and stories of a forgotten era.

In the heart of the chamber, a serene pool of water shimmered with crystal clarity. Tunnel offshoots branched out in every direction, presenting the dilemma of which tunnel to explore.

'We're in an underwater chamber,' Zander explained as he arrived by my side, a hint of joy in his voice. 'Each passage leads to a labyrinth of caves nestled within the mountains, where many communities thrive. They enjoy the freedom to worship a God of their choice, speak their native languages, and live lives guided by free will.'

'What's all this?'I asked,' pointing to the carvings.

A wistful expression washed over Zander's face. 'It started with those who first fled here, wanting to narrate and preserve a true record of history. Generations have added their story so that nothing is ever forgotten.'

Mary had openly shared stories about her life on the mainland, but had never hinted at how vast it was. Surveying the shadowy entrances of the offshoot tunnels, I wondered which one led to her people.

'This is barbaric,' Rowan said, her gaze sweeping across the cavern walls. 'Pax will obliterate all of you and quash your rebellion.'

'Keep telling yourself that,' I replied, hoping she'd choke on her words. 'So where do we go from here?' I enquired, shifting my focus to Zander.

He pointed the way, a subtle smile on his lips as he brushed past and strode ahead. After a few minutes, he stopped, bending down to indicate rows of slender, silvery cords. 'Be careful of the tripwires,' he warned, straightening himself and gingerly stepping over each one. 'I don't want to alarm my people. Our defence mechanisms could prove fatal before they realise my identity.'

I gestured for Rowan to follow Zander. 'I assume you're capable of walking unassisted now,' I remarked. 'I'll take up the rear. Let me be clear – if you think about triggering any of those wires, I'll end you before the mechanisms have a chance to react.'

She followed Zander without protest, walking with a slight limp as she favoured the side of her stumped arm.

The descent had been gradual on our trek to this point, and now, as we scaled a steeper path, I felt the strain burning the back of my calves. The subdued glow of electric lights gradually faded, replaced by the warm, flickering flames of torches set into the rugged stone walls. Their fiery illumination cast dancing shadows that seemed to breathe life into the ancient passageway.

'Why switch back to firelight instead of electric?' I called out to Zander. Rowan would be dead soon, so I didn't worry about her discovering their secrets.

Zander must have shared my sentiments, his reply carrying the knowledge of a life I could only imagine. 'It's our contingency plan for plunging our home into darkness in the event of a government raid. We've established a water system linked to the sea, primed to douse the flames and convert certain passages into submerged chambers. Our enemies would meet a watery demise before reaching us.'

Distant chatter drifted down the passage towards us, accompanied by the rich, smoky scent of cooked meat. It hung heavy in the still air, causing my stomach to growl.

A bulky shadow appeared from around a sharp bend, casting an imposing silhouette in the firelight. His gruff voice boomed through the cavern. 'Who goes there?'

Zander's voice rang out with triumph as he replied, 'It's me, Zander, Saxon's son.'

Rapid footsteps thundered towards us, bodies bursting forth from the shadows, their faces aglow with astonishment. Surging forward, they flocked to Zander in a whirlwind of excitement. They hoisted him into the air as a chorus of hoots and ecstatic hollers bounced off the walls.

Rowan and I trailed behind the procession that led us into an expansive cavern. It was a breathtaking sight. The walls were decorated with a riot of colours - painted pictures and vibrant tapestries. We were surrounded by children's laughter, their carefree joy tugging at my heartstrings and bringing a tear to my eye. The smell of countless herbs and spices floated in the air, teasing my tastebuds, and joining the smoky scent I recognised from the passageway.

Fire pits dotted the cavern, bathing the space in a comforting light. Around them, partitions outlined seating areas, with tables and chairs cut from solid stone. It felt as though I had stepped into a whole new world, one where beauty, warmth and camaraderie flourished.

As I watched more people rush to welcome Zander, a gentle tap fell on my shoulder. I turned, and there he was – Cooper, my friend. His face lit up with a wide grin that mirrored the happiness in my heart. He opened his arms wide, an invitation I gladly accepted.

'Cooper,' I said, feeling as if no time had passed at all. His presence was like a lifeline to my soul, flooding me with an intense sense of belonging. 'It's so good to see you,' I whispered, my voice choked.

As we stood there, wrapped in each other's arms, I knew that no matter what trials lay ahead, having Cooper by my side would make everything alright.

'Who is your friend?' he asked, scanning Rowan from head to toe.

Although Rowan showed no emotion, her gaze swept around the room, absorbing every detail as if she were cataloguing information to take back to Malus. 'We're not friends,' she said, her eyes fixing on Cooper. 'I'm her prisoner.'

I nudged her forward. 'This is Rowan,' I said, my voice

carrying a hint of pride. 'Do you have a safe place we can hold her?'

Cooper's jaw practically dropped to the floor. 'Rowan, the one who told all those lies about you at your trial.'

Nodding, I replied. 'She was with a group setting up camp to measure an earth tremor. I wanted to kill her but it was Zander's idea to kidnap and bring her here.'

Cooper's eyes widened. 'We've never captured one of their agents before. Come on, I'll show you where she'll be properly secured.'

Following Cooper's lead, we left the large cavern and entered a maze of corridors and connected caves. Eventually, we arrived at a dimly lit chamber, where a hole punctured the floor.

The three of us stood on the brink, peering into the depths below. The stony rock face bore the scars of time, its surface smoothed and weathered over the centuries.

Cooper's voice cut through the eerie silence. 'Throw her down there.'

'I don't want her dead just yet. I need information from her first. After that, you can throw her off the top of your mountain for all I care.'

He chuckled. 'It's not bottomless, but deep enough to keep her caged. She won't be scaling her way back up. Especially with only one hand.' His gaze settled on a neatly coiled rope, one of its ends tied securely to a ring fastened to the wall. As he approached, he unfurled its length. 'We can lower her down with this,' he suggested. 'The hole serves as a place for those in need of a swift reality check. After spending a few days down there, they often emerge with a newfound sense of community spirit.'

He tied the rope around Rowan's waist. 'Hold on with your hand too, and I'll lower you down. The distance might seem longer due to the darkness. It plays tricks on the eye.'

Rowan raised her stumped arm, her eyes meeting mine in a silent exchange that spoke volumes. When she spoke it was directed at Cooper. 'I suppose going down the hole is better than having my leg cut off. You barbarians seem to take great pleasure in such acts.'

With steady fingers on her left hand, Rowan ensured the rope around her middle was securely fastened before taking a firm grip on the length that would lower her down. As she settled on the lip of the crag, her body tensed, and she pushed herself off.

'Don't worry, I won't let go,' Cooper reassured her, feeding the rope through his hands inch by inch. The silence stretched, broken by the faint thud that echoed from below. 'Are you okay down there?' he called out.

Her response was brief. 'I'm fine. Give me time to untie the rope.'

A sense of hope remained in me – that deep within her subconscious, the true Rowan was grappling with fear in the darkness, struggling to break free from the prison inside her mind. It was a twisted desire, wishing her to match the nightmare Lily and Willow had suffered. Once I got the information I needed, I would make sure her end was just as horrific.

20

The caves were just as Mary had described. I watched fascinated, as figures huddled around a modest fire, their faces illuminated by its gentle glow. They were engrossed in conversation, their laughter infectious. Amidst them, some carved tools from pieces of wood, the rhythmic scraping and tapping adding a musical lilt to their words. If only I could have spoken the old language.

As I approached, their friendly smiles and nods made me feel welcome and accepted. Despite my outsider status, there was an undeniable warmth in their gestures. Yet, even amidst their camaraderie, I couldn't shake the feeling of being an outsider.

'Jasmine,' a voice called out. It belonged to an elderly man, his deeply lined face making him appear older than Mary had been. 'Come and join me, bonnie lass,' he beckoned, his words reminiscent of Saxon's. 'Come, warm yourself by my fire.'

I clasped his hand in greeting before settling down, crossing my legs beneath me. 'Thank you,' I said, holding my hands out over the grill, feeling the heat from the flames below.

'I've heard all about you, and have been eager to meet you.

You can call me Pops,' he said, his smile revealing a few missing teeth. 'Thank you for bringing Zander home.'

'Actually, it was the other way around. If it weren't for Zander, I'd still be wandering the wastelands alone.'

As if hearing his name, Zander appeared, passing me a small jug of cloudy liquid before taking a seat beside Pops. 'I see you've met my grandad.'

A jolt of recognition swept through me, realising I was sitting next to Saxon's father. Studying the ageing contours of his face, I couldn't help but see a glimpse of my old friend reflected in his features. 'I'm so sorry about Saxon,' I said, my voice quivering. 'He was like a father to me. I wouldn't have survived the mines without him.'

Pops placed a bony arm around Zander's shoulder. 'Cooper told me all about you on his return. But, I never thought I'd see this lad again,' he said, pulling Zander in close to plant a kiss on his forehead. 'At least I have my grandson back, and for that, Saxon would be grateful.'

Zander didn't seem fazed by his grandfather's display of affection. He raised his jug, tapped it against mine. 'Let's toast to our return,' he suggested, 'And to the assurance that, no matter what challenges come our way, we'll always find our way back home. My dad will be watching over us, ensuring our safety.'

'To Saxon,' I said, swirling the liquid around in the jug. 'What is it?' I asked, wrinkling my nose at its pungent odour.

A low rumbling chuckle escaped Zander's lips. 'Root beer. It's made from lingonberries and any spare herbs. We sometimes add moonshine, but you'd need something in your stomach first before I let you try it.'

I shuddered, remembering the taste and awful after effects of the moonshine Spindle had given me. It reignited thoughts of his kiss, a sensation I quickly suppressed. Now, as a leader, I had to focus on my role, leaving no space to entertain hopes or dreams.

As I scanned the cavern, my eyes locked on Cooper. He leaned casually against a large wooden barrel, his attention captivated by a slender, graceful young woman. Their animated conversation hinted at a bond beyond friendship, igniting a spark of curiosity. It was only when she departed, leaving behind a trail of shared smiles, that I noticed a bundle strapped to her back.

At first glance, it appeared to be nothing more than a collection of fabric, draped in muted tones, blending with her tattered cloak. As she shifted, the bundle stirred, unveiling the precious cargo nestled inside – a tiny baby, cradled securely against her back.

My heart seemed to expand within my chest, as if trying to contain the flood of emotions threatening to overflow. It was a captivating sight, reminding me of the fragile purity existing within our harsh reality.

'How's little Nova doing?' Pops asked as Cooper ambled over.

'She's keeping her mother up to all hours of the night, but apart from that, she's doing just fine,' Cooper replied, then turned to me. 'You must be hungry. Come, let's get you some food.'

My jaw dropped. 'Never mind food. You didn't tell me you were a father. How could you keep this from me?'

A wistful grin spread across his lips. 'Little Nova's my niece. Her mother, Freya, is my sister.' Mary had tried to explain the concept of family to Coral and me. While we didn't fully understand it, witnessing it firsthand amplified the sense of wonder about being part of this community.

'I've already eaten, but I'm happy to tag along,' Zander said, his hand resting on his grandfather's shoulder as he rose. 'Is there anything I can bring for you?'

Pops shook his head. 'I'm fine, for now. Go and enjoy yourselves while you can.'

Zander downed his root beer, wiping his hand across his mouth. 'You can drink while we walk, Jasmine. There's plenty more too, if you're thirsty.'

I took to my feet before taking a sip. 'It's spicy ... and sweet,' I said, smacking my lips at the strange but intriguing taste. 'I hope the food is just as good.'

As we threaded through the bustling cavern, the aroma of sizzling meat wafted through the air, enticing my senses. It was the familiar scent from earlier, now carrying a rich, smokier essence, infused with the distinct char of an open flame.

'Did you find the others?' I asked as we waited in line for our food.

It was Zander who answered. 'They're out scavenging, but will be back soon. I can't wait to see their faces when they return to find us here.'

I was brimming with excitement at the thought of seeing Astrid, Felix and Minx. I missed them so much, and I knew they'd be overjoyed to see Zander was safe.

Cooper handed me a meat skewer. 'Here, eat it while it's still warm. It doesn't taste as good cold.'

'Is it chicken?' I asked, my teeth sinking into the meat.

'I wish it was,' Cooper chuckled. 'It's rat meat. Not the most appetising, but it's our primary source of protein, unless we stumble upon snakes. Unlike your people, we don't have access to cloned poultry or beef.'

The mention of cloning stirred memories of Coral, rekindling my determination to find her. Even if it meant finding a version of Coral different from the one I once knew. This was a point I intended to make clear to Spindle when we crossed paths again.

As if seeking my approval for kindness, Zander announced, 'I lowered a bucket with some food, water, and painkillers to

Rowan. She might encounter some rats and spiders down there, but they tend to keep away from you.'

He turned to Cooper. 'Once Felix, Minx and Astrid return, we should travel to all the communities to organise a gathering. Perhaps atop Ashen Ridge? There's ample space for everyone from all parts of the caves to come and hear what Jasmine has to say.'

Zander and I had relayed every detail of our journey to Cooper. We explained my deteriorating health, the Resistance's plot against me, and Spindle's daring rebellion. We briefed him on our successful capture of Rowan, with Robinia's invaluable assistance. Cooper listened with a grave expression, realising the urgency of our situation.

Cooper bit his bottom lip. 'Honestly, I'm worried about the others,' he admitted. 'We didn't feel the earth tremor up here in the mountains. But what if Felix, Astrid and Minx were caught up in a network of tunnels that collapsed? They could be trapped underground again. Until we assess the damage, we won't know. And as you mentioned, Zander, the government soldiers will soon be aware of our underground network.'

Zander's face reflected Cooper's worry. 'It'll be difficult to explore with the army out in force doing the same,' he said, tensing his shoulders. 'We should send some men out to monitor the soldier's movements and warn us if they come close.'

With the government soldiers closing in on the underground network and no sign of Astrid, Felix, and Minx returning to the caves, the mounting tensions were undeniable. Each unfolding event fuelled my growing apprehension, leaving me anxious about what might go wrong next.

We strolled through a section of the cavern where stools and brightly embroidered cushions were scattered on the floor, forming an inviting gathering space. Murmurs of conversation floated in the air as well as the scent of root beer.

Suddenly, a figure with dark, tousled hair caught Cooper's attention. The man beckoned him over, prompting Cooper to gesture for Zander and me to follow.

'Allow me to introduce you to Orion. He's Freya's husband, and that makes him Nova's father,' Cooper said, his explanation clear. 'Jasmine is still getting used to all our terminology.' His eyes flitted between Orion and me.

I held out my hand in the customary greeting. 'It's lovely to meet you,' I said, with a warm smile. It seemed as though Orion was not particularly eager to respond. When his hand finally met mine, the brief contact felt forced, as if he couldn't wait to release it.

'Likewise,' he replied, wiping his fingers against his trousers as if rubbing away my touch.

'Please, take a seat.' He pointed towards the vacant stools. 'The entertainment is about to begin.' With a nod towards the table behind him, he signalled to a man and woman seated there. 'Klin, Jaz.' He called over to them, his eyes then drifting towards me. 'This is the girl, Jasmine, that Zander brought back.'

Jaz's sharp blue eyes locked onto mine, a hint of disapproval flickering from them. The glint of her nose ring caught the firelight as she scrunched her face, and my eyes were drawn to the ancient language tattooed along her neck. The hair on one side of her head was shaved close to her scalp, while the other side, in stark contrast, cascaded down in vibrant multi-coloured locks.

Klin, slightly older than Jaz, sported a long boldly dyed beard - similar to the vibrant hues of Jaz's hair. His short-sleeved shirt proudly displayed muscled arms packed with inked writing. Others nearby, in the same fashion, formed a formidable group and I couldn't shake the feeling I was the topic of their conversation.

Amid Cooper, Zander, and Orion's chatter, laughter rang

out frequently. Although I was only welcomed into their conversation occasionally, it lessened my feeling of being left out. Gradually, my wariness of Orion melted away, replaced by a budding connection as we chatted more easily.

From amongst the gathering, a young girl stepped forward clutching a slender wooden flute. She delicately lifted the instrument to her lips breathing life into it, coaxing forth an enchanting tune.

As the tune drifted through the cavern, it acted as a beacon, summoning others to come and see. From every corner, individuals emerged – girls and boys, men and women – with a unique palette of skin tones and facial features. As they gathered around the young flautist, their voices blended seamlessly, singing ancient words in beautiful harmony.

'What's it about?' I asked, captivated by the song.

'It's a story of a world lost and a new world to be born,' Cooper said, and began to hum the tune too.

Orion's expression darkened. 'It's a world we could have reclaimed generations ago if your people hadn't betrayed us.'

Jaz patted him on the back. 'Well said, Orion.' Her tone brimmed with hostile bitterness. 'They'll wipe us out if we give them the slightest opportunity. Never again will we align ourselves with such evil. Zander has a cheek bringing *her* here.'

Those who aligned with Jaz closed ranks around her, their murmurs of agreement rising to reach me. Their faces, lit with fervour, created a barrier of support that pulsed with loathing.

Cooper's jug crashed onto the table, its thud breaking through their antics, bringing silence. 'This is not the time for such conversation,' he declared, asserting his authority. 'If we're to collaborate with the Resistance and secure our freedom, we must rise above our prejudices.'

Orion appeared poised, his posture straight, as if he were ready to argue the point and have more say. He was silenced by the disapproval rippling from those at nearby tables, their exasperated glances cutting the air like shards of glass. He clenched his jaw, and returned his attention back to the performance.

Jaz and her group retreated into the shadows, their figures melding with the darkness like phantoms. I could still feel their chilling presence, their sly glances and hateful stares. It was as if they revelled in the discomfort they instilled - their smirks hidden in the gloom but unmistakably felt. Even as I turned away, focusing on the song, their malicious energy clung to me. I did my best to shake them off.

A heavy sigh slipped from my lips, realising the burden of countless sorrows and shattered dreams. It was all before my time and not of my doing. 'I hope it won't be too challenging to persuade your people to join forces with the Resistance,' I murmured to Cooper, my gaze falling on Orion. 'We all want a better life.'

Cooper leaned in close, his voice barely a whisper as his lips grazed my ear. 'I have no doubt you'll have your army, but convincing some, like Orion, will require patience. He's a decent man deep down. Don't judge him too harshly. The same goes for Jaz and her group. Once trust is earned, you'll find they're good people.'

The weariness of the past few days filled every fibre of my being. Yawning, I stretched my tired limbs. 'I don't think I've ever felt this exhausted.'

'The adrenaline that's kept you going is wearing off,' Cooper said, rising to his feet. 'Tomorrow, I'll show you our ecosystem and how we've thrived here for generations. Then we can start building your army.' He took hold of my hands and pulled me up. 'We've readied a small chamber for you to rest. I'll show you to it, and you can get some sleep.'

Zander rose too, pulling me into a tight embrace. 'We did it. Can you even believe it?' he said, his voice bursting with pride. 'And to top it off, we've captured a prisoner – a first for our people. That alone will rally the masses behind you. Sleep well and tomorrow we'll strategise.'

* * *

The cavern given to me had been meticulously carved into the rugged rock, creating a homely retreat. A humble bed crafted from woven fibres and plush moss awaited me, nestled snugly against the stone wall. Soft candlelight illuminated the small space with a soothing warmth.

My head had barely grazed the pillow, when thoughts of Rowan stole the need for sleep. I imagined her isolated in the frigid darkness, accompanied by the scuttling of rats and silent spiders. Her accusation against Lily remained at the forefront of my thoughts. I needed answers. Moreover, I was driven to uncover her connection to Malus and find his motives for having Coral cloned.

It could take weeks - perhaps even months - for Control's effects to fully fade, but time was a luxury I couldn't afford. With the stun gun still in my possession, I intended to pull her from the pit in the morning and extract the information I needed from her.

If this meant risking her life, so be it.

21

I cradled Nova in my arms, gazing down at her with awe; she was the most beautiful thing I had ever seen. Her little fingers wrapped around one of mine as if she didn't want to let go. Leaning down, I pressed my cheek against her soft skin, savouring the pure fragrance of innocence and new life. A wave of warmth spread through me as I watched her gentle breathing, syncing with my own. Holding her was an entirely new experience for me, one filled with awe and tenderness.

A mist of water clouded my eyes as I leaned close to Freya, my voice barely a whisper. 'She's so beautiful,' I said, breathing in her scent. 'She's the most amazing thing I've ever seen.'

Freya's gaze softened as she glanced at Orion. 'Yes, we are blessed,' she said, her voice carrying a quiet hope. 'Perhaps she'll come of age in a world where equality prevails over oppression. She'll hear the story of the great warrior queen who once cradled her in her arms.'

Orion's tone was full of scepticism when he spoke. 'Assuming the warrior queen's Resistance fighters don't betray us. It's all good and well that Cooper vouches for you. But, I'm wary of your associates. Don't take it personally, Jasmine, but like me, there are many you'll need to persuade.'

A flush of colour rose to my cheeks, my lips parting slightly as I met Orion's gaze. 'I'm not sure about this whole warrior queen thing,' I replied, feeling the weight of uncertainty settle in my chest. 'All I know is that I've been tasked with preparing you all for battle. But I can make one promise – I'll fight alongside you. If anyone from my faction plans to betray you, it will also be a betrayal to me.'

Freya's back stiffened as she turned to shoot Orion a withering glare. When she spoke, it was aimed at me. 'You've come bearing a message of hope, and that's what counts.' Her voice carried a note of earnestness. 'Don't judge Orion or the others before looking at the inscriptions on our cave walls. Have Cooper translate them. Then, you'll understand how many times we've been disappointed by those who come and claim to oppose the government.'

I longed to find the right words to persuade him of my loyalty. 'I'm sorry for what happened in the past. Orion, I swear on Nova's life.' I said, glancing down at the precious bundle in my arms. 'I'll do everything possible to unite us in our struggle against Malus.'

As Nova gurgled, a tiny bubble of saliva formed at her lips. My heart swelled with love so profound, it took my breath away. How could I ever have imagined I would feel this way? 'I promise to make a better world for you,' I said, passing her back to her mother. 'And when freedom comes family will reign above all else.'

Cooper, who had been sitting in silence, now rose and gestured for us to leave. 'We should get going. We've much to organise, and I have a nice surprise waiting.'

Bidding Freya and Orion farewell with a casual wave, I followed Cooper out of their chamber. 'Thank you,' I murmured, as we strolled through the narrow tunnel. 'Holding Nova was the best thing I've ever experienced.'

Cooper chuckled softly. 'Who knows, after we win the war, you might find love and become a mother.'

My mind was crammed with thoughts of Spindle, and I couldn't shake the question – did he ever dream of becoming a father? On Ruin, nurture was never taught and love was a foreign concept. How could we learn to be like Freya and Orion, with their loving instincts, when we never felt that kind of warmth ourselves? 'The chances are I won't live long enough,' I said, my voice loaded with regret. 'Even if I survive the war, being given Control from an early age has wreaked havoc on my health. I don't think I've much time left.'

Cooper appeared shaken by my frankness, his composure faltering. 'I'm sorry, Jasmine. I wasn't thinking.'

I forced a chuckle, hoping it sounded sincere. 'Let's not dwell on it. Our main goal is bringing down the government.'

We pressed forward through the winding tunnel, our shadows stretched out like elongated ghosts. Cooper often had to stoop low, the ceiling height fluctuating along the passage. There were moments when it even brushed against the top of my head.

As we entered a new cavern, my eyes widened at the vast space unfolding before me. It stretched beyond my sight, its grandeur overwhelming. Mirrored glass hung from above reflecting faint light filtering through small holes in the stone wall.

It formed as a mesmerising glow, flowing across the rocky walls to the floor, and bathed long rectangular boxes with a form of sunlight. The boxes were dotted all around the ground, each covered with a delicate netted cloth woven from metallic threads.

Cooper lifted one of the covers to reveal the crop growing beneath. 'This is lavender,' he said, brushing his fingers over their tiny purple heads. The sweet floral scent it released made me sneeze. 'Bless you,' he said, before continuing. 'We grow loads of different herbs and vegetables down here.'

'This is amazing,' I said, bending my head to sniff the purple clusters. 'Our saplings on Ruin rarely took hold. All our herbs and root vegetables are grown in a lab. Yet, you've managed all of this,' I said, my hand sweeping around the cavern. 'Without the technology we have.'

'Generations of learning.' Cooper said, leading me through the chamber past thriving crops. The earthy scent mingled with the distant drip of water, the sound growing louder as we ventured deeper into yet another tunnel.

'Those who came before us searched for the cleanest, purest soil in the valleys and crevices around these mountains,' Cooper said. 'They learned to recognise the spots where internal spring waters gifted us with uncontaminated earth. You know the soil is good if it bustles with earthworms and other tiny creatures, each playing their part in our ecosystem. So, our crops thrive despite the state of the world outside.'

Listening to Cooper unveil the intricacies of their underground world stirred a sense of wonder. Yet, it also sparked my frustration at the ignorance of our government toward these resilient cave dwellers. They had been labelled as savages - cast aside and denied the recognition they deserved. It was a tragic oversight, a missed opportunity for the advancement of all humanity.

The sound of water grew into a deafening roar as we entered the next cavern. A beautiful sight of crystal-clear torrents plummeted from the heights above, forming a shimmering pool at our feet. The sight was mesmerising.

Bending down at the water's edge, Cooper scooped up a handful of the pristine liquid in his palms. 'Go ahead, give it a try.'

The water had a refreshing, icy flavour, distinct from the

metallic tang of the sanitised water I was used to. 'So, this isn't the same as black rainwater. Where does it come from if it doesn't come from the sky?'

'We think it comes from clouds but is cleansed by many of the minerals concealed inside the rocks as it falls through,' Cooper said, his face glowing with a sense of wonder. 'All we know is it's here, a ceaseless gift that never runs dry, even when the world as our ancestors knew it came to an end.'

As I moved to sit up, I noticed several carved openings in the rock just below the water's surface. 'What are those for?' I asked.

'Water from here flows into our pipelines, feeding every corner of our communities with what they need. While some groups have separate water systems, we aim to provide enough vegetables and water to sustain everyone in the caves, regardless of location.'

I was speechless, unable to find adequate words to express the deep respect that was due. Their remarkable ability to thrive, creating a resilient community against all odds in the depths of the earth, left me in awe.

'Come on, let's keep moving. I'll show you where you can freshen up and wash your clothes and bedding to stay clean,' he said, leading me through another tunnel. 'Watch your step, though. The ground can get slippery around here.'

As the tunnel widened, the air swelled with warmth, its gentle waves of heat caressing my skin. The passage we traipsed over was narrow, flanked by a hazardous drop on one side. I clung tightly to the sturdy wooden rail for balance. Peering downward, I saw a sluggish river of molten yellow and orange sizzling and crackling over a jagged bed of rocks.

Cooper's eyes fixed on the same sight that captivated mine. 'That's lava,' he explained, watching the molten flow. 'We've harnessed its power, and it heats the pools. Be careful around it.'

As we approached the entrance to the next chamber, the sound of laughter greeted us. The cavern pulsed with humidity, causing moisture beads to gleam on every surface. A watery sheen coated the walls, gathering in crevices, giving the chamber a surreal quality. Wisps of steam rose from the aqua pools, twisting gracefully into the air.

The laughter belonged to a woman surrounded by three lively children. They splashed and played in one of the smaller pools, their excitement filling the chamber with echoing delight.

In a nearby alcove, a cluster of elderly women gathered around what appeared to be a makeshift laundry station. They scrubbed garments on rigid wooden boards, their hands moving the material swiftly over its surface. Suds of soap bubbled from their fabrics as they rinsed them in the sparkling water of a pool next to them.

'Feel free to dip your toes in,' Cooper said, nodding towards the pools. 'This chamber's reserved for the womenfolk. The men's area is through one of the other passages.'

'I'll come down later,' I replied, torn between the allure of the water and the tasks ahead. 'If you have any spare clothes I could borrow, it would be a great help. I could wash the clothes I've on, so I have a spare set.'

'Sure thing. Freya will get you some. Ready to keep exploring?'

Cooper led me through a series of caverns, each unveiling its unique wonders, methodically crafted for specific tasks. We passed through the busy kitchen, where individuals prepared rat meat with spices. Further ahead, the soft chatter of children sounded from a classroom, where they absorbed lessons in the old language.

Cooper's eyes sparkled as he tugged me along, his steps quickening as he pulled me forward, back through the main bustling chamber. We arrived at an offshoot where he stood behind me, his hands cupping my eyes. Blinded, he guided me forward. 'Welcome to our bar,' he said. 'Here, we raise a toast with our moonshine, celebrating every success, no matter how small.'

'Come on, let me see.' I laughed cheerfully as I tried to peek through his fingers.

'And now for your surprise,' he said, his excitement barely contained.

'Surprise!' they chorused in unison as Cooper released his hold.

A wave of warmth spread through my chest as Felix, Astrid, Minx, and Zander encircled me, their arms entwined in a tight-knit embrace. A sense of belonging washed over me, reassuring and serene. In their presence, I found solace, and in that moment, I knew I had finally found a way of life – a home, with people I loved. I would do everything and anything to protect them.

'Shall I whip us some moonshine to celebrate us all being together again?' Zander asked.

My words rang out with conviction, daring anyone to challenge my command. 'We'll have plenty of time to drink later. For now, let's focus on getting Rowan out of the pit. I need answers by the end of today, no matter what.'

22

Rowan emerged, her trembling hand barely able to grasp the thick rope. Her tattered nightdress clung to her gaunt figure and her blinking emerald eyes struggled to adjust to the sudden brightness. Despite Control's effects, she looked terrified.

Cooper dumped her onto a chair that Zander brought with him from the bar, its legs creaking under the sudden weight. Rowan slumped into it, her body limp.

Astrid leaned into Rowan, their faces inches apart. 'Wow, she's nothing like the person you described during your trial. Where's her beauty and confidence now?'

Rowan's eyes widened, the dark circles underneath highlighting her exhaustion. Her gaze darted nervously between each of us, her left hand fidgeting with the frayed edges of her nightdress. 'What do you want from me?' she asked, her voice laced with uncertainty.

I stepped into Rowan's line of sight, my grip tightening around the stun gun's trigger. Electricity crackled from its nozzle, casting an eerie glow and filling the air with a sharp, burning scent. 'Hello, Rowan. Remember me?' I asked, my voice sharp with contempt.

She regarded me warily. 'You kidnapped me while I slept. You do realise you'll be cleansed for this when you're caught.' Her gaze flitted to Zander. 'It's not too late to turn this around.'

I moved swiftly, administering a sharp jolt to her arm. Her body jerked in response. 'Malus won't find you.' I couldn't help but gloat. 'The only cleansing you'll face is the one I'll ignite if you don't start remembering,' I said, waving the stun gun at her face. 'Tell me,' I pressed, my voice sharp. 'Is Coral alive?'

Rowan's brow knitted together. 'Who is Coral?'

Electricity sputtered against her skin once more, sending shivers down her spine. Her body shook with its intensity. 'Coral,' I said, jabbing her again. 'My dear friend, sentenced to die on the Island of Mortem as a sacrifice to your false Goddess, Pax.' I paused, letting the gravity of her situation sink in. 'Coral's only crime was helping me rescue Mary stranded on Ruin's shore. But you know all of this.'

Rowan's tremors gradually stilled, her breath slowing as she fought to regain control. 'I'm trying to remember,' she whispered, her voice shaky. 'If she was taken to Mortem for sacrifice, the ritual would have been carried out.'

'Why has her microchip suddenly come to life?' I asked.

Rowan shook her head, her wide eyes fixed on the gun. 'I'm sorry,' she replied, the frustration evident in her tone. 'I've no idea why this could be happening.'

With a firm hand, I pushed the gun against her right shoulder and held it there, feeling the continuous jolt vibrate through her body as she convulsed violently. Blood trickled from her bitten tongue, staining her lips crimson. 'Has Malus cloned her? I shouted, over the crackling zap. 'What twisted purpose could he have to do such a thing?'

Rowan's head slumped to the side, and a foul stench filled

the air as she lost control of her bladder, all bodily functions giving way.

Zander shot me a pointed glance. 'Stop with this cruelty. She's reached her limit. Knocking her out won't help. Plus, we should check her wound. It might need attention.'

I rushed over to him, my fist clenched and thrust towards his face. 'Cruelty? You're worried about cruelty?' I spat the words out. 'Were your ears closed when I told you what she did to me and Coral?'

Zander raised both hands. 'I understand you're upset and angry,' he said, his voice soft. 'We're all feeling it. But it's crucial to stay level-headed and to think logically, rather than let your temper dictate your actions.'

Cooper's hand landed on my shoulder. 'Zander's right. Let's give her some time to come around. She'll need food and water, then we'll figure out our next steps.'

Zander's tense expression softened, his shoulders relaxing as a flicker of relief flashed across his face. 'How about we take some time to contact the other cave settlements?' he suggested, his tone lighter. 'We could request a meeting at Ashen Ridge.' Turning to face me, his eyes regained their usual warmth. 'Your time would be better spent meeting with people, rallying their support and uniting them under your cause. Focusing on this would serve your purpose far more effectively than torturing Rowan.'

His words struck a chord, a reminder of the darkness threatening to consume me. I met his gaze with a sheepish look. 'Put her back in the pit for now.' Even though I had stopped, I didn't want to admit he was right. 'I'll deal with her later. But if she's of no use to us, then she should be dead.'

Inhaling deeply, I composed myself. 'Give me a few hours, and then meet me at the bar. We can discuss our ideas on how to deliver my message throughout the different communities then.'

As I strode away, their stares fell heavy on my back. Hurrying onward, I headed toward the only destination to quell the simmering rage burning all through my body.

* * *

After soaking in the warmth of the hot springs and changing into clean clothes, I felt more at ease, as if I could finally begin to think more clearly. But there was still one place I needed to be. I set out to find Freya, knowing that holding Nova would ground me and help make sense of everything.

Freya was in her quarters, feeding the little one from her breast. As my breath caught in my throat, I managed to whisper, 'I had no idea.'

Her smile washed away my embarrassment, as she motioned for me to join her. 'She's nearly full and content. Look how heavy her eyes are getting,' she said, wiping Nova's tiny mouth with a cloth. She passed her to me. 'Here, have a cuddle before I put her down for a nap.'

The same feeling of love from before overwhelmed me once more as I breathed in her sweet baby scent. With a touch of shyness, I asked, 'What was it like for you, becoming a mother?'

Mary had shared Laura's story with Coral and me, the tale of Ash's birth, which tragically claimed her life.

She screwed up her face. 'It was hours of pain, but the moment I held her,' she paused, love shining from her face as she looked at her daughter. 'The pain vanished, replaced by the most incredible feeling I never knew existed.'

'There you are,' Cooper announced, as he entered the chamber. 'I've been searching high and low for you, Jasmine.' He joined me at the bed to look lovingly at his niece.

I glanced up at him and smiled. 'I needed some time to cool off. Zander was right. I should've been more careful.'

Cooper nodded. 'Rowan will be fine. I'll make sure someone checks in on her soon. The others are gathered at the bar. Are you ready to join them?'

I didn't feel great and was at odds with myself, but I knew I had to push through. Kissing the top of Nova's head, I gently placed her in her small box bed. 'Okay, let's go,' I murmured, my gaze fixed on Nova's peaceful face as I brushed her cheek. Her tiny eyes opened and met mine. At that moment, all the pain and suffering seemed to fade away. 'I'll come back soon, little one,' I whispered.

'You can visit anytime,' Freya said, pausing from folding Nova's clothes. 'We love having you around.'

Parting from them felt like battling an unseen force. I longed to remain in their presence, drawing strength from the bond we were forming, and to forget I was preparing for the impending war.

* * *

As I made my way to the bar, raucous laughter and the clinking of jugs filled the air. Moonshine flowed freely, while rowdy rebels crowded every corner. Fists pounded on tables, and voices rose in in shouts of boastful defiance. I couldn't hep but notice the complete absence of order or discipline among them.

'While I was sulking, you've been busy drawing a crowd,' I said, turning to Cooper.

He gestured toward Zander with a nod. 'You have him to thank. He's determined not to let you down.' Taking my arm, he guided me forward into the centre of the chamber. 'Now, it's time to introduce yourself to those you aspire to lead.'

I could feel my pulse racing in my ears, each thump resonating like the call to battle. I rubbed my forehead with a shaky hand and took a deep breath. 'Hello everyone,' I said, my voice quivering despite my efforts to sound confident. 'I've come here to be with you, to fight alongside you for what's right.'

But my words were swallowed by the boisterous chatter of the crowd, their attention scattered like sand through an hourglass. I strained to project my voice, each word a battle cry in the tumultuous sea of sound. 'Together, alongside the Resistance, some hiding within the government ranks, we can bring about the freedom we seek,' I shouted, my conviction adding strength to my words.

It took several moments for the chatter to settle down, their voices fading into a low murmur. Nods of approval rolled through the groups as they began to listen. Among them, an older man with steely eyes rose from his seat. 'We welcome you, Jasmine,' he said, his voice gruff. 'Pops speaks highly of you, said you're a beacon of hope in these dark times. We'll stand by your side and help pave the path to victory. But it's the other cave settlers you need to convince.'

His speech ignited an outpouring of cheers and raised fists around the chamber. Cooper and my other friends joined in on their enthusiasm, their faces alight with happiness. I noticed Jaz and her group of followers, their features twisting with sneers as they rose from their seats and marched out of the chamber, their departure a silent protest.

'Where are they going?' I asked, upset at their obvious dislike of me.

'Don't worry about them. They'll come round,' Cooper said.

I lifted my hand, signalling for silence, my voice cutting through the echoes of their cheers. 'If anyone thinks this fight will be easy, they're in for a rude awakening,' I declared. 'We've only one shot to catch our enemy off guard. If we blow it, it will be a long, bloody struggle. That's why we must rally the other settlements to our cause.'

Pausing, I scanned the faces before me, meeting their eyes

with a determined gaze. 'I'm calling for scouts to head out and gather our allies on Ashen Ridge.' I continued to shout, even though the noise from the crowd had settled. 'And we need leaders – those willing to step up and command. If that's you, come and find me after this meeting.'

Volunteers bustled around afterwards, speaking with myself and Cooper. We took their names, and thanked them for their willingness, as they chatted in excited tones of freedom. Among the flurry of activity, whispers spread rapidly carrying the news of the upcoming gathering atop Ashen Ridge. Noon the next day was set as the time to unite everyone and have us all stand together.

'That went well,' Cooper said, as the crowds dispersed. 'Let's grab some rat skewers before we call it a night.'

'It felt a bit too easy,' I said, unease stirring my gut. 'If you don't mind, I think I'll go and spend some time with Freya. She mentioned she's tired, and I can lend a hand with Nova so she can get some rest.'

'I've noticed how fond you are of my niece,' Cooper said, his expression softening. 'Freya will be delighted, especially tonight. Orion's on scavenge duty.'

With weary smiles, Cooper, Astrid, Felix, Zander and Minx exchanged goodnights. In that fleeting moment, our eyes conveyed a shared understanding, a silent promise to confront whatever trials would follow together. As they departed, I felt honoured to have them on my side.

As I made my way toward Freya's quarters, the myriad challenges we faced raced through my mind. Approaching a junction of tunnels, a sinister figure suddenly blocked my path. My heart skipped a beat, and I froze in fear. The black cloak billowed ominously, its large pointed hood obscuring its features in the darkness. A voice, in an unrecognisable whisper sent chills down my spine. 'Leave the caves while you can. If you go to Ashen Ridge, you won't make it down alive.'

23

Back at Fraya's chamber, Cooper's composed façade wavered, disbelief flashing across his face. 'I'm baffled. How could you not see their face? If someone leapt out at you as you say, surely you'd notice some detail about them, wouldn't you?'

Squeezing my eyes shut, I strained to summon any tiny detail that might help. 'They wore a long black cloak, draped from head to foot. The hood covered their face and neck too.'

Cooper's shoulders sagged, his face masked with disappointment. 'And the voice?' he pressed, hoping for a more fruitful outcome. 'Was it male or female?'

A heavy sigh escaped my lips. 'Cooper,' I murmured, unable to hide my frustration any longer. 'How many times do I need to repeat myself? It was a whisper.'

'Long black cloaks are common,' Freya murmured, her gaze fixed on Nova's tear-streaked face. 'With just that to go on, we can't narrow down a suspect,' she added, lifting the child from her box bed to soothe her. 'I think she feels your distress, Jasmine.'

'I don't get it,' Cooper said, scratching his chin. 'You've

barely been here, and haven't had time to stir up any trouble. Why would someone want you dead? Are you sure you heard right? Maybe it was the moonshine messing with your head . . .'

'Hang on,' I interrupted, halting his train of thought. 'I swear, I didn't even take a sip of moonshine. I'm being straight with you about what went down. Perhaps it's a bluff. They could've killed me right then and there if they'd wanted.'

Cooper raised his palms in surrender. 'I'm only trying to see it from all angles. It seems like a threat rather than someone messing around.'

As if things couldn't get any worse, Felix burst into Freya's quarters. His eyes were wide and his chest heaved with each breath. 'Jasmine,' he gasped out. 'It's Rowan . . . she's gone.'

I jumped from the small stool, its legs scraping against the floor with a sharp clatter as it toppled over. 'Is it possible there's a government spy living among us?'

Every pair of eyes in the chamber fixed on me, their gazes reflecting sheer disbelief. It was Freya who who spoke. 'The government's goal is to eradicate my people, not spy on them. I'm sorry, Jasmine, but what you're implying doesn't add up.'

I whipped around to face Felix and barked, 'Fetch Astrid, Minx, and Zander. Tell them we'll meet in the bar in ten minutes. We need to track Rowan down before she slips away, and find out who helped her.'

* * *

The tension in the bar was unmistakable. Zander shifted uncomfortably, his shoulders slumping under an invisible weight. His eyes darted around everywhere, avoiding mine.

Cooper's voice came low but firm as he confronted him. 'Are you going to tell her, or should I?'

'Tell me what?' I snapped.

Zander's body tensed. 'I'm sorry,' he said, faltering for a

moment. Cooper nudged him, urging him on. 'I helped Rowan,' he confessed, his words coming out in a rush. 'I took her to the hot springs and let her wash. After giving her fresh clothes, food, and painkillers, I returned her to the pit, hoping her absence would go unnoticed.'

I closed the distance between us in just a few strides, my hand connecting sharply with his cheek in a stinging slap. 'How dare you go behind my back.' I seethed, my tone furious. 'You had no right.' My body shook with uncontrollable anger, making it difficult to find the right words. I inhaled deeply trying to calm the storm raging inside me. 'Did you threaten my life last night?'

Zander's eyes widened. His lips trembled before he managed to speak, his voice wavering. 'I . . . I don't get it,' he stammered. 'Someone threatened you?' His eyes darted back and forth. 'Seriously, you think I would threaten you?'

My glare could have shattered steel. 'Don't mess with me, Zander.'

Cooper intervened, shaking his head. 'That's enough, Jasmine. Zander didn't threaten you. All he's guilty of is compassion. Whoever's pulling malicious strings here is succeeding in their scheme. This is what they want – us fighting amongst ourselves.'

Even though I knew Cooper was right, my anger toward Zander compelled me to retaliate. I pointed my finger at his face. 'If you ever betray me again, you'll join Rowan in the pit.' Rage simmered on my face as I issued the warning.

Zander's next words struck me like a lightning bolt. 'She's not as bad as you'd like to believe,' he said, his uncertainty of my reaction making him blurt his feelings out. 'Remember, she's also a victim of Ruin, just like I was a victim of Spindle's torture.' He paused, then continued when I remained silent. 'I had a lengthy conversation with her, and she's willing to meet with you, and will try and remember everything she can.'

'So, at least on one front, we've made progress,' Cooper said, giving Zander a hearty pat on the back. 'We should go and see her now before she has second thoughts.'

Zander opened his mouth to speak, but his words faltered. A fleeting glance of hesitation crossed his face, his fingers twitching nervously at his sides.

'What is it?' I asked, my tone still defensive.

'You should take her some oranges,' he said, avoiding my gaze. 'She liked them. Claimed the ones on Ruin didn't match up, not as zesty or juicy.' He paused, finally meeting my stare. 'I asked her how she remembered the oranges but not what happened at your trial. She reckoned the distinct taste of ours was what jogged her memory.' He grew more confident. 'Giving it a try this way might bring better results. Well, that's my take on it, at least.'

'You understand what happens next? Once we've gathered all the information, we can't just set her loose,' I said, concerned Zander was forming a forbidden attachment to her.

His jaw tightened. 'I'm not a fool,' he said, his fingers now clenched into fists at his side. 'I know exactly what needs to be done when the time comes. 'But,' he continued, his tone softening, 'We must handle it with dignity. Don't let hate consume and strip away your humanity, Jasmine. I see you changing before my eyes, becoming as ugly as the scars on my face. The last thing we need is to become like those we seek to free ourselves from.'

I knew he was right but I wasn't ready to admit it. 'After everything she's done, she deserves to suffer.'

Reaching out, he gripped my shoulder, his eyes silently pleading. 'If we're going to forge a new path of existence, it starts right here,' he said, his gaze sweeping over each of us. 'All of you, more than anyone should understand this.'

Acknowledging the truth in his wisdom was the right thing

to do but the festering hate inside me held sway. It robbed any ability I had to find a voice of reason.

Zander continued, 'Mercy isn't a weakness. It's the strength of a worthy leader – one who wields both authority and compassion.' He paused, a sad smile tugging his lips. 'It's what my father always saw in you.'

His words hit me hard, stirring up a tsunami of conflicting emotions. 'I understand, Zander,' I began,' trying to rein in the hate controlling my feelings. 'But how can we choose mercy when our survival is on the line?'

'Listen,' Cooper said, his voice reassuring. 'We've got this. Trust in us, Jasmine. Trust in yourself too, but take time to consider that perhaps Zander's right. Why not let him question Rowan?'

With a sceptical glance at Zander, I relented. 'Fine, let's do this, but don't be too lenient,' I said, 'I still need answers.'

* * *

Despite Rowan having washed, remnants of dirt still clung to her skin. Her pallid face bore the weariness of her ordeal, and she grimaced as she eased herself onto the familiar stool. Her movements were cautious as if every action jangled her body with pain. Hunched to one side, she seemed to be in search of a comfortable position.

We stood outside her line of vision while Zander kneeled in front of her, pouring hot soup from a flask into a small jug. 'Here, have some of this. It'll warm you up,' he said, handing it to her.

'Thank you, Zander. You're very kind,' Rowan murmured, her cracked lips barely moving. She sipped slowly, savouring each mouthful, the warmth slowly creeping into her chilled bones.

He gently massaged the stump and the remaining part of her arm. 'Did the ointment I put on earlier help with the pain?'

Despite her considerable suffering, her eyes shimmered with gratitude. 'It numbed it a little and the the fresh bandages eased the discomfort.'

'How's the soup? It's a blend of onions and carrots, seasoned with a touch of oregano for added flavour,' he said, helping steady the jug in her shaking hand.

Zander waited patiently while she finished supping. 'You said you'd like to help Jasmine with the information she needs.' He took the empty jug from her hand and dabbed her mouth with a cloth. 'Has anything come back to you that you'd like to share?'

Her fingers brushed against the side of her temple. 'Whenever I try to remember, there's a stabbing sensation here. It's as though the memories want to surface, only to be pushed back by the pain.'

Rowan's words resonated with me, evoking memories of my struggles to recall our shared past. That same ache she described was all too familiar, a constant companion when I delved into our early years on Ruin. Each attempt felt like wading through murky waters, where fragments of memory lay hidden, waiting to be discovered.

'Close your eyes and empty your mind,' Zander said, his voice smooth and velvety. 'Don't force anything but allow memories to surface of their own accord.' Each word rolled off his tongue like a soothing balm.' Don't panic if nothing surfaces immediately - sit still, and listen to the sound of your breathing. Big deep breaths in and out.' He lulled her into a tranquil state as if he were weaving a spell. 'Tell yourself there is no pain.'

Reluctantly, I found myself in awe of Zander. He was kind and patient, allowing Rowan the space and time she needed to collect her thoughts.

As she opened her eyes, her gaze wandered past Zander until it met mine and a fleeting moment of recognition flickered across her features. 'Jasmine,' she murmured. 'We knew each other once. I can't quite grasp the details, but I believe we were friends.'

Despite her acknowledgment, I couldn't rid myself of the nagging suspicion it was a ruse to distract from her present situation - that she was simply toying with me.

She touched her fingers to her mouth, and a look of shock crossed her face. 'I remember our lips meeting, and the whirlwind of sensations it awakened in me. It was something entirely new. Every day, I struggled to win your attention from Ash.'

This revelation caught me off guard, leaving me feeling exposed beneath the watchful eyes of everyone in the chamber. I shifted uncomfortably, feeling as if I were being judged by all.

Sensing my discomfort, Zander asked, 'Why did you make up stories during Jasmine's trial? What made you say those things?'

A look of confusion settled over her features, and I could see her deep in thought, trying to remember her actions and the conversations. After a few minutes, she answered. 'We were all under so much pressure. Malus wanted a conviction, dangling promises of prestigious positions on the mainland. Spindle resisted, though.'

She shook her head, trying to sort through her memories. 'He always despised you. Or maybe I'm getting it all mixed up?' With a frustrated sigh, she buried her face in her hand. 'I can't take this anymore,' she muttered. 'My head feels as if it's being bashed with a club.'

Zander reached out, squeezing her shoulder. 'Breathe deeply and let the pain drift away,' he murmured, his voice low and melodic. 'Don't let it consume you. Now, think back - Why did Malus have Coral cloned?'

Rowan faced me again. 'I can't seem to recall who Coral is,' she said, her brow knitting. 'Remembering you, and . . . Lily, is hard enough.' She paused, tears welling at the corner of her eyes. 'Oh, my goodness, poor Lily. She was getting lost and I was awful to her.'

I blurted out before I could think, 'You remembered Lily the other day when we travelled through the tunnel.'

'Did I? I'm sorry, but I don't feel I've remembered her until now.'

Zander shot me a piercing look, urging me silently not to interfere. He switched his focus back to Rowan. 'Did Lily report finding an old woman in the Black Cave to the authorities?'

She squinted, straining to dredge up the deep recollections locked away in her subconscious mind. 'I'm not sure,' she said, a look of uncertainty crossing her face. 'Lily mentioned the old woman, but I didn't buy it. She'd been babbling on about finding dead children, spinning wild tales. It was like she was unraveling - going crazy. Where is she now? Why don't you ask her?'

My words sliced through the air. 'Lily was cleansed, Rowan. It happened back on Ruin during mine and Coral's trial.'

Rowan's complexion turned even more ashen, her mouth falling open. 'She can't be dead,' she whispered, her voice quivering. 'Not Lily . . . it can't be.' She fell into a stunned silence for a moment, but then, without warning, a primal scream erupted from her, raw and guttural. Tears poured down her face, her anguish spilling in an torrential flood.

'What's happening to her?' I asked, as Zander held her in his arms.

It was Cooper who replied. 'Perhaps the shock of kidnapping, losing a limb, enduring torture, and being confined in darkness has shaken Control from her system.

We stepped back, giving her the space she needed to grieve. Zander stayed by her side, embracing her tightly while uttering words of comfort. His warmth was a silent promise - she wasn't alone in her sorrow.

When her tears finally subsided, her eyes remained red and swollen, a haunting reflection of the turmoil she had just endured. 'You were asking about Coral,' she said, her voice hoarse. 'I remember her now.'

I could feel a knot tighten in my stomach. 'Go on,' I said, bracing myself for what Rowan was about to reveal.

'Malus and Aconite were concerned when Spindle swayed the crowd to his way of thinking during your trial. Their unease deepened as they contemplated the consequences. Determined to prevent any child from stepping out of line again, they concocted a plan - one that would install fear and ensure compliance, no matter the cost.'

My thoughts spiralled into a maze of potential scenarios. 'What does this have to do with Coral being cloned?'

It seemed as though Rowan was absorbing the information while sharing it with us. A flicker of horror swept across her face. 'Each year, on the anniversary of your trial,' she paused, as if the weight of her next words was overwhelming. 'A cloned Coral would be offered to Pax as a sacrifice so that the events of what happened would never be forgotten. Additionally, the cloned Coral would have to choose a child from Ruin to be sacrificed alongside her.'

Cooper's brow furrowed as Rowan's revelation sank in. 'Wait, none of this makes sense. A cloned Coral would still be an infant. Nowhere near the age needed to replicate a yearly sacrifice.'

Rowan leaned towards Cooper. 'You wouldn't believe the cutting-edge technology we have in reproductive and biotechnology. We can place embryos in artificial wombs and enhance their growth hormones. Our government can reproduce anything and anyone to the exact age in just a matter of months. Coral was supposed to be the first sacrifice, but there are plenty more of her waiting.'

'Wait a minute,' I said, backtracking on Rowan's last comment. 'What did you mean by Coral was *supposed* to be the first.'

'Jasmine, the sacrifice never happened,' she said, matter-of-factly. 'I remember Coral now. Her notes show that she did leave for Mortem, but a storm blew her watercraft against the rocks at Hazarded Bay. As far as we know, Coral drowned.'

24

More than ever, I needed to speak with Spindle. Countless narratives swirled around, each one adding weight to my growing dread. Neither Spindle, Aspen, Ash or Robinia offered any hint regarding Coral's absence from the sacrifice on Mortem. The uncertainty ate away at me, gnawing its way into every thought.

Not only that, Robinia had spoken of Coral's arrival at Mortem before I departed from Ruin. She couldn't confirm Coral had been sacrificed but had intimated it was highly likely. I felt as though my sanity hung by a fraying thread, threatening to unravel at any moment. I wanted answers.

The bar stank of sweat and spilt moonshine; and drunken laughter snapped me from my thoughts. I turned to Zander. 'Someone needs to clean this place up,' I said, watching the rest of my friends mingle. Segments of their conversations floated past, and it was selfish of me to begrudge any one of them happy moments. We'd be at war soon.

Zander's voice cut through my foul mood. 'Rowan could be making it all up.'

I mulled it over, surprised his statement reflected my earlier suspicions. It was as if he had plucked the doubt I first felt straight from my mind. 'She knew too much about other stuff - the kiss. She could be still be playing us though.'

'In any case, we have good news. The scouts we sent out with invites to meet at Ashen Ridge proved fruitful. I think we'll have quite a crowd.'

'You should go and celebrate. Go on, join the others. They'd be better company. I don't need babysitting, Zander.'

Leaning back in his chair, he crossed his arms. 'I won't be leaving you alone anywhere,' he said, his loyalty evident. 'If someone here aims to harm you, they'll have to go through me first.'

His words warmed my heart, a reminder of the unbreakable bond we'd forged. A faint smile tugged at the corner of my lips. 'Thank you,' I murmured, feeling the knot of anxiety lift from my stomach.

With a relaxed grin on his face, he added. 'Besides, I'm not keen on moonshine. It rots your gut and triggers flatulence. Not a good mix for enclosed spaces.'

His humour brought a chuckle, providing respite from the turbulence in my mind. I felt grateful for his friendship, a life-line in such traumatic times. Yet, I also felt guilty for the way I'd treated him recently. 'Does it hurt?' I asked, focusing on the burns on his face and neck.

'It's nothing, doesn't hurt much anymore,' he said, his fingers tracing the scars on his face and neck. 'Did you suspect I was running off with Rowan for the skin grafts she promised?'

I reached across the table and took his hand. 'I'm sorry,' I said, meeting his gaze. 'Please forgive me.'

'There's nothing to forgive. You're under so much stress.'

'You should see the scars on my back - big ugly welts. If we win our freedom . . .'

He cut me off, slamming his fist light-heartedly on the table. '*When* we win.'

'When we win, you'll be first in line for those skin grafts,' I teased, my tone light but sincere. Then, with a deep breath, I took a more serious approach. 'My apology extends beyond plain words,' I said, looking at him in earnest. 'My behaviour was appalling. You're right – I harbour a darkness, one I struggle to control. The anger prompts me to lash out, but what I did to Rowan . . . it brought an unsettling pleasure I can't seem to fathom.'

Zander leaned forward, his elbows resting on the table. 'It's understandable after all she did to you. But I won't have you turning into her, or her kind. Your compassion is what sets you apart.'

I pressed my teeth into my bottom lip. 'What if I can't control it? What if it consumes me, and the darkness takes over?'

He took my hand in a firm grip. 'I'll be your conscience,' he said with a half-smile. 'Just try not to slap me quite so hard the next time I try to talk some sense into you. You're like a sister to me, so please, be the sister I need you to be.'

'You've stood by me since we left Spindle's camp. My judgment was clouded, making me believe you were against me. I was foolish, and too proud to admit it. Saxon would be incredibly proud of you, Zander.' I squeezed his fingers.' I'm heading to bed. I'll let this lot run riot tonight,' I said, my gaze sweeping across the scene of merriment until it settled on Minx. She was now the centre of attention, dancing clumsily on a table. 'But tomorrow, we begin to act like soldiers.'

'I'll walk you to your chamber and stand guard in your passageway,' he said, pushing his chair back and rising to his feet. 'I promised Cooper I wouldn't let you out of my sight. We're all going to take turns to watch over you.'

'The last time you stood guard was in the tunnel, and you nodded off.' I replied, with a light playful punch to his chest.

A grin spread across his face, accompanied by a mischie-vous wink. 'That was before we became soldiers.'

Hooking our arms together, we made our way out of the bar. The clinking of jugs and hearty laughter faded into the back-ground. As we walked towards the confines of my sleeping quar-ters, a sense of unease settled over me, but I found comfort in Zander's presence at my side. Our conversation remained light, as we savoured the passing tranquillity – a calm interlude before the war. One thing was certain, I would never doubt his loyalty again.

At the threshold of my chamber, a small wooden box was placed on the floor. I picked it up, noticing the outline of inscriptions etched in the ancient language. 'What does it say?' I asked, showing it to Zander.

'It's your name, Jasmine,' he replied, taking the box from me, and prising the lid open. A curse escaped his lips. He tipped the box upside down, spilling its contents onto the ground.

It scurried away from us, its tail arched high, its dark, glossy armour glinting briefly in the firelight before it sought refuge in the shadows. It was fascinating; I had never seen one before. 'What type of insect is it?' I asked.

Zander brought his boot down upon it, the creature meeting its end beneath his heavy heel. 'It's not an insect,' he said his tone grave. 'It was a scorpion, and its venom is highly poisonous. Hardly the kind of gift you'd want left in your sleeping quarters.'

* * *

Ashen Ridge sprawled beneath jagged peaks, its open terrain blending seamlessly into the rugged landscape. We shivered as we trudged through the thick frost, which transformed the landscape into an enchanting wonderland, where every laboured breath pierced our lungs.

Freezing moisture penetrated my boots leaving my toes tingling and numb.

After the endless gloom of the caves, I squinted as the brilliant light outside hit my eyes. No matter the chilly air, it felt good to be outside.

Individuals gathered, all dressed in unique furs and vivid colours, creating a breathtaking display of diversity, not only in clothing but in race. Despite the evident variations in appearance, their camaraderie portrayed an image of unity, where difference was celebrated rather than feared.

Yet, there lingered a sobering reminder of the misguided ideals perpetuated by our government leaders – a notion of racial purity that sought to erase the richness of all other cultures standing before me.

As Cooper and I strolled through the crowd, the air buzzed with a melody of languages and accents, each group emitting its distinct tempo and sound. 'How many variations of the old language is there?' I asked.

'After the End of Days, many countries were wiped out. But here in the caves, we have fifteen varied groups. We move freely among our communities,' he said, with a hint of pride. 'And try to learn a bit of each other's native tongue. Most, but not all, speak Echelon, the language you speak. This was favoured by the one-world government when they emerged from bunkers to rebuild the world.'

It never dawned on me that the language I spoke had a name. The mainland still felt foreign to me, but I could see an abundance of possibilities worth fighting for. With a newfound sense of hope, I made a solemn new vow – not driven by vengeance but rooted in the promise of a brighter future. I would lead these people to victory.

'Cooper, could you teach me all the different languages?' I asked, realising the task would be enormous. 'It would be amazing to converse with the people in their native tongues.'

He nodded, and I detected a note of admiration when he answered, 'I can help with some, but there will be others more qualified than I am.'

Minx approached, her step weary, her eyes dulled and bloodshot. 'Zander told me about the scorpion,' she said, her voice rough. 'I swear, when we find the culprit, I'll beat the life out of them for planting it in your quarters.'

I didn't want to dwell on internal enemies at this moment, so I shifted the conversation. 'How's the head?' I asked. 'That was quite a bit of moonshine you knocked back last night?'

Minx Shuddered. 'I've had better mornings.'

Cooper refused to let the matter of my safety rest. 'Don't worry,' he said, his eyes sweeping over the surrounding crowd. 'If anyone dares to cause you harm, we'll be ready for them.' Turning to Minx, he ordered, 'You stay here with us. Astrid and Zander are mingling, keeping an eye out for anyone behaving suspiciously.'

Jaz, Klin, and their group arrived, bringing with them an air of tension, settling nerves on edge among those gathered. Their boisterous behaviour drew glances and whispered speculations, as murmurs rippled through the crowd.

'Why did they come if they're here only to cause trouble?' I asked, feeling my heart sink.

'Hopefully, they're here to listen and not make waves.' Cooper replied. 'Jaz and her group are not dangerous, they're just all show. They've always been the same way.'

'Do you reckon it's time for me to begin? I'm worried if we wait any longer, people will leave.'

Cooper nodded. 'Whenever you're ready.'

As I strode to our makeshift stage, a nervous chill ran down my spine. Cooper's confident smile reassured me a little. The solid wood of the table beneath my feet felt like both an anchor and a reprieve from the cold slush below.

'Thank you all for gathering here this afternoon.' I shouted out with as much volume as I could. 'For those who don't know me, I'm Jasmine and was born on the mainland from the breeder programme. On the day of my birth, I was transported to the Island of Ruin and grew up in a harsh and unloving society. Convicted for a simple act of kindness, I was sentenced to toil in the mines – working until death would see fit to claim me.'

A collective murmur arose from the crowd as a hooded figure pushed its way forward, parting the gathered bodies like a cresting wave. People shifted uneasily, heads turning to catch sight of the disturbance and follow the figures path. Whispers of discontent swelled, growing louder with each step. The figure pressed on through the throng like a cleaver slicing through flesh.

From the corner of my eye, I glimpsed Astrid and Zander, moving swiftly, poised to intercept whoever it was. As the figure emerged at the front, I shielded my eyes from the harsh light, squinting for a better view. A hushed silence fell over the crowd, broken only by the sound of their uneven footstep on crutches. The figure balanced on one leg, waving one of his sticks in an attempt to push past Astrid and Zander.

'You said you were found guilty of an act of kindness.' His voice boomed, drowning out the mutterings. 'Did it involve providing shelter and food to an elderly woman named Mary?'

The question caught me off guard, sending a rush of adrenaline racing through my veins. 'Let him pass,' I shouted, signalling for Astrid and Zander to stand down. They stepped back and allowed him through.

Clambering down from the table, I made my way to him. 'Did you have a connection with Mary?' I asked.

'Mary was the mother of the woman I loved,' he said, pulling his head free from his hood. His brown eyes met mine. 'She journeyed to Ruin to find my son, but never returned.' His gaze was steadfast. 'There's a rumour circulating it was you who helped her. Please, tell me if there's any truth to this, or if it's simply a myth?'

Mary had never hinted that Larch was alive, leaving me to believe, that like Laura, he'd passed away. Yet here I stood, facing Ash's father, caught between disbelief and astonishment.

25

The meeting exceeded our expectations, although a few settlements remained cautious about aligning with the Resistance. Despite their apprehension, those with doubts voiced a willingness to reconvene at Ashen Ridge in two days to provide a definitive answer.

Back in the bar once more, and with moonshine now off-limits, we all sipped on herbal tea.

When do you think Spindle will come?' Cooper asked.

'He said I would recognise the sign when I saw it but assured me it would happen soon.' I said, struggling to mask my frustration. Robinia had mentioned looking for signs back on Ruin when she initially discussed the group opposing the government from within. It was an inefficient approach, and I would address this with Spindle when I spoke to him again.

'Larch's arrival made an impact,' Astrid remarked. 'Seeing him stride through the crowd, one wouldn't have guessed he was on crutches. He did us a tremendous favour. Did you hear the cheers from the crowd when he embraced you, hailing you as a hero?'

Orion's eyes dropped to the ground, his cheeks tinged with

a faint red as he shifted awkwardly. His mouth opened slightly, then closed again, as if he didn't know what to say. Finally, he asked, 'Did you really go against your laws to help one of us?'

'It wasn't just me. My friend Coral helped Mary too.'

He still couldn't look me in the eye. 'I made Klin and Jaz's group dislike you on purpose, hoping to cause problems for you here,' he confessed. 'As we left Ashen Ridge, I spoke with her. Had we known the extent of your sacrifices for one of ours, our attitudes would've been different towards you. Some of her group might remain sceptical, but you'll find hearts have changed. I'm so sorry, Jasmine.'

'Don't worry. We're on the same side now and that's all that matters,' I said, glad I'd no longer need to endure Jaz's icy stares whenever our paths crossed.

Zander drummed his fingers on the table. 'You were too modest, claiming it was me who captured Rowan. We did it together, so never underestimate your contributions again.'

Felix asked, 'Where do we go from here?'

His question drew all eyes to me. It dawned on me I couldn't keep riding in the passenger seat, relying on others to lead the way. It was time for me to step up and take charge. I rose from my seat, bracing myself against the table's edge. 'I'll personally visit the settlements who remain unsure for our next gathering at Ashen Ridge. Felix, let me know if I'll need interpreters, and if so, have them prepared to come with me.'

Cooper leaned back in his chair, eyeing me thoughtfully. 'That's quite a task,' he remarked. 'You've only got two days until the next meeting.'

'I'll manage, even if it means going without sleep until then. Can we swing by Larch's community on the way? I believe he could be a valuable asset to our cause. Mary shared information with me before she passed – about government leaders residing in private homes rather than Midpoints. He may know their whereabouts. Striking them here would catch them off guard.'

Astrid raised an eyebrow. 'Shouldn't Larch have disclosed this information before now?' she said, unable to conceal her bewilderment. 'If he's been part of our cave community for a long time, why keep this information to himself?'

I pondered her question. 'Let me speak with him before we jump to conclusions,' I said, rubbing my chin. 'After Ash was born, Mary was arrested. There's a chance Larch could've been detained as well. Let's find out more information before making any assumptions.'

Zander leaned forward, his eyes narrowing. 'What about Rowan?' he asked. 'Should we consider questioning her again? If not, then we all know what needs to be done. But I insist on one thing. He paused, fixing his gaze on me. 'The deed will be done, but not by your hands, Jasmine.'

A shift had taken root inside me; the desire for her demise no longer brought any pleasure. 'Yes, let's give her another chance, and you lead the process again, Zander.' I adopted some humility, valuing their thoughts on the matter. 'Afterward, depending on the information she offers, we can vote on what to do with her.'

Each of us drifted into quiet contemplation as a sobering silence settled over us.

Eventually, I asked, 'Have we received word back from the spies dispatched to monitor the soldier's movement at the camp?'

Zander coughed into his sleeve, before answering. 'They've located the fissure, but it seems they're not actively digging or utilising ground x-ray to pinpoint our passageways. Their camp remains active, but nothing shows imminent danger. Perhaps they're waiting on orders, or for specialised equipment.'

At least this news brought a sense of relief. Perhaps Robinia had diverted their attention, providing us with more time.

'Here's the plan,' I began. 'If Spindle doesn't show up following our meeting at Ashen Ridge, I'll take charge and lead a team to Robinia's camp to eliminate the threat. We can't afford to wait any longer.' I turned to Cooper. 'Round up a group of volunteers who are willing to join me for our initial assault.'

Astrid perked up. 'I'll head to the armoury and take stock of our weapons. If we're lacking anything, I'll arrange for the blacksmith to make the necessary preparations.'

'We have an armoury?' I asked, my curiosity piqued. 'Why am I only hearing of this now?'

'I thought you knew,' Astrid said, with a look of surprise. 'While our swords, spears, and arrows may not match the laser power of our enemies – we do take pride in what we have. We've adapted our fighting techniques with traditional weapons, and they've kept us alive so far.'

With a wry smile, Zander remarked. 'We call it hit and run.'

'On that note, let's pay Rowan a visit now then make a quick exit,' I said, trying to keep the mood light.

'I'll compile a list of the settlements you want to visit, and scout for interpreters,' Felix said.

Cooper shifted in his seat, his gaze flickering between me and Zander. 'Shall I come with you?' he asked.

'Actually, why don't you stay here and oversee the weaponry and manpower with Astrid? Zander and I will manage fine.'

The change in pace brought a refreshing shift, from waiting to taking action. It seemed to elevate the spirits of my companions, except Orion. He had been quiet most of the time, his face sullen. Perhaps going to war as a father was more difficult for him than for the rest of us.

* * *

Rowan appeared distressed, a sight that strangely gratified me. It was clear I still held a darkness that I thought was lost. When it came to Rowan, my moods appeared to be as changeable as the weather.

Despite her worn exterior, fear etched into her features, revealing an unmistakable mark of vulnerability. Her complexion remained drained of colour, while a faint tuft of auburn hair covered her head.

What struck me the most was the look in her eyes. Wide and glassy, they conveyed a stark awareness that her life could end anytime soon. I stifled any hint of satisfaction to avoid another scolding from Zander.

She devoured the small pear he offered, its clear juices dribbling down her chin. No part was wasted, as she consumed the core and stem too.

'What do you know about Malus?' Zander asked, handing her a cloth to clean her sticky face.

'I don't know much. I just followed his orders and reviewed statistics and data. There's nothing I can tell you that would be of help with whatever it is you plan to do.'

'Did you have access to his diary?' I asked.

Eyeing me warily, she gave a slight nod. 'Yes, but how relevant would that be now? Time has passed since I last laid eyes on it.'

I studied the black mole positioned above Rowan's lip. Minx had one too, almost identical in size and position. Their eyes shared the same shade of green. My mind raced with possibilities as I contemplated their likeness. Re-shaping Minx's eyebrows would further add to their likeness, not to mention if we shaved her head. The resemblance would be uncanny.

The notion felt far-fetched, bordering on the impossible. Still, a persistent thought remained – what if we could leverage Minx's resemblance to Rowan to confuse our enemy?

'Jasmine,' Zander said, snapping me from my daydream. 'Did you catch what Rowan just said?'

'Sorry, I was thinking of something else, but I don't think we could pull it off. What did I miss?'

Rowan's fingers flexed and curled before she rested her hand on her lap. 'I feel like the inside of my head is a jumble,' she said, her voice strained. 'I'd like to help you, but I can't guarantee the truth on anything I say because I'm unsure if it's true or false. I feel so confused and when I try, the pain in my head is worse than the agony from the stump you've left me with.'

'Do you need more painkillers?' I asked.

'That would help. But, I'm going to say what I think I know one last time, and then I'm done. I can't take much more. So, do what you intend to do, rather than put me back in that hole.'

Despite my hate, I felt a flicker of empathy for her. 'Okay,' I said, keeping my tone even. 'I promise, this will be the last time.'

Closing her eyes, she inhaled deeply, holding her breath before letting it out. 'Lily was scared, convinced she found a dead child on Ruin. But no one, including me, took her seriously. She told me she stumbled upon the old woman when she went to the beach, but I brushed it off as another hallucination. Lily reported it to her section command and was devastated when you were locked away. She couldn't forgive herself.'

Her eyes flew open. 'I've just remembered Salix. Oh no! Salix killed himself.' She buried her face in her hand, tears streaming down her cheeks. 'What did they do to us?' she murmured, between sobs.

'Rowan, it's okay.' Zander comforted her, his hand kneading her shoulder. 'Let all your grief out.'

She wiped her nose with the cloth Zander had given her and cleared her throat. Her lower lip trembled. 'Can I ask you a question, Jasmine?'

I nodded. 'Sure, what is it?'

'Did they carry out experiments on us?'

Her question hung heavy, ladened with implications of the horrors we endured. Horrors that were locked away in the vaults of our subconscious.

'Yes, but we were conditioned not to remember.'

Rowan's gaze darted from me to Zander, her body tensing. 'There were rumours of children going missing while we were on Ruin. I think I know where they take them.'

'How could you possibly know this?' Zander asked.

Rowan's eyes bore the burden of shame. 'If I am remembering correctly, I used to meet children from Ruin at the port and take them to a place called Omen's Keep. This was part of my duties given by Malus.'

A primal wail escaped her, as she pounded her head with a clenched fist. Zander seized her wrist pulling her up from the chair and holding her to his chest in a tight embrace. 'It's alright,' he said, as she crumbled against him. 'Everything's going to be just fine.'

She clung to Zander, her voice cracked and raw with emotion. 'You have to save them,' she begged over and over. 'Terrible things are being done there.'

26

As we made our way back to the main cavern, each step felt like a battle against the passage of time. The urgency to take action pulsed like a drumbeat calling me to war. 'Damn it, Spindle, where are you?' My frustration bubbled to the surface in a muttered curse, his name becoming a bitter taste on my lips. But even as I resented his absence, I knew my instinct to press forward was the viable option. Remaining in a state of limbo would erode any advantage we might have over the government camp.

A searing pain lanced through my skull momentarily blinding me to everything. I staggered, my hand shooting out to grasp the coarse wall for support, the other holding my head. The world spun around me, threatening to pull me into its chaotic dance.

I winced as a sharp cramp shot through me, my muscles tensing against the onslaught of pain. My vision blurred, wavering like a candle flame in a gust of wind. It was as if a hammer were pounding on my head, trying to break down the walls of my consciousness.

Zander's voice cut through the haze of pain. 'What's wrong?' His hand closed around my waist in a firm grip.

I struggled to form the words. With great effort, I managed to lift my gaze to meet Zander's worried eyes. 'Headache,' I managed to rasp out. 'Help me back to my chamber. Medication – it's on the shelf.'

The trip back seemed to stretch on indefinitely. Eventually, Zander guided me to my bed and I sank gratefully onto its softness. He lit the candle on the shelf, his brow furrowed. 'Jasmine, your medication's not here?' Looking around, his fingers brushed the corners of the floor. 'They're gone. Someone must have taken them.' His cold hand touched my clammy brow. 'Hang in there, I'm going to fetch Ella. She'll be able to make one of her herbal potions.'

I must have blacked out. When I came to, Zander was there, propping me up while someone else poured liquid into my mouth. I spluttered and coughed, struggling to keep the bitter taste down. It spread through me, its effects slowly seeping into my weary body. It didn't eradicate the pain, only dulled its sharp edges and mute the ferocity.

My voice sounded croaky. 'What did you give me?'

Ella's ageing face drew nearer to mine, her gentle touch coaxing my eyelids open as she peered at them. 'It's a concoction known as Lavender's Lull,' she explained, in a calming tone. 'You'll feel better soon. Zander mentioned your pupils had constricted, but they're dilating back to normal now.'

I drifted of to sleep listening to the soft murmur of Zander and Ella's voices, the sound wrapping around me like a protective cocoon. There were no tormenting nightmares, only a serene expanse of peaceful darkness.

As I stirred awake, my eyes fluttered open to find Zander slouched at the foot of the bed. 'Seems you dozed off too,' I mumbled, disturbing his gentle snores. 'Where's Ella?' I asked, as he sat up.

'She left a short while ago, only when she was confident you'd be fine.'

Swinging my legs over the edge of the bed, I said, 'We need to start moving. Are you ready to go?'

Zander didn't try to hide his concern. 'Are you certain you're up for this? We could send the others.'

'I'm fine. I bet Minx has felt worse after a bucket full of moonshine. Anyway, it has to be me who goes,' I said, slipping on socks and boots. 'People need to see me to believe in me.' I looked up at him. 'Did you tell the others about my episode?'

'No, because I knew you wouldn't want me to. Cooper will be angry when he finds out.'

I thought about it for a few seconds, contemplating the implications. 'If Ella tells him, we'll be long gone by the time he finds out. Did Felix pass you the list of communities we need to visit?'

Zander nodded, 'Yes, and we don't need interpreters as they have folk among them who speak Echelon.' He picked up a flask from the table by my bed. 'And Ella made some extra Lavender's Lull. What do you think brought on your attack?'

I thought about it, trying to understand its sudden appearance myself. 'Perhaps it was the shock of Rowan's revelation. Coral suspected children were going missing, but I put it down to an overactive imagination.'

'Talking of Rowan, we need to decide what we're going to do with her?'

Rowan still posed a dilemma for me. I found myself torn in two, one part of me yearning to rid the world of her, while another part overruled that desire. 'Let's keep her alive for the time being. There's a chance she might recall more, and her cooperation is promising. She's completely changed from the Rowan I once knew. If someone had told me she'd shed a tear for anyone, I would never have believed them.'

'She didn't want to be kept alive if she were going back down the hole. Could we not move her to a chamber and have guards watch over her? She could also do with a bath, and her arm should be looked at, to make sure there's no infection.'

I cast a final glance around the chamber, taking in the familiar surroundings before hauling on my back and making my way towards the passageway. 'We'll see about making her more comfortable when we return.'

* * *

Stepping over the familiar tripwire safety measures, we ventured into the bulbous room decorated with cryptic writing. With the faint odour of minerals seeping through the walls, we continued into the complex network of tunnels.

After what felt like an eternity of twists and turns, we reached an opening and clambered through. Outside, the path stretched before us, flanked by towering sandstone cliffs looming like sentinels. Their imposing presence seemed to guard our route.

'We're almost there,' Zander said, catching his breath as we re-entered the mountain with branching paths ahead.

'How can you be sure we're heading in the right direction?' I asked, struggling to match his brisk pace.

Pride sounded in his voice. 'When you're born in these caves, it becomes ingrained in you, a way of life. We all know these tunnels like the backs of our hands,' Zander explained. 'Even though we live in separate settlements, we're all connected. We interact, mingle and often collaborate in scavenging and work. Though our homes may be divided, we're united as one people, looking after and making the most of the space we share.'

As we neared the entrance to the main cavern where Larch's community resided, a sentry's voice rang out, asking for our identity.

'I'm Zander, representing the Ember Enclave,' he announced, chuckling at my astonished expression. 'It earned its name from the lava flowing through it.'

'I didn't even know it had a name,' I said, realising there was still so much I had to learn.

As we approached, three men emerged from the cavern to meet us. The eldest among them stepped forward, extending his hand. 'Welcome,' he said with genuine warmth. His smile widened as his face shifted towards me.

'This is Jasmine who spoke at Ashen Ridge,' Zander said, wrapping his arm around my shoulder. 'She's come to speak with Larch.'

The elderly man grasped my hand in a hearty shake. 'I'm Falconer, and I'm very pleased to meet you. Come, we have food and drink to share. We'll let Larch know you're here.'

As we entered the main cavern, it bore a striking resemblance to our own at Ember Enclave. Flickering torches cast dancing shadows on the walls, illuminating the space with a warm, golden glow. A patchwork of colourful tapestries lined the walls and the overdone smell of grilled rat meat mixed with the chatter from many voices.

News of my arrival spread throughout the cavern bringing a sense of excitement. As we moved along, heads turned and whispers grew louder. Eager faces strained to catch a glimpse of me as people drew closer, their hands reaching out.

'I think it might be better if you met in Larch's chamber.' Falconer said, parting the crowd. 'We can arrange for refreshments to be brought to you there.'

It took a few minutes to reach Larch's chamber from the directions Falconer gave us, and as soon as Larch spotted us, he hopped over with a wide smile. 'Jasmine, it's wonderful to see you again so soon. I planned to attend the next meeting at Ashen Ridge, but having you here makes it more special.' He pointed toward a pile of cushions on the floor. 'Please, make yourselves comfortable. Are you hungry?'

'It's good to see you too,' I said, relieved to take the weight off my feet after our long hike. 'Falconer is arranging for food to be brought.'

A still moment hung in the air between us, a silent exchange speaking volumes as we acknowledged each other's presence. It was me who broke it.

'I hope you don't mind me asking, but what happened to your leg?'

A deep sorrow reflected in his eyes as he spoke. 'After Laura passed away,' he began, his voice weighed down with resignation. 'Mary was arrested and taken to one of the prison camps. Thankfully, she was eventually rescued by her people.' He paused, the words catching in his throat as he struggled to continue. 'I wasn't as fortunate.'

Larch's burden of pain was unmistakable, evident to even the most casual observer. As much as I hated pushing him, I had a feeling it was important to know. 'Why? What happened to you?'

'My father was a powerful man,' Larch revealed. 'I was put under house arrest where my memory was erased. 'But deep down, I felt a void in my life, a missing part of who I was. I escaped from his clutches without a clear destination or knowledge of who or what I sought. All I knew was something was missing, and I had to keep searching.'

Leaning forward, I reached out and took his hand, offering what little comfort I could. His hand felt warm in mine, but as he continued to share his story, I let go and settled back on the cushions. My heart filled with empathy listening to what he'd endured.

'The soldiers discovered me,' he said, his voice quivering. 'And returned me to my father's house. I suffered several beatings and underwent further mind experiments - as my father believed I retained memories of Laura and our child.' Remebering brought tears to his eyes. 'It was a recurring cycle, until the final time I was captured.'

A shudder passed through him. 'That's when my father ordered the removal of my leg. He hoped to stop me from escaping to the place I so desperately tried to find – but couldn't remember where or what it was.'

Zander's voice came in a whisper, but loud enough for us to hear his disgust. 'Monsters . . . your father was a monster.'

'How did you manage to find your way back to the caves?' I asked.

Larch let out a heavy sigh. 'If you ever experience true love, you'll understand what I'm about to share.' He paused, gathering his thoughts. 'No matter the efforts of the medics to fix my brain, my heart triumphed over their treatments. Despite having only one leg, I crawled deliriously from the hospital bed and along the cold, sterile floor of the medical bay. I was fortunate – the medic who discovered my attempted escape was part of the Resistance,' he explained, a note of gratitude laced through his words. 'He arranged for a brave soul to transport me to the foothills of these mountains, where I was left abandoned, but free.' A ghost of a smile touched his lips. 'The cave dwellers recognised me as Laura's lover, took me in, and saved my life.'

As remarkable as Larch's resilience was, it was also heart-breaking not to have the happy ending he deserved.

'Why did your microchip not lead the army to your hiding place?' I asked.

A hint of irony laced his tone. 'The elite and their families don't have microchips, Jasmine.' He pulled the collar of his sleeve back to show me his mark, nearly identical to the one on Ash's wrist. 'We're branded to keep a record of bloodlines, but still have freedom.'

I could only imagine the turmoil Larch must have undergone. To search for something erased from his mind, yet fuelled by love – persisting above all odds. His hand trembled as he reached into his pocket, his fingers struggling against the fabric.

He revealed a heart-shaped locket with a gentle pull, its surface catching the candlelight in a soft, ethereal glow.

'Mary was rescued from the camp and helped to heal my mind. It took a while, but the memories returned.' The sense of longing in his words could not be denied. 'She insisted on travelling to Ruin herself, confident in her ability to find my son and bring him home. But alas, you know the rest.'

His features softened as he held up the locket. 'I gave this to Laura when we fell in love, and she kept it hidden beneath her prison uniform. I managed to retrieve it after she died.' Leaning forward, he placed the locket in the palm of my hand. 'Mary would want you to have this,' he said, his voice filled with a mixture of sadness and hope.

Tears welled in my eyes, Larch's kind gesture stirring memories of Mary's small wooden cross, lost in the depths of the mines. 'I'll cherish this and keep it close,' I promised, gratitude flooding my heart for this precious gift.

As a young girl entered the room, balancing a tray of food, our emotionally charged feelings began to thaw. Larch's shoulders relaxed, as he greeted her with a smile, a stark contrast to the sombre expression he wore moments ago. Even Zander, who'd been silent for most of the conversation, leaned back in the cushions with a sigh. The clinking of plates and the smell of freshly brewed herbal tea signalled a subtle shift in the mood in the chamber.

As we ate, the conversation flowed smoothly, shifting between happiness and sorrow with each story Larch shared about Mary. He spoke of her with a tender fondness, recounting how her love, kindness and patience were the medicine used to guide him to his lost memories. Yet, a shadow veiled his expression when recalling Laura, advising when his memory of her eventually returned, he had to face the grief of losing her all over again.

I teetered on the brink of asking about his childhood. If he could summon to mind the opulent homes where the elite and their families resided, worlds away from the Midpoints or settlements.

'Jasmine,' he implored, before I had the chance, his face beseeching as he asked, 'Before she passed away, did Mary manage to find my son?'

His sudden question startled me, and I struggled to find the right words, my mind racing to formulate a response.

27

W hat could I say? Ash didn't deserve this family who loved him immensely - without ever having met him. Despite Larch enduring unimaginable hardships, I dithered to answer. Perhaps it was my hesitancy which gave him hope.

'I'm sorry,' I said, with regret. 'Mary's mission to find your son was an impossible challenge.' I grappled with the lie and my inability to forgive Ash. 'I wish it could have turned out differently.'

Larch's shoulders slumped, his chest heaving with each ragged breath. He buried his face in his trembling hands. Between muffled sobs, he choked out, 'Mary died for nothing.'

I sprang from the cushions, his distress propelling me forward. Dropping to my knees, I grasped Larch's hands firmly in mine. 'That's not true,' I said, asserting a truth. 'Mary's journey to Ruin led me to you and the people of the caves. Together, we'll fight for our freedoms. And when our battle ends, no child will be bred as a commodity, but born out of love.'

Larch released a deep breath. 'If he survived, he'd be of age now, and it's possible he could be a soldier fighting against us when our battle begins.' His gaze fell from my face to my wrist. Tenderly, he turned my right hand over to inspect my mark. 'You bear elite colours too,' he said, meeting my eyes again. 'Your lineage comes from an affluent bloodline.' he added, his thumb racing over the colours and shape.

'So, colours also signify a hierarchy. A sign of superiority,' I said, taken aback by the revelation. It was puzzling to think I could be born from such a high-ranking status.

'Indeed, purple, red, and also dark blue symbolises heredity of elite importance. It's quite likely I might have crossed paths or known your father. The resemblance of our ink is apparent, yet not substantial enough for a close kinship, perhaps more of a distant connection,' he speculated.

'I was born from a breeder,' I admitted, my eyes fixed on my mark. 'Why would an elitist couple with a woman of such low standing?'

'There's no simple explanation,' he said, releasing my hands. 'The government's thirst for slave labour knows no bounds. Some men, driven by ambition to climb the political ladder, would enter into such unions. Those at the pinnacle of power are ruthless. They'll resort to any means to maintain dominance and prestige, even if it means fathering a child they'll never acknowledge or care for.'

The desire to rid the world of these psychopaths burned fiercer with each new revelation. 'What do you know about a place called Omen's Keep?' I asked, my voice dripping with disdain.

Larch thought for a moment. 'The name doesn't spark any significant recollections, he said. 'I'm not saying I haven't encountered it in the past, but there are still gaps in my memory. Imagine it like a computer wiped clean, needing to rebuild its database from scratch.'

I had hoped larch would provide valuable insights, shedding light on the mystery surrounding the abducted children and the purpose of their captivity. Nevertheless, with Rowan still in our custody, there remained a glimmer of hope she might divulge further information about Omen's Keep.

Struggling to contain my frustration, I unclenched my fists, pleading against all odds for Larch to remember, for the puzzle pieces to fall into place. 'Can you recall anything about your childhood or the homes you lived in?'

'I believe I was content,' he mused, his brow furrowing deep in thought. 'My father was often absent, occupied with government duties. But when he returned home, he'd bring gifts, which brought joy to my mother.' His expression darkened as he continued to unravel memories. 'Growing up, I was shielded from the harsh realities of how others lived. I was taught to view the rebels from the caves as filthy beings, animals who consumed their young. It seems the medics who tampered with my brain wanted these perceptions to remain. I chose not to follow in my father's footsteps and instead trained as a medic.'

My eyes held a glimmer of hope as I asked, 'Can you recall the place where you spent your childhood? Would you be able to show me on a map?'

He answered with a touch of melancholy. 'Many years have slipped away. It's all a blur now. When I was brought to the caves, I was heavily medicated. Mary told me I'd travelled to them before when she helped rebuild my memory. Laura was pregnant, and I needed help to coordinate an escape for her and our child. But without Mary's help recalling that fact, I would never have known this.'

Mary's approach mirrored Zander's methods of healing, offering Rowan kindness and sustenance. It triggered fragmented yet precious pieces of information, albeit incomplete and hazy.

I raised the stakes, presenting Larch with a compelling proposition. 'Imagine being granted the one thing you desire most in the world. Do you think it could unlock your memories?'

'What could I possibly desire?' he asked, with a hint of intrigue. 'You can't bring back those I loved, can you?'

I locked in on his gaze. 'What if I could reunite you with your son?'

'But . . . but you said Mary didn't find him,' he stammered.

'Yes, that's true,' I said, acknowledging the fact. 'But Coral and I did. We didn't get the chance to tell her we'd found him before she was imprisoned. I know your son, and I'll have the opportunity to reach out to him soon.'

Larch's face lit up with hope. 'Why didn't you tell me this before?' he asked, his words rushing out. 'And how could you possibly have access to him?'

'His name is Ash, and he works with the Resistance.'

Speaking those words aloud marked a key moment, a turning point stirring deep emotions. It was a declaration signifying more than a change in perspective. It ignited a flame of forgiveness within me, not only for Ash, but for the sake of the man sitting before me. It carried hope for the future.

'Ash,' he murmured, his voice trembling. 'My son is alive.' The words froze him in place - as if their meaning was too much for him to comprehend. He repeated the name over and over, convincing himself of its truth. Then, shaking himself out of his stupor, he looked at me with newfound purpose. 'When are you planning to head back to Ember Enclave?'

Zander reached into his backpack, pulling out the list of communities Felix had entrusted to him. 'We plan to visit these settlements first,' he said, unfurling the paper and handing it to Larch. 'To persuade them to join forces with us and support the Resistance.'

'Count me in,' Larch said, manoeuvring off the bed and hopping over to an alcove in the rockface. Despite his single leg, he moved with surprising agility, using the wall for support.

From the alcove, he retrieved a rucksack and began packing clothes tucked under his bed. 'I'm coming with you. Wherever you go, I'll be by your side, ready for the moment you can take me to my son.'

Zander and I exchanged glances, a silent conversation passing between us. I wrestled with conflicting feelings – on one hand, the desire to be inclusive and honour Larch's commitment - on the other, a concern his disability might impede our progress.

'Do you think the journey might be too strenuous for you?' I asked. 'Maybe staying here, mapping out locations of the elite's residences, could be a more manageable task for you?'

He looked at me as if I had a horn growing out of my forehead. 'Do you honestly believe I'd sit back, knowing my son is fighting alongside us?' he said. 'Now, more than ever, I need to be part of this. I'll think about the residential sites along the way; after all, exercise expands the mind. My one leg has never hindered me before, and it certainly won't now.'

'Having a face from another settlement might not hurt,' Zander said, focusing on the potential benefits. 'But if you hamper our progress, Larch, we'll have no choice but to go on without you.'

He threw back his head and laughed, and when he spoke, the lilt of his voice was upbeat. 'I've trekked many a passageway through these caves, keeping pace with the fittest of men.' His gaze flickered towards me, a glint of anticipation in his eyes. 'And you can tell me more about my son as we go.'

'It seems the decision has been made,' I said, rising from the cushion. 'The sooner we set off, the quicker we can return to Ember Enclave. We've much planning to do, especially with the gathering at Ashen Ridge looming ahead. Our priority is to rally as many committed fighters as possible by then.'

28

On our return to Ember Enclave, crowds lined the walkways. Their thunderous applause echoing throughout the main cavern and beyond. Heartfelt chants accompanied the cheers, creating an atmosphere of celebration. Banners with my name in ancient script hung from poles, while colourful streamers danced and fluttered alongside them.

Larch's unexpected decision to join us made a significant impact, and our mission had been a resounding success. The news of our achievements had reached Cooper's ears, who met us on our arrival with open arms.

'Welcome back,' he said, patting me on the back. 'We've received reports that all the communities are behind us, offering their full support.'

'To be fair, Larch made our job much easier,' I said, nodding towards him. 'He's staying with us, hoping to provide information on the elite's residential areas.'

'I'll make sure a chamber is prepared for you,' Cooper said, turning to Larch. 'We need all the insight we can get.' His focus returned to me. 'The others are in the bar. Do you want to rest for a few hours before we call a meeting?' Like me, he knew we had to act swiftly.

Before I could reply, Zander chipped in. 'I'll go and check in on Pops, and I'll meet you all there.'

On the way, I noticed Jaz sitting with her with friends warming herself by an open fire. Although she didn't shoot me an icy glare, I couldn't overlook the hint of distaste on her face. I made a mental note to talk to Orion about it later - to make sure all was still good.

As we stepped into the bar, a further wave of cheers burst from the crowd. Mugs clinked together, and hands pounded the tables in a lively beat. The chamber stunk of root beer and moonshine as if the festivities had been in full swing for some time.

Cooper weaved his way through the tables.'Sorry folks, we need this space for a private meeting,' he said, encouraging everyone to finish their moonshine and vacate the chamber. 'Come back in a few hours.'

Most left willingly, but grumbles of discontent could be heard by some, mainly Jaz's group as they departed. Klin rose from his seat, the scraping of his chair against the floor drew all eyes to him. He loomed over the table, his gaze fixed on me. Despite their initial protests, his companions filtered out, leaving him to stand alone. He hovered menacingly before departing.

I called Orion over. 'Do I still have a problem with Jaz and Klin?'

Orion shrugged and shook his head. 'Not that I'm aware of,' he replied. 'According to Jaz, she was good with you and was going to speak with the rest of the group. I'll catch up with the two of them later and have another word.'

Cooper merged two tables and dragging chairs, we hurried to sit around them. I studied their faces, the architects of our

destiny. Cooper, Zander, Felix, Astrid, Minx, Orion and Larch –
each name poised to etch itself into the chronicles of history.

The words spilled from me thick and fast. 'We'll strike them
at three strategic locations,' I announced. 'We space our
assaults hours or days apart, depending upon our ability to
mobilise to each site.'

I leaned in towards Zander. 'To succeed, we must find the
location called Omen's Keep, where Rowan took the children
from Ruin. I aim to rescue all of them. Additionally, we need
more intel on Malus's movements. Rowan may know more than
she realises. Make sure she's bathed, fed and relocated to a
secure chamber with guards posted in the passageway.'

Zander clasped his hands on the table. 'Your presence in
these interactions proves invaluable. Rowan has a connection
with you, and when you're calm, she responds well.'

'I'm happy to help,' I replied, without hesitation. 'Let me
know when you need me.'

Astrid's hand shot up, her voice clear as she posed her question, 'If Rowan was the one who took the children to Omen's
Keep, why is she unaware of its location?'

It was Zander who explained. 'They were transported in an
armoured vehicle, completely windowless. Rowan never saw
the journey from start to finish. We can try to work it out by
looking at the time she spent in the vehicle from the port to the
site, and the look of the landscape when she arrived.'

I shifted my focus to Larch. 'Any progress on locating the
residential areas with the maps Cooper provided?'

He rolled his eyes. 'I've only managed a quick glimpse so
far,' he said, pulling the map from his pocket, unfolding it, and
placing it on the table. 'The terrain looks plain with a few
distinguishing features. I'm certain they were built deep inland,
far from any settlements or Midpoints. Perhaps with more
detailed maps, I might have a better chance.'

Cooper tapped his chin. 'There might be some old maps in the classroom. I'll see what I can dig up.'

Surprisingly, it was Felix who raised an issue I anticipated coming from Cooper. A sense of concern replaced his usual laid-back manner as he ran his hand through his tousled blond curls. 'How do you plan to get us to each location, once you know where they are?' he asked, with more than a hint of scepticism. 'We've struggled with single roadside jobs, let alone managing three specific sites we've no clue how to get to.'

My smile widened. 'You never asked where the third site was?'

Felix chuckled. 'Let's hope it's one within walking distance.'

'We'll use the tunnel Zander, Rowan and I travelled through,' I said, leaning over the table and seizing the map Larch had laid out. 'If memory serves, we entered the underground network at this rocky outcrop.' I traced the route with my finger. 'The camp we took Rowan from is located here. This site will serve as our initial assault. Once secured, we'll have all their vehicles, allowing us to transport our fighters and captives.'

Cooper leaned forward, his brow furrowing as he absorbed the details. 'They won't be expecting us,' he remarked, his voice low but confident. 'We'll catch them off guard at night.'

Felix nodded in agreement. 'That gives us the element of surprise,' he added, his hand tapping against the table.

'There's a crucial detail you must all be aware of,' I said, pausing to let the significance of my next words sink in. 'Robinia, a woman in the camp, must remain unharmed. She's one of us, fighting for the Resistance within the government administration.'

Nods of understanding flowed through the group. Zander, ever the strategist, interrupted. 'It's a brilliant and daring plan. But, besides not knowing the locations of two sites, we have another problem; none of us know how to drive.'

Larch's voice cut through the murmurs. 'Driving was second nature to me before I lost my leg,' he said. 'I can sketch diagrams of pedals and gears, and I'll be ready to assist when we seize the vehicles.'

Zander still wasn't convinced. 'Do you think we'll get the information we need in time from Rowan? To execute a three-pronged attack with only a few hours between each assault is a big ask.'

A hush fell over the bar, the tension mounting as they absorbed my plan. Cooper scratched his head, his brow furrowed, while Astrid exchanged glances with Zander, Felix, and Minx. Orion sat with his elbows on the table, his fingers entwined in his hair. Amidst all the uncertainty, Larch's was the only face that shone brightly.

I felt a growing need to secure their support. Reaching out I gently tapped Zander's hand. 'You calmed my fears during Rowan's capture. I thought it impossible, but your faith prevailed. You echoed your father's words – anything is possible if you truly believe. I believed in you, Zander, and look what we accomplished. And now, I need your belief in me.' Rising from my chair, I addressed them all. 'I need all of you to believe in me.'

'You're right,' Zander said, as he straightened his shoulders. 'We're too focused on the flaws in the plan rather than looking for ways to fix them.'

Cooper offered a quick salute. 'I'm with you. Even if we don't take down three sites, I'll gladly settle for the camp. But, where do you intend to hold any captives? We can't have microchips bringing the full force of the army to us.'

'We'll transport them to the outpost up North, the same one where Spindle took me,' I said, envisioning our potential success. 'Robinia will be with us, guiding the way. With any luck, she might possess information on the other sites.'

'Okay, let's do this,' Cooper said, thumping his fist on the table. 'Are we all in agreement?'

'We're in,' they chorused in unison.

I felt a wave of relief wash over me. 'Thank you,' I said. 'I would never have gotten this far without all of you.'

The low murmur of voices outside the chamber grew louder, accompanied by the shuffle of footsteps as people filtered back into the bar.

'Looks like we finished right on time,' Cooper said, offering them a welcoming smile. 'Can I fetch anyone a drink?'

Zander shook his head. 'I'm heading off to see Rowan. I want to begin working with her immediately.' He shot me a glance. 'Will I be seeing you soon?'

'Sure,' I said, 'I'll pop along shortly.'

From the corner of my eye, I saw Orion leave without a word, his face sullen. I hurried to catch up with him. 'Is anything wrong?' I asked.

'I'm exhausted, that's all,' he muttered, rubbing his eyes. 'It's tough with a baby, you know? The constant lack of sleep. Anyway, I was heading off to find Jaz and Klin. To see what's going on with them.'

'Thank you, I appreciate it,' I said, meaning every word. 'Do you mind if I go over and pay Freya and Nova a visit? I always find strength when I'm holding your beautiful daughter.'

'Yes, of course,' Orion replied, with a nod. 'Freya always enjoys your visits. I'll update you on my conversation with Jaz if you're still there when I return.'

Approaching our table to bid farewell, I found Cooper, Astrid, Minx and Felix gathered around Larch, who was happily sketching pedals and gears in the dust with one of his crutches. 'I'll leave you all to it,' I said with a smile, wishing them a goodnight.

* * *

As I entered the chamber, Freya balanced Nova on a mat, the baby squirming and wriggling as her mother attempted to wipe her clean. 'Can you fetch me one of her sleep suits from the alcove over there?' she asked, pointing with a free hand to a gap in the wall concealed by a curtain. 'If I leave her to her own devices for a second, she'll be off on all fours down the passageway.'

'I'm happy to help,' I replied, sliding the curtain aside and selecting a beautifully stitched baby gown. As I glanced at the neatly stacked clothes, my attention was drawn to a plastic box nestled in the corner. It was the same one that had been stolen – the container holding my pills.

I lifted the box from its hiding place and showed it to Freya. 'How did these end up among Nova's clothes?' I asked, presenting her with the tablets. 'They were taken from my room. So, how did they end up here?'

Freya wore a puzzled expression as she took them from me. 'I've never seen these before. I've no clue how they got there.'

Orion strode into the cavern, stooping down to scoop up a crawling Nova. 'Our little escape artist was making a run for it.' His words trailed off as he caught sight of Freya, engrossed in an object settled in the palm of her hand.

'Have you seen these before?' she asked, passing him the box. 'Jasmine claims they were stolen from her chamber. She found them in the alcove where we keep Nova's clothes.'

He handed Nova to Freya, swapping her for the box, turning it gingerly in his hands. 'I've never seen this before. Where did you say you found them?'

I felt a sheen of sweat form on my brow and my hands felt clammy. 'In the alcove, near Nova's baby gowns,' I said, as a sickly feeling churned in my gut. 'Do you happen to own a black cloak?'

'No, this is absurd!' Freya's shout startled Nova, making her cry. 'Orion would never wish you harm, no matter how it looks.

He's being set up. Think about it. Why would he leave your medication where I could easily discover them? They've been planted here to frame one of us.'

Orion passed the box back to me. 'Despite our differences, Cooper is like a brother to me. His belief in you is everything to him and he'd be devastated if I betrayed you.' He shifted his attention to Freya. 'Can you please go and fetch Cooper? We need to figure out what's going on here.'

They returned within minutes, and Cooper's expression showed he was fully informed.

Glancing inside the alcove, he shook his head. 'The hiding spot is odd. It's as if it was chosen deliberately for Freya to stumble upon.'

Freya settled a now sleeping Nova in her in her box bed. 'They weren't there this morning, or I'd have noticed them,' she said.

Orion's face took on a puzzled look as he absently rubbed the back of his neck. 'I'm glad I came back when I did. Had I managed to find Jaz, I'd have been away longer. This situation needs to be dealt with.'

'Do you think Jaz did this then bolted?' I asked, unable to contain my suspicions. 'I saw her earlier, and she seemed . . . off. She wasn't hanging out with Klin in the bar. Maybe she stashed them here, then vanished, worried we'd see through her plan.'

'Jaz is like a sister to me,' Orion said, shaking his head. 'I don't believe she'd try to frame me or Freya. She can be wild, go against the rules – but I doubt she'd stoop to this.'

Cooper paced back and forth across the small length of the chamber. 'Who all knew about the theft?'

'Only Zander and Ella. I fell ill, and when we realised the medication was missing, Zander had Ella whip up some Lavender's Lull.'

Orion's eyes met mine. 'How do we begin to untangle this mystery with everything else we're dealing with?'

An idea sparked in my mind, its feasibility entirely dependent on Orion's willingness. 'Orion,' I began, wondering how to put it. 'What are your thoughts on spending a night down in the pit?'

29

The atmosphere was thick with suffocating tension as Cooper, gripping Orion's arm tightly, dragged his weary companion towards the pit.

Orion yelled out in desperation, twisting his neck to catch a glimpse of Freya. She struggled to keep pace, cradling a wailing Nova in her arms.

'Jasmine, please,' he begged, craning his neck to find me. 'You have to believe me. I didn't steal from you.'

His plea fell on deaf ears. 'Move, thief,' Cooper shouted, his voice booming for all to hear.

A murmuring crowed trailed behind, their voices blending into a restless hum. They followed the trio into the smaller cavern, their curiosity and unease adding to the toxic energy of the space.

Freya's voice rang out. 'Don't do this. He's innocent. I swear he didn't steal anything.'

Gasps of disbelief swelled from the astonished crowd as Cooper propelled Orion towards the edge of the pit's lip. He snatched the rope and hurled it at Orion. 'Tie this around you now, or I'll push you in myself.'

'I'm innocent. Please, believe me, Cooper,' Orion said, kneeling on the ground. The rough fibres of the rope coiled in his hands as he secured it around his chest and middle. 'You have to believe me.'

'Get in now, and I'll help you down,' Cooper snapped, his jaw clenched tight.

Orion steadied himself at the edge, staring into the darkness below. With a deep breath, he braced himself, scaling down the wall, and disappearing into the darkness.

Breathless, Freya caught up with Cooper. With an anguished shriek, she unleashed a searing slap across his cheek. Her eyes blazed with fury. 'How could you do this to us? To me?' Her voice trembled with a blend of hurt and outrage. 'Orion has never stolen anything in his life.'

Cooper shoved Freya aside. 'Go to your chamber and look after your child.' His voice was stern and demanding. 'The shame of it, Nova having a thief for a father.' When he faced the assembled spectators, his tone took on a chilly authoritative note. 'Behold the fate of thieves,' he bellowed. 'Let Orion remain in the pit until he confesses his crime and explains why he saw fit to steal from Jasmine.'

Cooper leaned in, whispering in my ear. 'I could use a drink. Care to join me at the bar?'

'I'd rather go from chamber to cavern and look for Jaz. There's still no sign of her.'

As we passed, people congregated in small clusters, their hushed gossip drifting from group to group. The cavern was alive with curious glances and speculative theories about what Orion might have stolen.

The bar bustled with rumours too. We settled into our seats alongside the others, our drinks already waiting for us. A pang of guilt hit me as I glanced at Orion's empty chair. 'I hope he's okay,' I said, feeling my stomach twist.

Minx tipped her drink in my direction before lifting it to

her lips. She took a hearty swig. 'The moonshine's flowing, just like you ordered.'

'So, what do we do now?' Zander asked.

I sipped some herbal tea. 'We wait,' I said, looking around. 'Sooner or later, someone will slip up and reveal they knew what was stolen. Once word spreads that it was my medication, we trace the source back to where it came from. Then, we'll have my would-be assassin, and Orion can rejoin us.'

'Freya packs quite a slap,' Cooper said, rubbing his cheek. His light-hearted comment served as a surprising break; the humour brought an outburst of laughter. Not that Cooper found it funny.

Zander gulped his drink, setting his jug down hard on the table. 'Right, I'm off to give Ella a break from watching over Rowan. She offered to organise a rota, thinking it would be good to involve some of the women. Might be less intimidating.'

The Rowan I knew back on Ruin would never be intimidated. If anything, she would have been a formidable presence, someone not to be underestimated. I glanced at each of my friends in turn. 'There's no use in me sitting around here waiting for whispers. I'll head off with Zander to see if we can press Rowan further on Omen's Keep.'

'Agreed,' Cooper said, his chin dipping in a nod of approval. 'We'll compile a list of the best fighters from each community for our upcoming attacks. Thankfully, we have a layout of the camp, and our spies have reported nothing has changed.'

'Remember to check in on Orion and pass him some food, water, and a blanket,' I said, in a hushed tone. 'He'll be cold down there.'

As Zander and I left the bar, I sensed all eyes tracking our movements. To my surprise, Klin offered a tight smile as we passed. 'Looks like he's not so tough without Jaz by his side,' I remarked, noting a change in his demeanour.

Zander's face creased with distaste. 'I tend to steer clear of that bunch. Many of our attacks on outposts failed because they charged in recklessly. My dad stopped taking them on scavenges too. They ended up being more of a hindrance than a help.'

'Do you think Jaz could be my enemy? She's never been fond of me?'

'It could be any one of her crazy gang.'

We contemplated the matter till we arrived at Rowan's chamber, with Zander having the last word. 'But we shouldn't jump to conclusions. We need solid proof. It's odd, though, that she hasn't been around. Usually, Jaz and Klin are inseparable.'

Rowan lay on the bed, blankets drawn up to her chin. Ella, perched nearby on a heap of cushions, hummed a melodious tune. The tranquil atmosphere was far removed from the cold dark pit.

Ella rose to meet us, her lips pressed thin. 'Rowan ate a bit of rat meat and drank some mint tea. She slept for a while, but was plagued with nightmares, so I brewed one of my remedies to help calm her down.' Leaning over the bed, she kissed Rowan's forehead. 'You'll start feeling better soon, love.'

Rowan's eyes fluttered open. 'Thank you,' she murmured, her voice heavy with sleep. 'You're so kind.'

A warm, infectious smile spread across Ella's face. 'I'll check in on you tomorrow to see how you're doing.'

As she was leaving, Ella beckoned Zander and me to join her in the passageway. 'She was talking in her sleep,' Ella said, her brow creasing. 'Kept repeating the same thing - *you have to save them, they're suffering.*'

'Did she mention anything about it when she woke?' I asked.

'No, she couldn't recall the dream, just a sense of dread and fear. The potion I gave eased her distress, but before that, you'd have thought she'd endured the depths of Hell. I'll leave you to tend to her, but do take care not to be too harsh,' Ella said, before taking her leave.

Zander returned to Rowan's side, lifting her head and adjusting the pillows. 'I won't allow anything bad to happen to you,' he said, as he tucked her blanket up to her chin. The sincerity in his tone carried a sense of genuine care and protection. 'You can trust me, Rowan. You know that, right?'

Her large green eyes locked onto his 'Don't make promises you can't keep. I'm not naive enough to hope for survival,' she said, with a note of resignation. 'Just make it swift and painless. I can't bear to suffer.'

Then, her gaze shifted to me, regret written all over her face. 'Jasmine, I'm sorry for everything. I truly am. If only I could turn back time and make different choices. Our upbringing moulded us, but it doesn't excuse my actions. You were the beacon of light in our darkness. That's why we all gravitated towards you.'

The glance I shared with Zander held a mutual understanding. Rowan deserved our utmost honesty. Despite my resentment towards her, a peculiar pang of sorrow grabbed me. 'I promise - when the time comes, it will be quick.'

She closed her eyes as if to shield herself from the finality of my words. 'I'll try and sleep now, but will attempt to recall every detail on Omen's Keep,' she whispered. 'Consider it my farewell gift, and I pray you'll find it in your heart to forgive me once I'm gone. If I can think of anything regarding Malus, I'll let you know. Though our wounds differ, Jasmine, I was a victim too.'

Felix's arrival shattered the solemn mood in the chamber. His face appeared flushed from exertion as he stood breathless at the entrance. He managed to choke out the words. 'You need to come now. Something's gone wrong in the pit.'

'Is Orion hurt?' I asked, my voice rising in panic.

'Go,' Zander said,' ushering me out into the passageway. 'I'll stay here with Rowan.'

As we dashed towards the chamber, Felix filled me in on the unfolding situation, his words tumbling out in a breathless rush. 'It's Jaz, she was down in the pit beside Orion. The others working on getting her back up.'

I couldn't conceal my confusion. 'Jaz . . . in the pit. Why on earth would she be down there?'

He slowed his pace, his fingers gripping my arm to slow me down. 'There's something else,' he started, his breath coming in short bursts. 'Just as you suspected, word is spreading that it was your medication that got stolen. We traced the rumour back to Jaz's gang. They're pointing the finger at her. They're saying she took them, and it was her who left the scorpion for you to find too.'

As we approached the scene, Cooper and Minx scrambled to secure the area, shooing away curious onlookers. Astrid knelt beside Jaz's still form, her fingers pressing against her wrist in search of a pulse. Off to the side, Orion sat shaking, cocooned in a fur blanket. The shock he suffered showing in his ghostly complexion and wide eyes.

Feeling a need to comfort Orion, I settled beside him wrapping my arm around his shoulder. 'Do you have any idea what happened?' I asked, after a few minutes.

My question seemed to take a moment to register with him, and when it did, his speech was slow and sluggish. 'Astrid passed me down a basket of food, along with a slow-burning flair - that's when I saw her. She must have been here before I was lowered down.'

Freya hurried into the chamber, her face waxen and eyes wild with panic. She scooped Orion into her arms, her comforting words muffled by the hair on his head.

I rose, offering Freya a smile of encouragement. 'I'll leave you to it. But let me know if I can do anything?' My sentiment was sincere and full of warmth. I loved them like family and would go to great lengths for them.

Astrid was still on the ground tending to Jaz. 'Her skin is so cold,' she said, glancing up.

With a heavy heart, I knelt down beside them. 'Is she dead?' I asked, studying the purple and blue bruise on the side of her head.

'She's alive - only just. Cooper's away to fetch a stretcher. We'll get her to Ella, who'll know what to do.'

'Larch should take a look too, he was a medic in a past life. Do you think someone threw her down there?' I asked.

'Did Felix fill you in on the rumours floating around about her being the thief?'

'Yes, he did. But why would she throw herself down the pit? Why not just leave?'

Astrid gestured towards the opening of the pit. 'There's a narrow hole and passage within the hole,' she explained. 'If you're agile enough, you can climb down to it, and crawl through on your stomach to an exit near the shorefront. My guess is Jaz was trying to escape but lost her footing.'

30

F reya fussed over Orion. He waved her off with a reassuring smile, insisting he was fine. I found myself pacing the room with a grumpy Nova cradled in my arms. Her cheeks were rosy and warm, and tiny droplets of saliva trailed down her chin.

Freya shuddered. 'I wonder how long Jaz was down there?'

'I'll have Zander quiz Rowan to see if she heard anything,' I said, pondering the situation. I looked at Orion. 'Jaz could have fallen in between the time Rowan was lifted out and you were sent down.'

Nova's gurning eased, her tiny body relaxing. As I settled her in her box bed, I ran my fingers over her delicate curls. 'I often feel like giving up,' I said, feeling the burden of our struggles weighing me down. 'But when I look at your beautiful daughter, I know we have to keep going.'

I turned to Orion, a lump rising in my throat as the weight of what I had asked him to do pressed on me. 'I'm sorry for what happened, but it worked.' My voice wavered under the burden I had placed on him. One day, I hoped to show him just how deep my gratitude ran, though today,

4

words felt insufficient. 'Thank you,' I added. 'I'll always be in your debt.'

'I don't get it,' Orion muttered, I honestly believed her when she said everything was fine between you two. She felt guilty after Ashen Ridge and told me she'd talk to you when you both had the chance.'

'Once she's conscious, we'll find out why she did it. Let's face it, she was never going to be my biggest fan,' I said, shrugging my shoulders.

I did feel a sense of relief knowing the threat posed by my would-be assassin had been neutralised. With that concern lifted, I could finally let go of the constant need to look over my shoulder.

'I'll check in on Jaz, and then see how Zander's doing with Rowan,' I said, hoping for progress. 'Cooper's probably filled him in on everything.'

'Has Larch made any progress with his memories of the Residential areas?' Orion asked.

We're still at a standstill,' I said, with a sinking feeling. 'It feels like we could use a breakthrough. At least we have one objective we can act on. The camp.'

Securing even one breakthrough felt like grasping at fragile straws of hope. To have a second would be a miracle.

* * *

As I approached Jaz's bedside, I found Larch and Ella stationed on either side of her, their eyes trained intently on her condition. 'How's she doing?' I asked.

'She's taken a nasty blow to the head,' Larch said. 'And is drifting in and out of consciousness. But her vitals are improving, so there's hope.'

Dry blood matted her hair and the purple and blue bruising now covered half of her face. A slender tube snaked into a vein in her arm, secured by tightly wound fabric. Suspended above the bed, a bag hung from a hook, delivering clear liquid through the tubing into her bloodstream.

Ella's eyes followed mine as I inspected the contraption. 'Larch made it,' she said, her admiration shining through. 'It's a saline solution, designed to hydrate her.' A hint of red coloured her cheeks. 'Having a doctor on our team certainly has its perks.'

'She's not to be left alone,' I said, desperate for her to recover. I needed to know her side of what happened with Klin and the others.

The sound of approaching footsteps echoed softly. I turned around to find Felix. 'We've rounded up Jaz's gang. They're confined in a chamber near the wash caverns,' he said. 'Cooper's with them, attempting to unravel who knew about Jaz's actions and whether the others pose any further threat.'

'Make sure they're closely watched for now.' I said, happy that action had been taken. 'If anybody is looking for me, I'll be with Zander and Rowan.' I turned to Larch. 'Send for me right away if Jaz wakens.'

* * *

As I wound my way through the labyrinth of corridors to reach Rowan, conflicting thoughts battled in my mind. Resentment simmered towards Spindle for his silence. Yet, I couldn't deny the comfort found in his absence, free from interference. Despite this, we remained ill-prepared, having squandered valuable time on fruitless conflicts and unnecessary drama.

The realisation hit me hard – earning unwavering trust from everyone was an impossible task. In every settlement, there were factions similar to Jaz and her group's sentiments. It was clear, they harboured deep-seated animosity toward the

Resistance because of their past wrongs. Forgiveness was out of the question - their mistrust ran too deep.

The only path forward was to press on with the trust I'd managed to earn. Delaying our assault on the camp only increased the chances of them fortifying their defences. With these thoughts, I knew I was doing the right thing. I needed to dismiss any nagging doubts about waiting for signs. We would make the first move, and it would be up to the Resistance to catch up.

As I rounded the bend toward her cavern, the distant murmur of Zander and Rowan's conversation drifted to my ears. Their voices flowed with a relaxed harmony, broken occasionally with bursts of laughter. I felt a pang of sadness, realising Rowan's inevitable fate loomed. Yet, I glimpsed a side of her I would have valued. But, trust remained an unscalable wall between us.

Her face lit up as she caught sight of me. 'Jasmine,' she said. 'You'll be pleased to know I've made progress.'

'Indeed we have,' Zander said, a bright smile spreading across his face. 'We've been chatting away like there's no tomorrow.'

'That's excellent news,' I said, glancing at Zander. 'Why don't you make your way down to the area near the washrooms? Cooper's there, and he'll fill you in on everything you've missed. After that, you should try and get some rest. We'll be mobilising soon.'

Zander didn't need words to reply, his expression said it all - a warning, to approach all matters with love and kindness.

* * *

I settled into the space beside Rowan on her bed, and a nostalgic smile played on her lips. 'This reminds me of the times we shared bunks back on Ruin,' she said, sighing at the memory. 'Back then, it was you who wrestled with nightmares. I wish I could have been more sympathetic.'

'Mine were often about Ash,' I said, with a soft chuckle. 'Not the Ash we knew, but a draconian version, with menacing eyes, a forked tongue, and his skin covered in grey reptilian scales.'

Her eyes widened, her lips forming a slight 'o' shape. 'No way. I thought you liked him. I always envied the way you looked at him.'

'Do you want to hear a secret?' I whispered, drawing her close as I linked my arm around hers. 'I used to have a bit of a crush on Salix too.'

'What do you mean by a crush?'

'It's from the old language,' I explained. 'It's used to describe feelings when you believe you like someone, and can't stop thinking about them. It comes before an emotion called love,' I paused, hoping my explanation was making sense.

Her face drew closer to mine, her voice low and filled with earnestness. 'Salix held values similar to yours and had a kind heart,' she murmured. 'It's hard not to have feelings for someone like that,' she sighed, her gaze becoming distant. 'It feels like losing them all over again. And realising how our emotions were suppressed . . . it's unsettling. We were set up for failure from the start.' Her voice wavered.

'I keep thinking about Lily, wishing I had been there for her. I truly believe she didn't intend to betray you.'

Tears trickled down her face, and in that moment, I longed to weave it into a memory of solace, a fragment of warmth she could carry with her into the next realm. Had this world been kinder, we'd have been two ordinary girls discussing boys and our dreams of motherhood.

'So, who was your biggest crush?' I asked, deliberately steering the conversation away from the lives that had been stolen from us.

She nudged me playfully. 'Oh, come on. You know it was

always you. Maybe that's why I acted the way I did. I never understood the feelings I had for you,' she admitted. 'It was easier to lash out than to be kind.'

I leaned the side of my head against hers. 'And all the time, I thought we were competing for Ash's attention,' I said, with a chuckle.

A moment hung in the air as we both drifted into our thoughts. 'You were my first kiss,' I said, breaking the silence.

Rowan's lips curved into a smile. 'You were my only kiss. So, go on - who else?'

'You must promise not to tell anyone?' I teased.

'I'll take whoever's name you give me to the grave.'

Her response caught me off guard, though I doubted she intended any hurt. I hoped she didn't notice my subtle flinch. 'Brace yourself,' I said, 'Because you'll be shocked.'

She released my arm and turned on her side, so she faced me square on. 'No more beating around the bush. Tell me who was it?' she asked, her tone insistent.

'Spindle,' I said, waiting for her to react.

She shot up into a sitting position, her eyes like saucers. 'Spindle? Seriously?' she blurted. 'I thought you two couldn't stand each other.'

I nibbled on my bottom lip. 'Yep.'

She sank back into her pillows, disbelief settling upon her features. 'I've heard it all now,' she said. 'Though, from his standpoint, it does make sense,' she added, mulling my revelation over.

'How come?'

Rowan sighed deeply. 'He treated you with even more contempt than I did. Perhaps he was grappling with his feelings for you while sensing your lack of interest in him,' she explained. 'In a way, Spindle found himself in a situation similar to mine.'

We lapsed into a comfortable silence, my heart lighter by

the connection we were finally forging. It offered a glimpse into the friendship that might have bloomed between us. I sensed Rowan felt it too.

With a hint of concern, her eyes searched mine. 'All this time, and you haven't asked me about Malus or Omen's Keep. As enjoyable as our conversation's been, I know you've more important matters to deal with. I want to help you, and I hope you believe me.'

'Zander will update me. Let's just cherish this time together. Unless you're tired, and need to sleep.'

Rowan responded with a wistful smile. 'I don't want to sleep. I want to stay awake for every moment I have left.'

31

J az's limp form slouched against the plush cushions, her head swathed in layers of bandages concealing her features. Her chest rose and fell in shallow breaths, the only sign of life in her otherwise still body.

'Is she any better?' I asked.

Larch's face was heavy with exhaustion, dark shadows lurking beneath his eyes like storm clouds. 'She's suffered a bit of a head trauma, so recovery will be a gradual process,' he said, rubbing his temples wearily.

Her eyelids fluttered open, and she tapped the surface of her blanket with a trembling finger. 'I think she's trying to tell us something,' Larch said, rising from his stool and steadying himself beside her bed.

Leaning closer to her, I met the depth of her gaze. 'If I ask some questions, could you nod for yes and shake for no?'

There was nothing. She remained lost, her vacant gaze fixed on me but not registering. It was as if I stood before a shell, her presence empty despite her eyes meeting mine. I was desperate to find a way to break through the invisible barrier that held her captive.

Her chest rose and fell slightly, and the tapping of her finger was the only sign of life.

I pressed my hand gently on hers to make it stop. 'Are you trying to tell me something?' I tried again. 'Did you threaten my life?'

Her body tensed, a tremor rippling through her limbs. Then, without warning, her muscles contracted, painfully contorting her body. Frothy Saliva bubbled from her lips, her breath heaving in harsh gasps.

Larch raised her head, holding a small jug to her mouth. Some of the potion slid down her throat while the rest dripped down her chin. 'It's Poppy Milk that Ella made. It will calm her down for a bit, and hopefully, you can try again later when she's more stable.'

Leaning on his crutches, he escorted me to the passageway. 'I need to apologise,' he said, with a tinge of sadness. 'With everything that's happened here, and preparing the others for driving, I haven't had a moment to review the maps Cooper found. I'm still no closer to pinpointing the locations you're searching for.'

'I know it's a long shot,' I said, 'But keep at it. We're going to launch an attack on the camp tomorrow evening regardless.'

He shifted uncomfortably. 'Will I meet my son soon?'

'If everything goes well, we can ask Robinia tomorrow where he is, and hopefully, we can arrange a meeting. In the meantime, I'll organise for someone to watch over Jaz to let you rest.'

Finding time to sleep was crucial. I found myself functioning on automatic, unable to remember the last time I had rested my head on my pillow. As I lay in bed, I pondered whether to pray. What rituals did the great leaders of history perform before embarking on the path of war? Did they seek solace in divine guidance, or did they rely on the strength of their convictions? Our cause was just, liberating people from tyranny.

I was haunted by restless dreams, filled with battle cries and the spill of blood. It was an unrelenting onslaught of gore and chaos, until I woke with a start. I washed quickly and changed clothes, then headed to the bar, relieved to find everyone already assembled.

Zander stepped forward, standing tall and commanding the room as he briefed us on his discoveries regarding Omen's Keep. 'It's an ancient white stone structure, predating the End of Days,' he explained. 'Their hidden agenda involves experimenting on children with specific genetic traits. Healthy children are taken for organ harvesting, destined to replenish the weakened organs of the elite's offspring. This occurs due to inbreeding, with them trying to keep their bloodlines pure. They also collect skin to repair burn damage,' he said, his hand tracing the marred skin on his neck and face. 'Due to the secrecy surrounding it, Rowan believes it's not heavily guarded; thinking only scientists and medics will be present.'

'Did Rowan provide any information on how to find this place?' Cooper asked.

'No specific details on the location,' Zander said, his lips forming a small grin. 'But wait for this one,' he said, pausing for effect. 'Rowan mentioned the vehicles at the camp have computers linked into the mainframe in the capital. If we can get our hands on them, and possibly hack the system, we'll have information on every site, building, settlement, and Midpoint on the mainland, and all over the other islands.' His gaze fell on Larch. 'Including the elite's residential homes.'

The relief was contagious, sweeping through us with infectious delight. We could pull this off.

Zander brought us crashing back to earth. 'There's just one problem, and Jasmine, 'he said, looking at me. 'You're not going to like it.'

'What is it,' I asked, chastising myself for assuming it would be smooth sailing.

'The camp we took Rowan from isn't heavily guarded due to a unique security protocol,' he explained. 'Every few hours, a code is transmitted to the capital in two halves by two different soldiers, each unaware of the other's portion. No one else in the camp knows this formation. If the code fails to reach the capital on time, they'll detect a breach, and the army will descend upon us without mercy.'

'So, why haven't they come looking for Rowan?' I murmured, the question more a whisper to myself than to the others.

Larch was the first to speak up. 'If they've lost the signal from her chip, perhaps they assume she's dead.'

'So, it seems we're back to square one,' I said, exasperated at the setback.

'Not necessarily,' Zander said, his jaw clenching slightly. 'What I'm about to say next is the part you're not going to like.'

I rolled my eyes. 'Are you telling me that wasn't the worst of it, and there's more to come?'

'What if we take Rowan with us? She's familiar with everyone at the camp and thinks she can identify the soldiers who logged the codes,' he said.

'And let me guess, she wants her freedom,' I replied, shaking my head in disbelief. 'Not only that, can we trust her? For all we know this could be a ploy – not only for her escape, but to sabotage our mission.'

'Her freedom, yes, but among us – free from her past life,' Zander said. 'She doesn't want to go back to them.'

My fist slammed down on the table. 'That's impossible,' I hissed.

Cooper agreed with Zander's sentiments, his disappointment in my stubborn approach clearly visible. 'Will your desire for revenge against Rowan jeopardise one of our greatest potential achievements?' he asked, his expression serious. 'Having Rowan with us might bring significant progress. We'll keep a close watch on her, and if she betrays our trust, we'll take the necessary action.'

I swallowed my anger, reminding myself of the vow I made to Zander – that he would be my conscience. 'Okay, I'll consider it. But if she dares deceive us, she can forget about the swift painless death I promised her.'

Leaning forward, Larch offered a ray of hope. 'When I first met Laura, I went to great lengths to connect with her. I hacked into my father's computer to track her movements in the prison system. I managed to arrange medical appointments so that I could be present. While things could be different now, I might still be able to assist. With Rowan's role working for Malus, she likely has insight into their systems as well.'

I shifted my gaze to Zander, fixing him with a serious look. 'I'll hold you accountable for her actions.'

We reviewed our plan, strategising how to move from tent to tent and neutralise any potential threats. With luck, Rowan would identify the soldiers holding the codes, ensuring their safe capture, along with Robinia. While uncertain of their cooperation, Rowan had assured Zander she could exert her influence. The stakes were high; any unexpected awakening could lead to chaos.

Zander continued his briefing. 'Our spies confirmed there are still five vehicles at the camp. Rowan mentioned they can hold around twenty of our fighters along with a driver.'

I turned to Cooper. 'Make sure all the fighters you've selected for this initial phase are prepared to move tomorrow.'

As our discussion circled back without progress, I relented and allowed everyone to share a single jug of moonshine. I hoped that a toast would lift our spirits among the approaching uncertainty.

'If you don't mind, I'm going to head back to spend time with Freya and Nova,' Orion said, declining my offer.

Knowing how difficult leaving them would be, I asked. 'Do you mind if pop round later to say goodbye?'

'You're family now. Drop in anytime,' he replied, stopping to hug me before leaving.

As I watched my friends mingle with family and comrades in the bustling bar, the weight of responsibility remained heavy on my shoulders. Despite wanting them to savour these final moments of peace, cautionary alarms blared in my mind. Deep down, I understood that our course of action was our sole remaining option.

But I couldn't shake Spruce's ominous warning he gave at the outpost - we had one chance for victory, or it would mean the end for us all.

My plans veered off course, fuelled by a sense of isolation while awaiting a sign from the Resistance. Our strategy evolved into a three-pronged attack – seizing their camp, liberating captive children, and dismantling the machinery of their private hell. Crucially, we aimed to capture and detain prisoners from their elite ranks. Would the government resist, triggering a full-scale battle, or would they surrender and seek negotiations for the return of their loved ones? Could the Resistance have achieved better results than my efforts?

No matter the outcome of our endeavours, we were committed to breaking free from the chains of oppression and building a better world for future generations.

32

The bar pulsed with bustling energy, now a hub for our fighters' preparations. Everyone moved with purpose, checking weapons and adjusting gear. Some polished blades while others tested bowstrings. The chamber cackled with anticipation as the fighters readied themselves to ignite a rebellion.

Rowan sat poised at a nearby table with Zander, her grip firm on a spear Astrid had entrusted to her. Amidst the whirlwind of activity, her conduct exuded a serene confidence that drew my gaze.

As I approached, she met my eyes with a knowing smile. 'Surprised by my weapon choice?' she asked, tapping the spear against the stone floor. 'I'm used to throwing with my right hand, but since Zander,' she paused, firing a wry smile in his direction, 'Chopped it off, my left will do just fine.'

Zander's expression wilted. Perhaps he felt a pang of guilt. 'Listening to you boast about your weapon skills isn't my priority,' he muttered, his frown deepening. 'I'll go and check on the others. I'll be back in a bit.'

'I should've known you'd chose that,' I murmured, sitting

across from her. 'I bet you'd still hit your mark if you threw it with your toes.' Our eyes met, and I tried to hide the distrust I still felt. 'Do you have any questions or anything you want to say before we head off?'

After a moment of contemplation, she let out a sigh. 'I've been trying to recall more about Coral.'

'And have you?' I asked, feeling my heart race.

'As I've said before, her boat crashed at Hazzard Bay. Neither her body nor the crew was ever recovered. If reaching her meant abandoning the Resistance and betraying those in the caves, would you do it?'

'What do you mean by that?' I asked, feeling the hairs rise on the back of my neck.

'It's a simple question,' she said, her tone serious. 'Let me simplify it. What would it be if you had to choose, saving humanity or rescuing Coral?'

I could sense my anger welling up, threatening to explode. I took a deep breath and asked, 'Tell me where she is, Rowan. Or I promise you, what happens to you next won't be pretty.'

Rowan's smirk twisted into a knowing grin. 'Perhaps I might know what happened to her, but that's not the crux of the matter.' She leaned in, her gaze piercing. 'Answer my question, and then I'll put an end to your torment.'

'Why are you bringing this up now, of all times?' I asked, my frustration rising.

'Because I need to know if you're willing to make tough choices,' Rowan replied. 'Going after Coral could put your whole operation at risk. Are you prepared for that?'

Thoughts of Coral tugged at my mind, but the weight of responsibility pressed upon me like a heavy burden. Surrounded by comrades willing to sacrifice everything for our cause, I stood at a crossroads, torn between conflicting paths.

'You've got until we seize the camp to make your decision,'

Rowan announced, reclaiming her spear from the floor and flashing Zander a sweet smile as he reappeared.

'Time to go,' Cooper said, sidling up beside me. 'There's a send-off crowd waiting for us in the main cavern. I'll get our fighters in formation, but you're the one who should lead us out.'

'Do you mind if I join you and Zander at the front?' Rowan asked, standing up. 'If I'm going to fight alongside you, I want to be recognised as part of the Resistance.'

Before I could reply, Zander swept his hand in front of him in a graceful arc. 'I'd be delighted to escort you into battle.'

An eruption of cheers greeted us as we strode into the main cavern. It teemed with jubilant faces, throngs lining both sides of the chamber, their voices raised in a chorus of support.

The cavern buzzed with life, laughter, and calls of farewell among those who cried for the safe return of their loved ones. It was a scene filled with hope and a promise, that even in the darkest of times, there was always light to be found in the heart of the community.

As the ethereal flute melody drifted in the background, a steady drumbeat joined its tune. Their combined rhythm and sound amplified by the stone walls stirred the depths of my soul.

From the corner of my eye, I saw Orion break away from his line to pull Freya and Nova into a tight embrace - holding them as if he feared losing them forever. Freya's tears flowed like a river, her delicate frame trembling as she sought solace in his arms.

As Zander stepped out to bid Pops farewell, a nightmare unfolded. From the shadows, a cloaked figure emerged, a spear gleaming in the flickering torchlight, raised high above his head with lethal intent.

With fluid precision, he launched the weapon, sending it hurtling towards me. It shot forward at blistering speed, yet I saw every twist in its deadly arc as if in slow motion. I yelled out, but it was useless - there was no time to dodge. If I moved, the weapon would find its mark in Astrid, standing defenceless behind me. My heart pounded as I braced myself, knowing I would never let that happen, no matter the cost.

I stood frozen, unafraid of death - my condition had long sealed its certainty. But then Rowan rushed in planting herself between me and the spear, a living shield against its deadly point.

Her eyes met mine, filled with purpose and sacrifice, and I could only watch in horror as she chose to protect me with her own life. The sickening clash of metal tearing through flesh and bone jolted me from my trance. Rowan collapsed to the ground, a ripple of horrified gasps sweeping through the crowd. I fell to my knees beside her, tears blurring my vision as I reached for her on the blood-stained ground.

I didn't need to see the face behind the hood to know it was Klin behind the treacherous act. His unmistakable multi-coloured beard betrayed him; the vivid hues spilling out form the shadows like a twisted rainbow.

He bolted from the scene, his footsteps pounding out a frantic rhythm. Behind him, a wave of fury followed, the crowd surging after him like a storm driven sea. Could Jaz have been innocent all along, her tapping finger a cryptic warning of the danger ahead? Had she been pushed down the pit to ensure her silence?

With Rowans's head cradled in my lap, I leaned down, our faces mere inches apart. My tears traced paths along her pale skin as I whispered her name. 'Rowan . . . what have you done?'

Her eyes fluttered open, a faint smile gracing her lips. With a trembling hand, she reached up to touch my cheek. 'Earlier . . . when I asked . . . would you give up everything for love? For one person alone?'

'Don't worry about that now,' I said stroking her head.

'I need you to understand . . . that's what I did for you,' she murmured, each word laced with fading strength. 'The moment Control started leaving my system . . . there was no turning back.' Her breath caught, and a tremor ran through her body. 'I'm so cold.'

Larch dropped to the ground beside us, his grim expression a silent acknowledgment of the harsh truth - there was nothing more to be done. He shrugged of his coat and gently draped it over her.

'Can you forgive me, Jasmine? I was horrible to you.'

'You'll need to forgive me too,' I said, 'At least you never cut off my arm.'

'Jasmine, I can see her . . . she's waiting for me,' she whispered, her voice trailing off, her breath slowing.

'Who do you see?' I asked, pressing a soft kiss to her forehead.

'It's Lily. . . Salix is there too. They look so wonderful,' she gasped, her voice filled with awe. 'I need to go now, they're calling me.'

'I'll be with you all soon,' I whispered, resting my forehead against her cold skin. 'Take care of them until then,' I added tenderly, as she released her final breath.

Grief consumed me like a storm, battering me to my core. Tears flowed freely, an unexpected outpouring of sorrow for Rowan. If anyone had warned me of such unbearable anguish for her, I would have dismissed it as impossible.

* * *

Back at the bar once more, I surrendered to the allure of moonshine. The burn in the back of my throat offered a brief respite from my emotional turmoil. With a bitter chuckle, I grumbled, 'Looks like our grand rebellion is off to a terrible start.' I downed the rest of the liquid in one quick gulp. 'Can't even give ourselves a decent farewell.'

Zander's distress mirrored my own, his eyes weary and bloodshot. 'I think you've had enough,' he murmured. 'We're pressing on with the attack. It's just a slight delay, that's all.'

'What about Rowan's burial?'

'Ella will take care of it. We'll pay our respects when we return,' he said, rubbing a hand over his face as if it would wipe away the sadness.

Cooper trudged over, his shoulders slumped and his face drained of colour. 'Klin managed to overpower the guard watching him, which is how he ended up in the cavern. The rest of the gang remains under close surveillance.'

'I want him dead,' I said, a cold, unforgiving hardness taking root in my heart. 'We need to get to the bottom of this, and when we do, all those involved will be punished.'

'He'll get what's coming to him. They all will.' Cooper said, with a steely resolve. 'Right now, he's stewing in the pit. Fully aware of his fate.' He glanced around, calling out to ensure his words reached everyone. 'We'll leave tomorrow, same time. But no procession this time on our way out.'

'How do we proceed with the attack?' Felix's voice cut through the tension. 'Do we take them all out now? Without Rowan's knowledge, we're in the dark about who holds the codes. Will Robinia know?'

The planning process became my sanctuary, a refuge from the raw ache of Rowan's passing. It provided a sense of purpose.

'I doubt it. Robinia came over from Ruin. I'm not sure what knowledge she has of the government's systems here on the mainland. If we secure her tent first, we'll find out.'

'We can execute a snatch and grab, similar to what we did with Rowan,' Zander said, regretting his words when my expression crumbled. 'I'm sorry . . . I didn't mean to upset you further.'

'It's fine,' I mumbled, my voice wavering. I rose from the chair, my legs unsteady. 'I think I'll go and lie down for a bit.'

'I'll escort you back to your chamber,' Zander said, taking hold of my arm. My head felt light and I leaned into him as we walked. Perhaps it was a sign of weakness, but at that present moment, I didn't care.

'Don't burden yourself with guilt. Celebrate her bravery. She died a heroine, sacrificing herself to save you,' Zander said, guiding me through the tunnel.

'I hated her for so long. Being here with her changed everything,' I admitted, my heart heavy with regret.

'I grew fond of her as well,' he confessed, his grip steadying me as I stumbled. 'Can you promise to keep a secret? I was never supposed to share this with you?'

'You can trust me with anything.' The words came out slurred, the moonshine taking its toll.

Zander's laugh was light. 'Rowan told me all about the first kiss you two shared,' he began, a playful lilt in his voice. 'She was so surprised that you had kissed Spindle and was peeved, seeing it as a competition.' He paused, chuckled. 'That girl, as bold as brass, she pulled me in for a long deep kiss. When it was over, she had the biggest smile on her face, happy she had evened the score.'

'That's so typical of Rowan,' I said, unable to hide the nostalgia I was feeling. 'She always had to be the best or have the highest score.' I paused, glancing at him with curiosity. 'Did you respond and kiss her back?'

With a wink, he replied, 'A true gentleman never tells.'

* * *

The darkness cloaked our movements, as we crept forward, seeking cover behind a stack of barrows. Using tactics similar to mine and Zander's past visit, we managed to take out all six guards. My breath shallow and palms sweaty, as we made our way to Robinia's tent.

She slept on her mat and crouching down, I covered her mouth. When my hand touched her lips, her eyes flew open, wide with surprise and alarm. It took a few seconds for her to realise it was me before her shock melted away. She sat up, pulling me into a relieved embrace.

'What are you doing here?' she whispered.

'Take us to one of the vehicles where we can talk without being heard,' I replied quietly.

She slipped on her boots, threw a jacket over her nightwear, and led us out of the tent, her eyes scanning the camp as we crept toward the nearest vehicle. It stood tall, its fortified metallic exterior marked by deep gouges, jagged scratches, and dents. She peeked around before sliding open the door and ushering us inside, sealing it closed behind us.

The interior held high-tech computerised equipment. Rows of seats lined the sides, padded in easy-to-clean material. Cutting-edge control panels and monitors were embedded within the walls. In the rear seating area, there was standing room for soldiers, with leather loops dangling from the ceiling to provide support during movement.

'What's going on?' Robinia asked, her gaze darting between Astrid, Cooper, and Zander.

'We can't wait any longer.' My words rushed out in a mixed-up jumble. 'Rowan shared crucial information, and Larch is with us now. He's been in the caves for ages, but he's on our side. And believe it or not, he's Ash's father. Our fighters are waiting at the edge of your camp, desperate to begin our revolution.'

Robinia silenced me with a raised hand. 'Slow down,' she said. 'This is a lot to take in all at once. You were supposed to wait for a sign from us.'

'But the sign never came, and we're ready,' I insisted. 'Spindle warned me it would be quick, so we prepared. What's Spindle doing anyway, and why is it taking so long?'

'Oh, Jasmine,' she sighed heavily, sinking into a seat. 'We've uncovered more about Coral. Spindle took off on a rescue mission to retrieve her, knowing it was what you'd have wanted him to do. His next move was to set explosives in government buildings all over the mainland. The explosions and smoke would have reached you. That was your sign.'

'But, we're here now,' I argued.

Robinia's brow furrowed. 'To do anything now will put Spindl, his men, and Coral in grave danger.'

Rowan's question came back to haunt me. What choice would I make if I had to decide between my loved ones and the fate of humanity? Once more, I stood on the verge of a crucial decision.

Cooper's face darkened. 'Retreating now will cause chaos among us. We've seen it happen over and over again, with every generation who stood with the Resistance.'

As the tension inside the vehicle reached its peak, the vehicle door slid open to reveal one of the camp's soldiers. His eyes widened, a mirror of our own shock, as his gaze locked onto us. For a heart beat, none of us moved, suspended in that shared moment of disbelief. Then, before we could so much as reach for our weapons, he jerked back, stumbling form the door, his voice tearing through the quiet as he yelled, 'Breach.' The sound ricocheted into the night.

Panic erupted as alarmed voices spilled from the tents,

shrill and frantic, signalling the breach. Soldiers emerged, half-dressed, their boots thundering on the dusty ground. Orders were barked while emergency light beams pierced the darkness revealing our fighters. They clashed with government soldiers, bodies and blades colliding in a frenzied chaos.

'Secure the vehicles.' Robinia's command sliced through the bedlam. 'If any are taken, they'll trigger an alert, and reinforcements will swarm in. Move fast!'

With swift precision, we relayed the order to each fighter we passed – the vehicles *must* be secured.

The initial upheaval was short-lived. Despite our sudden exposure, the advantage of surprise remained firmly within our control. Disoriented soldiers, shaken from sleep, scrambled to find their bearings in the mayhem. Our fighters were many, moving through tents, and striking before their sophisticated weaponry could be fully brought to bear.

As the first light of dawn painted the horizon, streaks of crimson and tawny hues reflected the colours of the battlefield below. Seated on the steps of the vehicle I had guarded, exhaustion flooded every part of me.

'Are you hurt?' Zander asked, approaching with a box brimming with medical supplies.

'No, it's not my blood,' I said, wiping my forehead.

'I found this in on of the tents.' He sat the box down and rifled through its contents. 'It will help for tending to the injured. But we need to make a list of our fallen. Their families will need to be informed on our return.'

'How many?' I asked.

'Ten, all good men.'

'I want every name recorded, and we'll honour their sacrifice,' I replied, watching him lift the box and hurry on.

The camp was a scene of disarray. Tents stood at odd angles, some ripped open, their fabric fluttering in the breeze. Shattered debris lay scattered across the blood-soaked ground, tangled with abandoned weapons that glinted dully. Wisps of smoke rose from dying campfires, casting an eerie haze over the area. The air was thick with the acrid scent of smoke and the metallic tang of blood.

Our fighters bore the marks of their struggle. Their skin streaked with dirt and sweat, and their clothes torn and blood-stained. Some limped from wounds sustained in combat, while others nursed bruises and cuts. They stood tall, their spirits unbroken, celebrating our success and ready to face our next challenge.

I rose to my feet and raised my voice, commanding everyone's attention. 'As satisfying as this victory may be, our mission continues. After we've cleaned up and eaten, those who are able should put on the clothes of the fallen enemy before we bury them. Gather all weapons, salvaging anything of value, and stockpile them in the vehicles.

Robinia approached, balancing two steaming tankards in her hands. 'Try this,' she said, passing one to me. 'It's called coffee, made from a black bean we cultivate in our labs. A rare find, exclusive to the mainland.'

As we sipped the bitter black liquid, I told her everything – the hardships, the challenges we faced, and the heartbreaking loss of Rowan. Robinia's presence was a solace; she held me close in my moment of sorrow, offering comfort in our shared grief.

'I'm worried about Coral and Spindle now, and the danger our actions have placed them in. But we had no option, with the soldier walking in on us. Why did Spindle rush off after her? He told me it was impossible. You all warned me, saying it might not even be her.'

'Back on Ruin, I led you to believe Coral had been delivered to Mortem because I was told this by Malus.' Robinia's smile was tinged with sadness, a soft and reflective curve hinting at the burden of her memory. 'But, her boat crashed off the coast

of Hazzard Bay, and somehow, she made it back to shore. It was
Ash who found this information in a file.'

'How has she managed to survive all this time? One of the
men at the outpost said her chip signal came from Mortem.'

'Her chip must have malfunctioned. Anyway, once Ash got
word to us, we searched the coastline for any sign of a wreckage. That's when we saw her. She was hiding out in the Black
Cave, probably surviving on insects and seaweed. Spindle took
off with a couple of men, without authorisation,' she said,
raising an eyebrow. 'And Ash is covering his tracks so's not to
arouse suspicion.'

'Spindle never told me how he came to be part of the Resistance. I don't know much of any of you when I come to think
of it.'

'One day, when time allows it, I'll share the story of his
recruitment. He, like you, possessed something special. But for
now, your focus must remain on leadership,' she said, drinking
her last dribble of coffee.

'We're vulnerable,' I said, glancing around.'Without those
codes, we're exposed and the soldiers will be upon us in a
flash.'

Robinia nodded, worry lines creasing her brow. 'Right now,
the government has no clue about this attack, but they will
soon. All the dead soldiers for starters - their signals will fade
from their systems. We need to figure out what to do quickly to
keep them from realising all is amiss. Cooper told me about
Omen's Keep and the residential area you wish to target.' Pausing, she mulled over the idea. 'We would need to move fast to
keep the advantage.'

'Larch is currently attempting to hack their systems to
access the maps. He's also working on creating a virus to
prevent them from tracings us, and hopefully block the signal
from your chip too.'

Robinia gave my hand a reassuring squeeze. 'It's hard to

believe Larch is Ash's father,' she said, her smile brightening. 'But let's focus on the task at hand. Finish your drink, and then we'll check on how he's doing.'

For once, a reassuring feeling settled over me, a belief that, despite all our trials, everything was finally falling into place.

34

The soft, eerie glow of the monitors bathed the vehicle, casting shadows on Larch's furrowed brow. With eyes fixed on the screen, his fingers clicked swiftly across the keypad as lines of encryptions scrolled rapidly before us. I stood behind him in tense silence, my heart pounding in my chest. Every passing second felt like an eternity. I held my breath, anticipation mounting with each flicker of the screen, waiting for the verdict of success or failure.

'I'm in,' he said, his fist pumping the air.

The absence of blaring alarms or flashing warnings was a welcome relief. Only the steady pale blue glow and a tiny dot appeared on the screen. From that dot, the government crest emerged, taking shape alongside a constellation of symbols below it, each representing different branches of government.

Robinia settled into a chair next to him, pointing to a file labelled Project Nexus: Secure Zone Mapping. 'This one will be more challenging to breach,' she said, pursing her lips. 'The firewall guarding this data is formidable. Hopefully, it will hold the key to locations of Midpoints, townships and active garrisons, not only here on the mainland, but on every island surrounding her shores.

'Will it give us the locations of the residential areas too?' I asked.

'I'm not sure,' she said, her gaze fixed on the screen. 'But they will be held on the systems somewhere. It may be more protected than the other strategic sites.'

'Keep working on it. Let me know as soon as we make progress,' I said, before stepping out of the vehicle, and leaving them to their task.

At least Cooper and his men's efforts could be seen. Shallow graves peppered the scarred landscape. Our fighters gathered around them, their hushed voices sharing memories of those we'd lost.

I called Cooper over. 'Select two of our men to guide our wounded back to the caves. Families need to be told of their lost loved ones. Tell them to say they didn't die in vain.'

Cooper looked around the camp, then said, 'We've gathered together everything that will be of use, but we want to move on quickly. If a passing patrol detects anything amiss, we're in trouble. Not to mention the lack of codes from the two soldiers.'

'You're right,' I said, shielding my eyes from the bright daylight as I scanned the landscape beyond. 'A patrol could pass by at any time. Select a few volunteers to learn how to drive, and begin following Larch's instructions. I'll send Robinia out to help.'

The air crackled with nervous energy as those selected to drive confronted a daunting challenge. I didn't know whether to laugh or cry at the dismal attempts. Shaky starts, abrupt halts, circling too fast, or moving at a speed where Larch could have overtaken them on his crutches. At times, the vehicles seemed unruly, as if determined not to be mastered.

Even with our frustrations, a sense of camaraderie blossomed as we tackled the task together. As the lessons progressed, some of us started to find our rhythm, our movements growing smoother and our confidence building with each attempt.

Zander hopped down from one of the cabs, a huge smile spreading across his face. 'I wasn't too bad that time, was I?'

'You did great,' I said, rewarding him with a hug. 'You can be my chauffeur once all this is over.'

A wave of exhilaration swept through the camp as we received another piece of good news. Larch had successfully implanted a potent virus into the government's main frame. A shield now concealed our movements and thwarted Robinia's microchip. With the camp poised to vanish from the government's radar systems, we stood ready and organised for action.

We loaded the vehicles, cramming them with as many of our fighters as they could hold. Two remained empty - a strategic reserve for those we'd collect along the way. The rest of our fighting force was sent back to the caves, but to remain on standby, ready to move if word came to them.

Armed with intricate maps and precise locations, we also unearthed a wealth of valuable information. We learned the names of evil puppeteers who pulled the strings of our world through representatives like Malus and Aconite. This was a revelation that caught Robinia by surprise too. But, who were they? And where did they hide?'

Despite these triumphs, a nagging fear gnawed at me – perhaps it had all been too easy?

At last, we were on our way, a convoy heading for Omen's Keep hoping for Rowan's intel on its minimal defences to be true.

The landscape unfolded before us, a vast expanse of barren earth stretching endlessly in every direction. The ground was uneven and treacherous, jostling our passengers with every bump and dip.

Orange dust billowed in clouds behind us, kicked up by the

colossal wheels as they churned through the wilderness. After a while, Omen's Keep appeared on the horizon. The engines rumbled to a stop, and we stepped out onto the grimy track to meet at the front of my vehicle. An acrid smell of oil emanated from the heat of the engines as they cooled. Passing binoculars between us, we peered through the lenses to study the fortress.

'Can you see any movement?' I asked, adjusting the view, honing in on the fortified steel doors. 'How do we get in?'

Robinia scrutinised the building's graphics on her hand-held monitor. 'We need to make it seem like we are here on a routine visit. Any hint of suspicion, and they'll notify the government,' she said, chewing her bottom lip. 'Will my microchip work on their locks?' she asked Larch. 'If I could gain access, and then let the fighters inside, we could round everyone up before they have a chance to react.'

'Your chip should work fine. What about the vehicles, though?' Larch asked. 'Do you think the camera on the barrier will recognise them from the camp that went dark?'

I couldn't stand the idea of waiting any longer with our objective within reach. 'Why don't we take one vehicle and give it a shot?' I suggested. 'If we make it through, the others can follow on. But if not, then we charge in and resort to brute force.'

A consensus was reached – Robinia would assume the guise of a government agent, gain entry, and hold the door for our infiltration. If the plan failed, it would be a case of fight and then flight.

As our vehicle drew closer to the ominous building, I watched our convoy shrink in the side mirror. 'Do you think there will be guards in those turrets?' I asked, turning my attention to the ugly greyish brick with towers jutting out like angry sentinels.

'We'll soon find out,' Cooper replied, as we rumbled closer to the imposing barrier.

Our engine hummed a low, mechanical growl before falling silent to its halt in front of it. For a tense moment, nothing happened. Then, with a metallic groan, the barrier began to lift inch by inch, allowing entry into a large gravelled area. It was only then that our convoy began moving forward to meet us.

'Let's hope this works,' Robinia muttered, lifting a small toolbox from below her seat.

My heart raced as she left our vehicle, her footsteps crunching on gravel as she moved toward the locked door. She pressed her right wrist against the keypad, a distinct metallic clink sounding as it opened. Before disappearing inside, she placed the toolbox down, ensuring the door remained ajar.

I was high on elation, with adrenaline coursing through my veins. As our convoy joined us, we sprang into action. Our fighters moved with lightning speed, now armed with hi-tech lasers instead of primitive spears and bows.

We advanced through the corridor, a stark passageway of shadows carved out by the glare of overhead strip lights. On either side, four laboratories stood, their massive glass windows offering a macabre display of the horrors inside. The medics inside froze mid-motion, their faces etched with disbelief at our sudden intrusion.

Our soldiers burst into each room, and scalpels, surgical drills, and forceps crashed to the floor. Astrid wrestled with a heavy-set medic, securing his arm in a vice-like grip behind his back. She forced him out of the laboratory, shoving him to his knees in front of me.

'How many scientists and medics work here?' I asked.

'Soldiers will be here soon,' he said, his voice calm. 'You should leave while you still have a chance.'

A further three were brought before me, their dishevelled white lab coats evidence of their scuffles. 'I'll ask again. How many people work here?' The sight of them unleashed a torrent of disgust that flooded my senses as I waited for one of them to respond. But all of them remained silent. I turned to Astrid. 'Have someone secure them in one of the vehicles, then come back and help.'

Zander stood at an open door at the end of the corridor, 'Jasmine, you need to see this,' he called.

I moved through the corridor to another, seeing our fighters take charge. The struggle from the medics paled in comparison to our previous battle. Rowan had been right, no soldiers or guards resided here. Those captured were bound and escorted out.

Zander stood by an open door, beyond it, a wooden stair-case descended into the basements. Each step down brought a mournful creak from the stairs. The air grew heavier with each level we passed, thick with the scent of must and decay on each new landing.

I could hear their whimpers long before I saw them. Drawn by their sorrowful cries, my heart plummeted as I witnessed their plight. Children, of all ages huddled together in a large cage. Their hollow eyes pleaded for freedom while their tiny fingers clutched the metal bars.

Filthy mattresses lay scattered across the floor, a patchwork of neglect and decay. Each one soiled and stained bearing witness to the suffering of those who slept there. In the corner lurked a toilet, its grime-encrusted bowl releasing a stench that clawed at my nostrils and made me gag.

'Jasmine, up here,' Cooper shouted from the landing above.

Zander placed a steady hand at my elbow. 'Go. Minx and I can deal with this.'

I bounded up the steps two at a time, my breath coming in short gasps. Reaching Cooper, I struggled to find the right words. 'I . . . I don't know what to say.' My voice choked with emotion. 'Those poor children . . . they must be traumatised.'

'It's a house of many horrors,' Cooper said, guiding me to a room adjacent to the kitchen and dining area. I shivered from the icy chill that permeated the air, coming from the colossal freezers lining the wall.

Cooper opened one of the large thick doors. 'Have a look inside,' he said, his tone solemn.

The shelves were stacked with harvested body parts – organs of all kinds earmarked for transplant. Rows of preserved skin meticulously rolled, each tagged and ready for dispatch.

Robinia plucked a glass jar from a shelf filled with an assortment of vividly coloured eyeballs. 'Collect any data we come across. It will serve as evidence against our leaders for their crimes against humanity.'

Felix wandered over, visibly shaken, running a trembling hand through his tousled blond curls. 'Robinia, there's a door leading out back, but it's locked. I need you to come and open it with your chip.'

Cooper, Robinia and I trailed behind Felix as he led us through a narrow passage where Robinia granted access to the outdoors. The landscape was a tapestry of undulating mounds, each one with a subtle variance in size to its neighbour. They weaved an endless pattern for what seemed like miles upon miles. It was as if the land itself was breathing, rising and falling in a hypnotic rhythm, mimicking life itself.

'What do you think this is?' I asked, straining to see the extent of their reach. 'It goes on for miles.'

'Mass graves,' Zander said, coming out to join us. 'One of the children asked if I could find her friend, claiming she was out in the back garden. I believe that's what the medics must have told them when they didn't return to the cage.'

Perhaps it was shock, but Cooper's words erupted in staccato bursts, 'This . . . has been happening . . . for generations.'

A tremor of cold dread slithered down my spine, its icy fingers clutching at my resolve. 'Once we've collected all the information we need, I want this building burned to the ground.'

35

The maps revealed several residential zones, each location a potential target for our attack. Because of our limited resources, we had to concentrate on the homes where the top officials' families might live.

After careful consideration, we settled on a well-defended compound, a formidable structure rising from the desolate landscape. Its towering walls looked impenetrable, reinforced with thick steel and equipped with intimidating automated laser weaponry.

As Larch extracted data from the computer, his brow knitted in concentration. 'This won't be straightforward,' he said, his fingers flying over the keyboard. 'I'm uncertain if I can disable their laser defences. We've been fortunate so far, but my knowledge in this field is somewhat limited.'

'How do the lasers work?' Cooper asked.

'If memory serves me right, they're programmed to identify unauthorised vehicles or visitors and initiate fire automatically upon detection.'

'What if we could input information into their system to legitimise our presence?' I asked, my mind working overtime for solutions. 'Maybe we could pose as a convoy conducting security checks. Would that prompt the gates to open and allow us safe passage inside?'

'There might be a way,' he muttered, more to himself than to me. 'Let me work on it and see if I can make it happen.'

Robinia's expression soured. 'It could be risky. Inputting data could trigger an alarm in their system. Until now, we've only retrieved information. If an operative notices data being added in real-time, it could alert them of our breach.'

'We don't have a choice,' I said, feeling her fear but not willing to give in just yet. 'We've come this far.'

Larch remained confident despite Robinia's concerns. 'When I hacked my father's computer back in the day, I would input data to tweak Laura's prison tasks.' He smiled, recalling his cunning with pride. 'I'd adapt them to areas in the prison where I'd be working, all without detection. I'm confident I can pull this off, and I don't think it will take long. Much easier than dismantling weaponry.'

'Go ahead,' I said, skipping the need for a second opinion.

Larch inputted details about a convoy scheduled to evaluate security concerns across all residential areas. The systems updated the data, treating the information as legitimate.

'I'm not so sure,' Zander said, mulling the situation over. 'Can we be certain we won't come under fire?'

There's only one way to find out,' I said, picking up the radio to connect with Felix. 'How are the children?' I asked, when he answered through the static.

'They're doing as well as can be expected. Are we set to go?'

I glanced at Robinia as I put my plan in motion. 'I'm sending Robinia over to your vehicle, to help you and Orion with the children. If this all goes wrong, she'll get you back to our outpost.' After clicking off, I contacted Minx. 'How are our prisoners doing?'

'They're not saying much, but I assume it's because of the gags in their mouths,' Minx replied.

'Keep the prisoners where they are but send all our fighters over and spread them out into all our other vehicles. Once you've done that, drive off a little so you're not too near everyone else. If anything bad happens when we try to get into the settlement, I want you to get out, and set the vehicle on fire. Robinia will get you all back to the outpost.

'Don't you want to keep them as hostages?' Minx asked.

I felt my fingers tighten around the radio. 'I'd rather they burn alive than put them anywhere near those children again.'

I turned to Astrid, Cooper, Larch, and Zander. 'If you could all step out of the vehicle, I'll handle this part alone. If I manage through, escort the other two vehicles in.'

They looked at me as if I had suddenly broken out in a swarm of festering boils.

Zander's voice rose in defiance. 'Do you honestly think I'm going to abandon you - for you to face this alone, then you're mistaken.'

Cooper and Astrid voiced their objections too, a hint of anger in their tone at the thought I'd even consider leaving them behind.

I wrapped my arms around Robinia, pulling her in close enough to feel the steady beat of her heart. 'I can't risk your safety,' I whispered. 'If anything happens to us, promise you'll get everyone back to the outpost.' I only let go when she nodded, her eyes shining with unshed tears.

Turning to Larch, I pulled him into a firm embrace. 'We'd never have gotten this far without you, and I owe you so much. Go with Robinia. She knows your son and can reunite you.' Pausing, I swallowed hard. 'If I don't return, tell him . . . tell him I forgive him. Let him know he always had a special place in my heart.'

Larch's eyes shone with a fierce intensity. 'Thank you,' he

said, his voice full of gratitude. 'I don't know him yet, but whatever he did wrong, I can't shake the feeling he'll carry those regrets with him forever.'

We watched them depart, Robinia, stealing a single glance back. Cooper settled into the driver's seat, bringing the engine to life and shifting the gear to drive. 'Strap in. It's time to party,' he said, keeping his tone light.

We moved forward, our pace steady. The sand-coloured wall loomed larger, casting a colossal shadow over us. The settlement was huge, making our midpoint on Ruin seem like a minuscule spec on the land. Its massive domed roof towered high, as if it pierced the sky - offering the elite who lived her direct access to the Goddess Pax.

'The weaponry hasn't fired on us yet,' Cooper said, as we arrived at the steel doors. He shifted the gear into the park position. 'That must be a good sign, right?'

The engine ticked over in a continuous hum while we waited. Suddenly, the gates stirred, and each massive slab slowly moved apart, the heavy metal creaking against its hinges. Relief swept through me and the taste of this small victory felt sweet and surreal.

'Shall we wait until the others catch up?' Cooper asked, watching in his rear mirror as they headed towards us.

'Yes, we'll all go in together,' I said, taking a deep breath as I tried to steady my racing heartbeat. Then a thought occurred to me. 'We didn't say how we were going to organise the transport for the hostages we take from here?'

Zander was a step ahead of me. 'We'll put all the women and children on the bus with Orion and Felix. Any men can be kept with the scientists and medics from Omen's Keep.'

'They're here,' Cooper said, moving us forward into what looked like a concrete holding pen. 'It must be some kind of double security.'

'It looks like the Cleansing Chamber on Ruin,' I said, with a shudder. 'What if they've lulled us into a false sense of safety?'

'Too late,' Zander said, rolling down the window and looking out the back. 'The gates have closed. Our other two vehicles are packed closely behind us.'

My heart dipped as panic tightened its grip with each passing second. 'What do we do?' I asked, staring wide-eyed at Cooper. 'We're trapped.'

A loud beep sounded, bouncing off the concrete walls, and a holographic clock materialised on the slabbed doors in front of us. Its digital numbers ticking down from three minutes.

'What happens when it arrives at zero?' I asked, finding Zander's hand, our fingers locking together. A lump formed in the back of my throat. 'I should never have let any of you come with me.'

Zander kissed the top of my head. 'We're together. That's what matters.'

I gulped in a deep, my heart galloping, as I squeezed my eyes shut, bracing myself for the moment when the numbers reached zero. The concrete slab opened smoothly granting us passage into a place different from anything I'd ever seen.

We were greeted with an abundance of breathtaking beauty, a striking contrast to the monotonous orange dust outside. Lush greenery stretched as far as the eye could see, interrupted by bursts of vibrant colours from flowers that bloomed in uniformed clusters. Each petal shimmered like precious jewels in the sunlight shining through the glass dome.

We passed by a jubilant welcoming committee, a group of children who waved excitedly from the side of the road. Some older boys kicked a ball back and forth in a grassy park.

'This is how Larch spent his childhood,' I murmured, my mind's eye comparing it to the dark gloomy confines we had on Ruin.

Zander's face hovered close to the window, his breath

forming a misty veil upon its surface. 'They must grow all the plant life in a lab and transport it here.'

Their homes stretched out spaciously, each showing their unique style and luxury with colourful and intricate details. Women in elegant dresses lounged on porches, sipping from crystal glasses, while their children played on the lawns. Laughter blended seamlessly into the tranquil atmosphere.

The smiles on the women's faces dissolved, their expressions turning suspicious, then to outright fear. Mothers sprang to action, their movements frantic as they sprinted towards their children. Panic gripped them as they gathered their little ones in trembling arms, desperation carved on their faces.

'They've realised we're the enemy,' Cooper said, pressing his foot on the brake.

I chuckled. 'It was probably our hair that gave us away. But asking all of you to shave heads would have caused a bigger war.' I picked up the radio, changing the setting to the loudspeaker mode. 'We are the Resistance, and are taking control over our governance.' My voice sliced through their startled cries. 'If you cooperate with us, no harm will come to you.'

Our fighters filed out from the vehicles and began organising the mothers and children on the grass, instructing them to kneel in family groups. Meanwhile, others fanned out, combing through the houses for those who'd sought to hide from us.

'We can't take them all. There's too many of them,' Zander said. 'And before you even consider it – we're not resorting to killing women and children.'

I shot him a bewildered glance. 'I wouldn't dream of it. Gather up some food and put it in the large building over there,' I said, pointing to the community hall. 'It seems spacious enough to accommodate a few hundred. Secure those we leave inside and burn the remaining buildings to the ground. We should also stock up on some supplies for our journey back to the outpost.'

'I'm happy with that,' Zander said, stepping outside. As he turned to leave, he glanced back. 'I'll contact our other two vehicles and tell them to meet us at the gate. We'll do our best to accommodate as many people as possible between them all.'

* * *

Back on the road, our vehicles groaned under their newfound weight. Cooper worried we'd run out of petrol but I assured him there were fuelling stations along the way. As well as programming our route, Robinia and Larch were busy trying to secure a safe channel to contact operations at our outpost.

'Jasmine, Robinia's voice eventually came over the static. She sounded excited. 'There is someone here who's eager to speak with you.'

My heart raced so fast, I feared it might burst out from my chest. I took the call with bated breath, anticipating Spindle's inevitable scolding for not waiting for his sign. However, I was sure he'd be delighted with our progress.

'I'm glad you're okay.' Aspen's words cut through the static. 'You're on loudspeaker, Jasmine. I'm here in operations with Spruce and his team and we all want to congratulate you on such an amazing accomplishment. Nothing like this has ever been done before.'

I made an effort to mask my disappointment. 'The real thanks should go to the people from the caves. They were fearless and bold at every turn.'

'Without inhalers or solutions, you and your travel companions will struggle when the oxygen begins to thin. Expect sickness, shortness of breath, and lung and chest pains. The key factor is to remain calm. Encourage everyone to take slow, deep breaths. We'll dispatch a vehicle with medics to meet you to help ease any problems.'

'That's good to know,' I said, feeling reassured.

Next, Spruce's voice came through. 'You've gone beyond our expectations, Jasmine. Could you provide more details about who you're bringing back so we can make the necessary preparations?'

Hearing his voice stirred my anger. His betrayal could have cost the lives of others around him. I pushed it aside for the moment. 'From Omen's Keep, we have six scientists, eight medics, two cooks, one cleaner, and twenty-two kidnapped children. We've also gathered loads of documents to look through. As for the settlement, I don't have a finalised count, but there are at least thirty women and potentially twice as many children.

The radio signal faded before I had the chance to ask about Spindle. My heart clenched with worry for his safety. Deep down, I knew our good fortune couldn't last forever.

36

Our convoy of vehicles thundered through the dimly lit tunnel, the noise from the engines bouncing off the walls as we approached. Spruce emerged from the shadows. With open arms he greeted Robinia, his face alight with relief at her safe return. Yet, as his gaze shifted to me, he appeared rattled.

'Jasmine,' he mumbled, his eyes trained on the ground. 'Welcome back.'

'Well, the last time we were together, you were transporting me to what should have been my death, had Spindle not intervened. My return might be a bit awkward for you.'

He squirmed uneasily, his speech faltering as he stuttered, 'I've . . . always . . . followed orders without . . . . question,' he said, his tone strained. 'You can count on me to obey your commands as faithfully as I did for those before you.'

'I'm relieved that no one was hurt in the accident,' I said, recalling the men dressed in camouflaged suits. 'But let me be clear - regardless of where your loyalties lie, if you ever attempt to take my life again, I won't hesitate to act before you get the chance.'

'Understood,' he replied, his posture straightening. 'In the meantime, is there anything specific I can assist with?'

'Speak with Larch, and consider him one of my generals,' I said, with an air of pride. 'He can demonstrate how he hacked into the government's systems, a skill the Resistance should have mastered years ago. Also, several documents will need to be sifted through for intel.'

With a quick nod, he turned, ready to leave without another word.

'Spruce,' I called, stopping him in his tracks. 'When will Ash return? Is there a way we can bring him back?'

'He's here now, but is preparing to return to the capital. The government is calling all their operatives back on duty because of the attacks. They're in panic mode. Nothing like this has affected them before. They believe their complacency was part of what went wrong.'

This presented a challenge. While I aimed to bring Larch and Ash together, the urgency of the situation demanded Ash's immediate return to his government post.

'Organise a private meeting room, and I'll meet Ash there,' I said, saddened time was against us, but knowing I had to prepare Ash for all that was about to be revealed to him. 'After Larch has briefed your operative on the hacking process, have someone bring him to me.'

As I left the tunnel, heading for the lift, I glanced back at the unfolding scene. Medics tended to those suffering from sickness, both to the captives and liberated alike. Some were ushered to temporary lodgings, and others to prison cells where they'd be held as hostages. Our principles included a clear policy – all would be treated fairly. Zander would see to it.

* * *

In the subdued lighting of the small room, I lowered myself into a chair, pouring myself a glass of water. Its tepid taste offered little relief compared to the crispness of the cave-filtered streams. With Ash's arrival pending, I mentally rehearsed what to say to him.

He lingered at the door, hesitant to step forward. 'I'm glad you've returned safely,' he said, with a deep sense of respect. 'And look at what you've accomplished.' He lowered his gaze to the floor, unsure of how his praise would be met. 'You wanted to speak with me?'

'Please, take a seat.' I gestured at a chair opposite. 'It's a relief to see you're unharmed too. You've been busy - helping Spindle's journey to Ruin to find Coral.'

'We both knew how much she meant to you. When the opportunity presented itself, we knew it was the right thing to do.'

'Thank you. It means the world to me.' Clasping my hands on my lap, I leaned forward. 'For such a long time, I hated you so much, Ash. But we were both victims of Ruin's circumstance. Our past shaped our actions. However, I've let go of that bitterness. I was wrong to accuse you of betraying me, but even so, you should never have told the lies you did. That only made me hate you more.'

His features relaxed. 'You have no idea how much I've longed for your forgiveness. There is not one moment that passes where I don't regret what I did to you. I've hated myself for so long,' he said, his voice shaded with a vulnerability I recognised sometimes in myself.

'I've since learned it was Lily who reported Mary to the Elders,' I said, my voice softening, 'When I looked for your mark on Birch's monitor, it was because I was trying to find Mary's grandson. Now that you're working with the Resistance, you're aware of the importance of family, and how it's been stolen from us.' Pausing, I took a deep breath before continuing. 'Ash, Mary was your grandmother.'

His features twisted in confusion as my words sank in. 'What . . . no. How?'

'You were the reason she smuggled herself onto Ruin. She wanted to find you and take you home,' I said, watching his face sift through so many emotions. 'Coral and I wanted to help Mary, and we traced the boy she was looking for back to you.'

He rose and paced the floor, his steps heavy with the weight of his words. 'I witnessed their brutality in the Justice of Pax,' he began, his voice thick with sorrow. 'I saw them beat and kick her. Jasmine, I watched my grandmother burn and didn't flinch. What kind of person am I?'

His shoulders sagged under the depth of his grief - as if the world's burdens had settled upon him. I moved without hesitation, reaching out and drawing him close into my arms.

'I wish I'd known then what I know now,' he said, pulling back and wiping tears away.

Reaching out, I stroked his cheek. 'We were conditioned not to love or form bonds. Somehow, feelings broke through and we all became friends. We've lost some, but their memory lives on.'

I thought of Salix, Lily, Willow - Rowan. I decided not to tell him about Rowan - not yet.

'I know this is all overwhelming, Ash, but there's more,' I said, with a positive tone. 'This time it's good news.'

Ash sighed, a sad smile teasing his lips. 'Only you could find something good among all this pain,' he said, as we returned to our seats.

'While living in the caves, I met your father. He's alive and well and working with the Resistance on our attacks. Without him, we'd never have had the success we did. He's desperate to meet you.'

Ash's face paled. 'I have a father?'

'Yes, his name is Larch.'

'Is he here with you now?'

I nodded, elated this moment had finally arrived. 'Yes, and he's an incredible person. He's been through a lot, but I believe he should share his story with you rather than you hear it from me.'

Ash hesitated. His voice carried a note of curiosity. 'Can you take me to him?'

'Wait here,' I said, 'I'll fetch him for you. The privacy of this room is better to meet him than in crowded corridors.'

I slid the door open to find Larch hobbling towards us as swiftly as his crutches would allow. As he reached me, our eyes met in a silent exchange. The reality of this moment was what Larch had lived for, and I was honoured to have helped make it happen.

As I sidestepped past him, a torrent of emotions tugged at my heartstrings. My thoughts drifted to Mary. It was as though her spirit lingered in the air, witnessing the long-awaited reunion of her family with a sense of joy and contentment. I could almost hear her laughter, echoing just beyond reach.

The serene moment shattered as Robinia rushed over, her face lined with worry. 'You need to come with me right now,' she said, tugging me along.

A cold chill crept over me. 'Why? What's going on?'

'It's Malus. He's found a way into our systems. He's live on the plasma screen and has specifically asked to speak to you.'

* * *

The tension was almost suffocating. Agents stood rigid at their workstations, focused and alert. All eyes were glued to the screen displaying a close-up shot of Malus's sinister face. Deep wrinkles carved harsh lines around his steely eyes adding an aura of menace to his expression. My friends - now my trusted generals, stood beside me, shoulder to shoulder.

Malus's mouth twisted into a crooked half-smile, exposing his yellow teeth. 'We meet again, Jasmine,' he said, the cruel note in his voice still present. 'I'm glad you didn't keep me waiting too long.'

Taking a steady breath, I summoned my resolve, making sure my voice stayed firm and calm. 'You must know that the Resistance has obliterated Omen's Keep and secured hostages. We have also captured women and children from one of your elite settlements. The time has come for you and your superiors to negotiate surrender to the Resistance and end your reign of tyranny.'

The sound of his laughter spilled from the screen. 'Do you believe you've played this game well, Jasmine? That you alone hold all the cards. There will be no negotiations other than one I will put forth to you. But first, let me show you something.' The screen turned black, and then into a swirling flurry of static.

When the picture cleared, it showed the mountain range, our majestic home. The sun's golden rays danced upon the rugged peaks, casting long shadows over the craggy rock formations below. It stretched endlessly, the rock-strewn beauty captivating and timeless, evoking a sense of wonder.

'Sending your soldiers into our territory would be a grave mistake,' I said, feeling a sense of dread. 'Our passageways are rigged, and any attempt to breach them would result in loss of life. Any harm that comes to those inside will have dire consequences for the hostages we have. I can only imagine the fury of your superiors should any harm befall their loved ones due to your recklessness.'

His hollow laughter boomed once more. 'Let me share a little secret with you. We could have extinguished the lives of those in the caves long ago without sending a single soldier into their domain. It served our purposes to keep them there . . . to have a boogeyman to keep people in line. And as for your threats of harming hostages . . . we'll come to that later.'

'I don't believe . . .'

'Enough,' he roared, the picture on the screen flickering. 'Let me show you who holds the power in this world.'

From afar, we heard a low forbidding rumble. My heart raced as we watched in horror, helplessly witnessing the ground shatter and split - swallowing everything in its path. The towering peaks trembled violently, their once-impregnable foundations crumbling to dust. Rocks and debris cascaded down the slopes, tumbling into the yawning chasm below.

Less than half remained standing, battered and dying, as molten lava dripped from shattered cracks, a fiery cascade flowing like a river of doom. Black smoke billowed out, mingling with dense clouds of dust, cloaking the skyline in a menacing veil of darkness. Then, abruptly, the screen flickered with static before plunging into blackness.

Terror gripped our hearts and minds, like an icy claw digging in deep to tear us apart.

Orion crumpled, his strength failing him, sinking into Cooper's arms. He called out for Freya and Nova, his voice hoarse with desperation. A tsunami of despair crashed over us all, our collective agony manifesting guttural wails, curses, and seething frustration. All the while, a haunting voice sounded in my head, relentless in its accusation. *This is all your fault.*

Once again, the screen flickered to life, and Malus's voice filled the room. 'We have a parting gift for you, Jasmine,' he declared, 'Have a look.'

The screen slowly materialised to the image of Spindle and Coral huddled together in a dim concrete room. The fear on their faces projected a sense of two lost souls seeking solace in the bleakness around them. Malus's chilling voice reverberated over the scene weaving dread into the atmosphere. 'If you harm any of the hostages you hold, Spindle and Coral will pay the price.'

My gaze fixed on Spindle's tired, worn blue eyes, fatigue carved deep within their depths. Upon closer inspection, I detected defiance in them rather than fear. It was as if I could hear his voice whisper telepathically, urging me to be strong – to embody the leader he knew I could be. His muscular arms held Coral, drawing her trembling body closer to his for warmth and comfort. It reignited the warrior within my soul.

While those around me sprang into action, planning the intricate details of a mission to rescue the survivors, I found myself rooted in place. We had suffered terribly, yet our struggle for freedom and justice was far from over. Though we had lost this battle, my resolve to win the war ahead was stronger than ever. All we had to do was keep fighting.

ACKNOWLEDGMENTS

Where to begin? Thank you to my wonderful husband, Martin, and my two beautiful grown-up children, Rebekah and Sam. For all you do for me, and for your love and encouragement.

Family and friends are everything, and for that, I am truly blessed. You all know who you are - too many to list.

Special thanks to my editor, Wendy H. Jones, who has supported me from the very beginning, encouraging me every step of the way.

A special shout out to all the writing organisations who have been a huge part of my writing journey. To name but a few - Ayr Writers' Club and History Writers. Not to forget my colleagues on the Council of the Scottish Association of Writers.

To Linda Brown and Kirsty Hammond for always being there, and bouncing ideas around.

Finally - all those who have played a part in writing journey - I extend my heartfelt thanks.

ABOUT THE AUTHOR

Having had a passion for reading and writing since an early age, this passion has only grown over the years. Marti M. McNair has been writing since she could pick up a pen, and after her children flew the nest she turned to writing seriously. Her main focus is writing for a YA audience, and her books feature dystopian settings, dark political undercurrents and places her characters in precarious situations which tests them to the limit. She was the winner of the prestigious Scottish Association of Writers, Barbara Hammond Prize. She is also a partner in Auscot Publishing and retreats and a graphic designer for Writers' Narrative Magazine. In addition she is the Vice-President of the Scottish Association of Writers.

ALSO BY MARTI M. MCNAIR

Island of Ruin

A Right Cozy Christmas Crime

Coming Soon

Rise From Ruin

Cozy Christmas Crimes Book 1

Printed in Great Britain
by Amazon